ALSO BY
ROBERT KROESE

THOMAS DUNNE BOOKS   ST. MARTIN'S PRESS ≈ NEW YORK

THE
LAST
IOTA

ROBERT KROESE

THOMAS DUNNE BOOKS.
An imprint of St. Martin's Press.

THE LAST IOTA. Copyright © 2017 by Robert Kroese. All rights reserved. Printed in the United States of America. For information, address St. Martin's Press, 175 Fifth Avenue, New York, N.Y. 10010.

www.thomasdunnebooks.com
www.stmartins.com

Designed by Anna Gorovoy

The Library of Congress Cataloging-in-Publication Data is available upon request.

ISBN 978-1-250-08846-8 (hardcover)
ISBN 978-1-250-08847-5 (e-book)

Our books may be purchased in bulk for promotional, educational, or business use. Please contact your local bookseller or the Macmillan Corporate and Premium Sales Department at 1-800-221-7945, extension 5442, or by e-mail at MacmillanSpecialMarkets@macmillan.com.

First Edition: May 2017

10 9 8 7 6 5 4 3 2 1

FOR ONE KRISTIN OR ANOTHER

ACKNOWLEDGMENTS

With thanks to Rob Blackwell, author of *The Forest of Forever*, for his invaluable help with fleshing out the mechanics and political ramifications of the iota virtual currency; and to Joel Bezaire, for helping me with the math.

I'll backtrack every move you made. I'll dig up everybody you ever contacted or used . . . I'll have the entire operation detailed down to the last iota and perhaps the civilized world will realize what kind of a terror they harbored.

—MICKEY SPILLANE, *THE LAST COP OUT*

THE
LAST
IOTA

ONE

"I'm not who you think I am," said the image of Selah Fiore on the screen in front of me. Her blond hair was wet and her dress hung damply from her exquisite form. "Some of the things I've done have been . . . questionable. But it was all for the good of the company. It was all for us."

The man holding a gun on her shook his head slowly. "You really believe that, don't you?" he said. He was grizzled, with a two-day beard and rumpled clothing. I got the impression he was supposed to be a cop, but he was a little too handsome for the job. I'd seen him in a few movies; I think his name was Ben something.

Needless to say, Selah Fiore was too beautiful to be whatever she was supposed to be. I'd come in at the middle of the scene, so it was a little unclear who her character was. Some flavor of femme fatale, no doubt. Selah Fiore had always excelled at the femme fatale. The two of them appeared to be standing in the rain in an alley dimly lit by neon signs.

"It's the truth," Selah said. "You knew that once. You and I—"

"No, Jessica," Ben What's-His-Name said. "There's no 'you and I.' Not anymore. You saw to that when you got in bed with GenoDyne."

"GenoDyne was a means to an end, Paul. Surely you see that."

"In the beginning, maybe. But you've changed, Jessica. So much that I don't think you can even see the end anymore."

"Good God," muttered the man standing next to me. "Who writes this crap?"

A ponytailed man standing behind a camera to our left shot a glare in our direction.

"Keane," I whispered. "You're going to get us kicked out of this place."

"I'm not seeing the downside," said Keane. "The screeching of feral cats making sweet love on the roof of a garden shed is *Casablanca* compared to this scene."

That earned us another glare, and I elbowed Keane in the ribs. He grumbled, but didn't continue his rant. I actually thought the scene was rather good, and in any case it was fun to watch Selah work.

We weren't watching the real Selah Fiore, of course. Selah Fiore was nearly sixty years old, and the woman on the screen appeared to be closer to thirty. This was Selah from her glory days, circa 2010. The voice was the real Selah's, but the image was a computer-generated facsimile combining Selah's appearance from thirty years ago, the real Selah's facial expressions, and the body of an android stand-in. Glancing at Keane, I realized the cause of the disparity in our reactions: I was watching the simulacrum on the screen to our right, but Keane was watching Ben What's-His-Name interacting with the android on the soundstage to our left. The android resembled a crash test dummy more than a human being, and it was a poor substitute for a fine specimen of femininity like thirty-year-old Selah Fiore. Watching the scene unfold with a faceless robot playing Selah's part definitely sucked the romance out of the experience. It was so unsettling, in fact, that I found myself deliberately ignoring the real-life scene to focus on the monitor. Meanwhile, Keane continued to forgo the illusion in favor of the robot. That was Erasmus Keane in a nutshell: always trying to get at the reality behind the illusion, even if it made him—and everyone around him—miserable.

"Then you'll have to shoot me," Simulacrum Selah was saying, her chin defiant but her lower lip trembling almost imperceptibly. The illusion was perfect: a computer was generating the composite image on the fly, transposing the real Selah's expressions onto a model of her face from thirty years ago and then transferring the resultant simulation onto the android's blank face. Presumably the real Selah Fiore was around here somewhere, acting out the scene, but I hadn't yet laid eyes on her. The soundstage was a large room, but the illusion of the rain-slicked alley extended just beyond the frame of the monitor. The director probably kept Selah in a soundproofed room nearby to ensure the sound was recorded properly and her movements were captured accurately. Of course, there was no reason she couldn't be in Paris or Hong Kong; with a high-speed data connection, the delay would be imperceptible. I only knew she was somewhere nearby because she had asked Keane and me to meet her here. The scene was supposed to be over by now, but evidently the shooting had gone long.

I say the director was "keeping her" somewhere offstage, but that wasn't accurate, either. There was no containing Selah Fiore. She was an actor in this scene, but she also owned the production company. The director—who was still finding time between his directing tasks to shoot disapproving glances at me and Keane—was just one of Selah's many employees. In fact, the company producing this film was only one small part of Selah Fiore's vast news and entertainment empire, Flagship Media. God knew why she still chose to star in the occasional film; she certainly didn't need the money.

I suspect it was some combination of vanity, nostalgia, and boredom. Keane and I were all too familiar with Selah Fiore's particular brand of vanity, thanks to a run-in with her on a previous case. In fact, as we learned on that case, *psychotic narcissism* was probably a more accurate description.

We had been hired to find a genetically modified sheep that had gone missing from one of Esper Corporation's labs. We ended up uncovering an illegal cloning operation, the end goal of which was Selah Fiore's own immortality. Selah had spent hundreds of millions of New Dollars and broken countless laws to produce clones of herself implanted with her own memories—and she might have succeeded if it weren't for me and Keane. She would have killed us if Keane hadn't outmaneuvered her. Selah Fiore was brilliant, beautiful, ruthless, and as close to pure evil as I've ever experienced. So to say that her call inviting us to the set of her latest movie was unexpected would be a considerable understatement. I think Keane agreed to come mostly out of curiosity. Ordinarily I would have resisted, but Selah had said something in her message that got my attention.

"Be reasonable, Jessica," Ben What's-His-Name, with the stubbly, too-perfect chin pleaded. I had to hand it to him; he made me believe he was actually addressing thirty-year-old Selah and not a naked, faceless android that looked like it had wandered away from a Macy's store window.

"I am being reasonable, Paul," said the Selah simulacrum on the screen. "It's the end of the road for us. This is how it was always going to end for you and I."

Keane, who had continued to fidget irritably next to me, could no longer contain himself. "You and *me*!" he shouted. "Clichés are one thing, but at least get the grammar right."

"Cut!" yelled the ponytailed man. "Everybody take five."

Ben What's-His-Name shrugged and walked off. The android put its hands on its hips and cocked its head at an odd angle, as if looking at something the rest of us couldn't see. The ponytailed man marched over toward me and Keane. "Who the fuck are you, and what are you doing on my set?" he demanded.

"My name is Erasmus Keane," answered Keane. "To answer your second question, I'm just a guy with a seventh-grade education and above-average attention to detail, which evidently renders me overqualified to be on your writing staff. Do you even know the difference between a subject and an indirect object?"

"Keane," I said, "I don't think that's—"

"In any case," Keane went on, "this isn't your set."

"The hell it isn't," the ponytailed man growled. "Security, get these two idiots out of here."

A heavyset man in a security uniform waddled toward me. I'd noticed him before; I'm in the habit of taking inventory of any potential threats when I enter a room. This guy was high on potential but low on threat. He wore a sidearm but I doubted he'd ever drawn it in the line of duty. Security on this set seemed to be an afterthought; we hadn't even been frisked before being allowed on the soundstage. We'd flashed our IDs, the man at the door had verified our names were on a list, and we'd walked right on. I wore a 9mm SIG Sauer on my chest and a Beretta on my ankle. Not that I'd need them for this guy. Still, I tried to avoid conflict unless it was absolutely necessary; the fact was, the guard had every right to eject us from the soundstage. If we resisted, we were likely to attract the attention of law enforcement, and that was generally to be avoided.

"Come on, Keane," I said. "Let's get out of here. If Selah wants to—"

"If Selah wants to what?" said a woman's voice behind the ponytailed man. Turning to look, I saw Selah Fiore approaching from a dark corner. She must have come in a side door while we were distracted. She was still beautiful at fifty-eight, but the contrast with the younger version of herself was striking. Even with the best plastic surgeons and anti-aging treatments, Selah was slowly losing the fight against her own mortality.

"If Selah wants to talk to us," I answered, meeting her gaze, "she knows where to find us."

"Indeed I do," said Selah. She turned to the ponytailed man. "David, take your goon and go get a coffee. No sugar for him; I see now where all the cafeteria donuts are going." She eyed the heavyset guard distastefully, and the man's face flushed red. God, I hated that woman.

"Come on, Tim," said the ponytailed man, David, sparing another glare at Keane. The two walked off the set, exiting through the door Keane and I had come through.

Selah clapped her hands twice. "Everyone out!" she shouted. A couple of technicians who had still been milling about exited as well, none of them saying a word. They all knew who Selah Fiore was, and they knew better than to question her. We were on the soundstage alone with her.

"It costs me a lot of money to have these people standing around, you know," said Selah, addressing Keane.

"Yeah, well, it costs me money to have this guy standing here," said Keane, jerking his thumb in my direction.

Selah laughed. "You two haven't had a case in three weeks," she said. She looked at me. "Is he even still paying your salary?"

In point of fact, he was, but only because I was in charge of the finances. We were four months behind on our lease, but I wasn't about to dock my salary so Keane could keep his office open.

"Keeping tabs on us, eh?" said Keane, before I could reply. "I didn't know you cared."

"It's in my interest to make sure you aren't causing mischief."

"You've been scaring our clients away?" I asked.

"Sadly, that hasn't been necessary," Selah said. "Maybe phenomenological inquisitors are just out of vogue these days." Keane insisted on calling himself a "phenomenological inquisitor" rather than "private investigator." I still wasn't sure what the difference was, other than Keane's ego.

"Like elderly actresses," Keane suggested.

Selah smiled without warmth. "Touché, Mr. Keane."

"You said you wanted to talk about Gwen," I interjected. "So talk. Do you know something you haven't told us?"

Gwen Thorson had been my girlfriend. I say "had been" because three years ago she had disappeared. Simply vanished, without a trace. I had spent much of the past three years trying to locate her but had been on the verge of giving up when Keane and I took the Case of the Missing Sheep. When that case ended, Selah had hinted that she knew what had happened to Gwen. The impression she gave us at the time was that Gwen had been murdered because of her involvement in a top-secret government program called Maelstrom.

Selah observed me impassively for a moment. "No," she said at last. "I'm afraid I misled you, Mr. Fowler. I mentioned Gwen merely to get your attention. I didn't want you talking Mr. Keane out of this meaning."

I sighed, hoping that I conveyed disappointment and resignation rather than what I was actually feeling, which was relief. If she knew something about Gwen that she hadn't told us, that was bad news. Because I knew something about Gwen that—hopefully—neither she nor Keane knew.

"Let's go, Keane," I said. "She's just playing us."

"Wait," Selah replied. "I want to hire you."

"Sure you do," I said. "What are you missing this time, a capybara?"

"A coin," she replied.

Keane cocked his head. "First a sheep, then a coin. You seem to be developing a theme, Selah. You don't have a prodigal son running around Sunset Strip, do you?"

"No sons that I know of," said Selah. "And the coin isn't mine. It's just something that I'm interested in."

"What sort of coin?" asked Keane.

"An iota," Selah replied.

"Iotas don't exist," I said. "Not as physical coins, anyway. They're virtual currency." I was somewhat familiar with iotas, as I had recently opened an iota account myself for some of Keane's off-the-books transactions. There weren't a lot of places that took them, but they could be handy for making untraceable payments—especially since the transaction could be conducted on a comm, without ever touching cash. Iotas had gone mainstream in the early 2030s, after the collapse of the U.S. dollar, and they remained a popular alternative to hard currency in many circles. There were other virtual currencies around, like bitcoins and XKredits, but the iota was by far the most popular. The idea of an iota coin, however, was an oxymoron. The whole point of iotas was that they were digital.

"Actually," said Selah, "there are nine physical iota coins in existence."

Keane nodded and rubbed his chin thoughtfully.

"Physical coins representing virtual money?" I asked. "How does that work?"

"It was a marketing gimmick," Keane answered. "There was a time when certain people were pushing iotas as an alternative to the dollar. It seems like a stretch now, but at the height of the Collapse, it wasn't at all clear there was a bottom to the dollar's fall. Meanwhile, virtual currencies like the iota were surging. At the height of iota fever, about three months into the Collapse, some savvy investors and tech guys got together to form something called the Free Currency Initiative. Theoretically, they were in favor of decentralizing currency—which is to say, taking it out of the hands of governments. These people blamed the government for creating a currency bubble, which burst, leading to the Collapse. They wanted a free-floating currency that couldn't be easily manipulated. Officially, the FCI took no position on any particular virtual currency."

"Unofficially," Selah added, "they were pushing iotas pretty hard. They hosted a big charity auction downtown, ostensibly for providing aid to families that had suffered financial hardship during the Collapse. Lots of high-profile celebrities and businesspeople attended. The usual stuff—get a picture with Priya Mistry, get the hat Cole Banning wore in *December Rain*. I wasn't there, but I knew many people who were. The proceeds went to several local charities. The catch was that all the donations were made in iotas."

"You mean people bid in iotas rather than dollars?" I asked.

"Yes," said Selah. "FCI representatives offered a demonstration of an iota trading app that would allow bidders to exchange dollars for iotas in order to bid. The iotas bid were then transferred to several local charity organizations. Representatives of several corporations—grocery chains, clothing stores, and the like—were on hand to work with the nonprofits to make purchases for their organizations. The businesses gave the charities steep discounts in exchange for the publicity of being involved in the event. All part of a larger scale PR campaign to mainstream iotas as an alternative to the dollar. Among the items auctioned off were nine commemorative coins bearing the iota logo."

"Physical coins symbolizing virtual money," Keane said. "A rather clever gimmick. The coins can't be worth more than a few hundred New Dollars, though. Why do you want them?"

"I only want one," Selah said. "It isn't important why."

"Of course it is," I said. "Presumably you've tried to locate one of these coins yourself and failed, which means that you aren't the only one who wants them. Why? Did someone just discover the coins have a chewy nougat center?"

"I'll pay triple your normal rate," said Selah, ignoring the question.

I groaned. Why did potential clients always play this game? Withhold vital information, making it that much harder to solve the case? "You realize we hate you," I said, trying a different tack.

Selah shrugged. "If I refused to do business with everyone who hated me, I wouldn't be a billionaire. And you'll be happy to know the feeling is mutual. However, it just so happens that Mr. Keane is the best at what he does. If anyone can get his hands on one of those coins, it's Erasmus Keane. Find me one of those coins and I'll wipe the slate clean between us."

I snorted. She tried to kill us, and now she was going to "wipe the slate clean"? Was Selah really that deluded?

Keane nodded absently. "Shake on it?" he said.

"You're not seriously thinking of taking this case," I said, turning to face him. He ignored me.

"I'm not much for physical contact," said Selah. "I'll have a contract sent to your comm."

Keane nodded again. "You're not fooling anyone, you know."

"Excuse me?" said Selah.

"Fowler, give me your gun."

I stared at him. "Why?"

"Just do it," he said. Selah seemed bemused by the demand.

I removed the SIG from its holster and handed it to Keane. He took it from me and pointed it at Selah. Before I could object, he fired two shots at her. Keane handed the gun back to me.

"What the hell?" I asked, taking the smoking gun from Keane.

Miraculously, Selah seemed unharmed. The bullets had left no mark at all. She looked at Keane curiously. "How did you know?" she asked.

"Security was too lax," said Keane. "You'd never have let Fowler get this close to you with a gun on him. You're keeping your distance, staying out of direct light. Your android double over there is still mimicking your movements, even though you don't appear to be near any sort of motion-capture apparatus."

Turning to look, I saw that Keane was right: even now, the android was standing haughtily, its arms crossed over its chest, as if facing down a phantom Erasmus Keane.

"Finally," Keane went on, "the android has only moved about twenty feet from where it was standing during filming, which would seem to imply that you suddenly appeared in this room twenty feet from where you're standing now."

"A hologram," I said, taking a step toward the projection. I could hardly believe it wasn't really her.

"Yes," said Keane. "A very convincing one, at that. The best I've ever seen."

"Cutting-edge proprietary technology," Selah said.

"But why?" I asked. "What's with the ruse, Selah? Or has it gotten to the point where deception is so natural to you that you don't need a reason?"

"It's a security precaution, as Mr. Keane indicated. I also have . . . other reasons for not wanting to be seen."

"That's your choice," said Keane. "But I'm not taking this job unless I can look you in the eye."

"Don't be ridiculous, Mr. Keane," said Selah. "There's no reason for us to meet in person."

"You're hiding something," said Keane. "That's reason enough."

Selah shook her head. "No," she said. "It's out of the question."

"Fine," said Keane. "Fowler, let's go."

I nodded, holstering my gun. I had no desire to work for Selah anyway. We'd find another way to make the rent. We started toward the door, and we were almost there when Selah flickered into existence in front of us. "Wait," she said, holding up her hand, which momentarily disappeared inside my chest. I shuddered. Even at this distance, it was almost impossible to tell she was a projection. Except for the fact that the lighting on her face was a little wrong from this angle—and the fact that her wrist ended at my sternum—I never would have known. "Please be reasonable, Mr. Keane."

"This isn't negotiable, Selah," said Keane. "Either we shake on the deal or Fowler and I walk."

Selah regarded Keane for a moment—or gave the impression of regarding him, anyway; although there were obviously cameras in the room, I didn't think the technology existed for her to see us from the hologram's point of view. Finally she sighed in resignation. "All right," she said. "Go through the door. Turn right. Surrender any weapons to the guard at the end of the hall. Tell him you're here to see Ms. Gray." The hologram disappeared.

"We can still walk out," I said.

"Aren't you curious?" asked Keane.

"Of course I'm curious," I replied. "But I don't want to

have anything to do with that woman. She tried to kill us, Keane."

"You can't take attempted murder personally in this business, Fowler. Come on, let's see what she's hiding."

TWO

Selah Fiore did not look well. Whereas her hologram could have passed for a forty-year-old woman—and a beautiful one at that—the actual Selah looked every bit of her fifty-eight years and then some. It had only been three weeks since I'd last seen her, and she appeared to have aged ten years since then. She was pale and there were bags under her eyes that even professional-grade makeup couldn't hide. She sat slumped in an easy chair, looking exhausted. A scarf covered her—bald?—head, and she wore an unflattering, tight-fitting bodysuit that was presumably part of the motion capture system.

"I took this part before I knew I was dying," Selah said, with no emotion in her voice other than exhaustion. "The voice work is no problem, but I may need a stand-in for the physical parts soon."

"A stand-in for your stand-in," Keane said. He and I were sitting on a plush leather couch across from her. Selah's dressing room was better furnished than most people's houses.

"Yes," said Selah. "No one will know, other than David and a few technicians, of course. It's important to keep up appearances is this business."

A smirk crept across Keane's face. "Even if it means hiring an actor to secretly pose as you to model your actions for an android that will be digitally modified to look like you from thirty years ago."

Selah shrugged. After a long career in Hollywood, these sorts of multilayered illusions were obviously old hat to her.

"What is it?" I asked. "Cancer?"

Selah nodded. "A rare form of leukemia. You'll appreciate this, Mr. Keane. The cancer seems to be a side effect of an experimental rejuvenation treatment I started a few months ago."

"Your quest for immortality is killing you," Keane said, nodding with approval. "I won't deny feeling a bit of *schadenfreude*."

"I was just trying to get a few more years out of this body while I worked out the details of my cloning operation. Now I've probably got less than a year to live, and thanks to you, I have no cloning operation. I trust that you'll keep this information confidential."

"You do realize," I said, "that at some point people are going to figure out you're dead? Or do you plan to 'keep up appearances' after death as well?"

"Thank you for your concern, Mr. Fowler," said Selah. "You'll be relieved to know I have a transition plan in place. I've got a few months left, though, and I intend to make use of them. My primary concern is securing my legacy."

"And somehow getting your hands on one of these iota coins is going to help you do that?" Keane asked.

"Something along those lines," Selah replied. "As I said, my reasons are not your concern."

"And as I said," I answered, "they *are* our concern. If we know the context of your request, we're more likely to be able to anticipate challenges we might face in fulfilling it. In any case, we're going to figure it out. We always do."

"Be that as it may," said Selah, "I'm not telling you any more. All you need to know is that I need one of those coins."

"Do you have a list of the auction bidders?" asked Keane. "Or any leads on who has the coins now?"

Selah shook her head. "FCI was dissolved in 2036. I've been unable to locate any records on bidders or attendees of the auction, other than some public news coverage, which I imagine you, with your prodigious detective skills, can locate as easily as I. Nor do I have any leads on current owners."

"Why won't you tell us why you want the coin?" I asked. "What's the harm in telling us?"

"I'm done meeting your demands, Mr. Fowler. You wanted to see me in person. Here I am, in all my glory. Will you take the case or not?"

"I have one more question," said Keane.

Selah sighed. "What is it, Mr. Keane?"

"If you're able to create such a convincing hologram, why not just film the hologram rather than filming the dummy and transposing your appearance onto it?"

Selah seemed relieved not to have to talk about her health anymore. "The hologram isn't as responsive to stage lighting," she said. "The technology isn't quite there yet to accurately modify the hologram's appearance on the fly in response to ambient lighting changes. Also, it casts no shadow. The android gives us a benchmark for shadows and reflected light. It's easier to combine the lighting effects on the android with a computer-generated image than to try to insert shadows and reflections after the fact. The computer actually erases the android's image from the scene, creates the new composite image on the fly, and inserts the new image into the scene. That's my layperson's understanding, anyway. My people at Empathix are constantly working to improve the technology." Empathix was another part of Selah's empire. They had started off as a market-research company, but had expanded into psychological testing, economic forecasting, and various types of computer modeling and simulation software. I'd heard that they had even developed an augmented reality system for military applications.

"Fascinating," said Keane. "So a physical object is necessary to create a more effective illusion."

"Exactly," replied Selah.

"We'll take the case," said Keane, getting up from the couch.

"We will?" I asked.

Selah leaned forward as if bracing herself to get out of her chair.

"Don't get up," said Keane, walking toward her. He stopped in front of her chair and held out his right hand. Selah took his hand and they shook on it.

"Excellent," Selah replied. "I'll have a contract sent to your comm shortly."

"Triple our normal rate plus expenses. And a ten-thousand-New-Dollar advance."

"Done. I need one of those coins, whatever it costs. Thank you, Mr. Keane."

"Understood," said Keane. "But don't thank me yet. You may yet regret hiring me for this case. As you know, I have a habit of uncovering uncomfortable truths."

"We'll deal with that eventuality when it arises," Selah replied. "I'm dead either way. Good day, gentlemen."

The Case of the Lost Coin was to be the twentieth investigation Keane and I worked together. Technically the coin wasn't lost, but I liked the symmetry with our previous case, the Case of the Lost Sheep. Hopefully this case paid better.

My association with Erasmus Keane had begun three years earlier, on the Case of the Mischievous Holograms. At the time I had been head of security for Canny Simulations, Inc., a company that creates artificially intelligent holograms of celebrities. CSI had the rights to most of the big names: Elvis, Michael Jackson, Beyoncé, Sheila Tong, the Weavil Brothers. A hacker had managed to get into our codebase and was projecting our celebrities all over town: at strip clubs, children's birthday parties . . . Bette Midler showed up at a bowling alley in Van Nuys. The hacker didn't seem to be particularly malicious, but the CSI board of directors was understandably concerned that having unlicensed versions of our biggest names crashing bar mitzvahs in Glendale was diluting our corporate brand. The feds had pretty much given up on trying to enforce piracy laws by this point (this was shortly after the Collapse, so the feds had their hands full with more important things, like domestic terrorism and the threat of Chinese invasion), and the LAPD couldn't be bothered to expend much effort to catch someone who was essentially a high-tech graffiti artist. The board hired Erasmus Keane over my stringent objections, and I insisted that I be present at all of Keane's interactions with CSI personnel. I ended up accompanying Keane during most of the investigation, and spent much of the next three days thoroughly documenting his unprofessionalism, lack of social propriety, neurotic behavior, inability to execute mundane tasks, and poor hygiene. He was like an idiot savant without the savant part. At one point during the investigation, he locked himself in a bathroom stall for over three hours. After I'd gathered what I thought was more than enough evidence to get Keane fired, I asked to address the next board meeting. When I got there, Keane was already in the conference room, laughing it up with the CEO and the rest of the board. With him was a fourteen-year-old kid named Julio Chavez, who was conversing animatedly with Obi-Wan Kenobi, Teddy Roosevelt, and Greta Autenburg, who was the latest teen sensation at the time. Keane had not only found the hacker; he'd convinced the kid to come work for CSI. He's the director of simulation development now.

I'd been so humiliated by this turn of events that I quit my job on the spot. Truth be told, I'd been bored stiff by the corporate security gig; I was basically a glorified mall cop. I'd only taken the job because it seemed like a cushy gig after three years of running security details for VIPs on the Arabian Peninsula. Anyway, it paid better than civilian law enforcement, and at the time I'd had some thoughts of planning for the future. But then Gwen disappeared, and . . . well, by the time dead celebrities started showing up around town, I'd pretty much given up on the future.

Three months after I quit, Keane showed up at my apartment with a job offer, saying I'd been "invaluable" on the hologram case. I almost punched him, thinking he'd come to my door with the sole purpose of making fun of me. Taking my reticence as a bargaining tactic, he upped his offer by twenty grand. When I balked at this, he offered me five grand for my notes on the hologram case. That's when it finally penetrated that he was serious.

I still probably wouldn't have taken the job, but Keane's timing—by chance or design—was fortuitous. I had spent every waking moment since leaving CSI investigating Gwen's disappearance, and had come up with exactly nothing. One day she simply hadn't shown up for work. I'd talked to her the previous night and she had sounded fine. We were planning to see Sheila Tong at the Orpheum that weekend, and Gwen was complaining that she couldn't stay out late because she had to work most of the weekend. She worked for the city-planning department, and they had been short-staffed ever since the Collapse, so she often took work home. She had called me on the way home from work on Wednesday night, and as far as I could tell that was the last time anyone had talked to her. It was unclear whether she ever made it home that night; her last documented location was the parking garage down the street from her office. I had talked to friends, family members, coworkers, neighbors . . . but nobody had a clue what had happened to her. She had vanished into the proverbial thin air.

In any case, by the time Keane showed up with his offer, I was out of leads, nearly out of money, and rapidly sinking into hopelessness and depression. I'm still not certain whether I took the job because I thought Keane could help me find Gwen or because I thought working with him would be an effective distraction from what I knew to be a lost cause.

My official title was Director of Operations, but it became clear in short order that my function was essentially to be Keane's tether to mundane reality. Keane's mind dealt in concepts and abstractions; when it came to routine tasks like keeping case notes or doing laundry, he was hopeless. He subsisted entirely on Lucky Charms, Dr Pepper, and insta-dinners. He dressed in rumpled, mismatched clothing that he bought by the palette directly from a Chinese wholesaler; he wore a set of clothes for a week and then threw it out. Ironically, my first task as Keane's employee was to locate the funds for paying my own salary. Keane possessed a bewildering array of bank accounts and investments, the value of which I eventually established at nearly a million New Dollars, but for those first few weeks I was basically writing myself checks and holding my breath. Thanks to a recent dry spell and Keane's penchant for immediately spending any money we acquired, we were now four months behind on our lease. Hopefully the Case of the Lost Coin would get us back on our feet. That would be small consolation for doing the bidding of the evilest woman on the planet, but money is money.

"I can't believe you agreed to work for Selah Fiore," I said as we waited for a car on the street outside the Flagship lot. Our own aircar had recently exploded due to a misunderstanding with a local gangster, so we were currently dependent on hired cars for transportation. I'd requested a car using my comm as we left the meeting with Selah; the iotas would be automatically deducted from my account.

"We need the money," Keane replied.

"That isn't the reason you took the case," I said.

"No, it isn't," Keane admitted, as the car pulled up. We got in the back. The car was driverless; most cars for hire were these days. It pulled away from the curb, having already been instructed by the app on my comm to transport us to our office.

"So why are we taking it?" I asked.

"Curiosity," said Keane. "I'm dying to know why these coins are so important to Selah. So to speak."

"Just one coin," I corrected.

"Yes, that's interesting as well. Why does she need one of them, but only one? Why isn't two better than one?"

"Has it occurred to you this is a wild-goose chase? Or worse, some sort of trap? Vengeance for us foiling Selah's designs on immortality?"

Keane shook his head. "Why make up a crazy story about wanting a novelty coin if all she wants is revenge? No, there's definitely something important about those coins. Some reason she wants to secure one before she dies."

"So you buy the story about her dying, too?"

Keane nodded absently, staring at his comm display and tapping buttons. "Selah's vanity trumps her mendacity. She genuinely didn't want us to see her in that condition. For whatever reason, she's desperate to get her hands on one of those coins."

"So what's the next step?" I asked.

"Research," Keane replied curtly, still buried in his comm display. I took the hint.

It was going to be a long ride back to the office, so I settled in for a nap. We didn't have the money to hire an aircar, which meant we were stuck taking surface streets around the DZ. The freeways had been gotten so hopelessly snarled with traffic during the Collapse that nobody'd ever been able to unsnarl them. In fact, nobody had even really tried. There seemed to be sort of a general agreement that the Los Angeles freeway system was an experiment that hadn't really worked out, like nuclear power or rap-metal. These days, if you wanted to get somewhere in L.A. you had to take the surface streets, pay to drive on one of the privately funded, ultrafast expressways known as Uberbahns that had been constructed on top of the old highway system, or—if you had the means—take an aircar. Our aircar was currently in a million pieces, as I've mentioned, and we couldn't afford to hire one. Using the Uberbahns was a bit cheaper, but the exits were at least five miles apart, so it wasn't efficient for a trip across town (which was the point, I suppose).

The office was a run-down, three-story building bordering the Disincorporated Zone. Nearly an hour after we'd left Selah, the car pulled up to our building. Keane got out and began to walk to the door. Realizing I wasn't following, he stopped and turned. "Coming, Fowler?"

"Meeting April for dinner," I said.

Keane nodded, still watching his comm screen. He turned, walked to the door, and disappeared inside. I closed the car door. "Secondary destination," I said to my comm, which would send the instruction to the car. "Thai Kitchen on Mission."

The car pulled away from the curb.

Technically, I'd been telling Keane the truth: I did have

dinner plans with my friend April Rooks. But it was only six fifteen, so I had time for another stop before meeting April at seven. It meant walking a few blocks from the restaurant and back, but I couldn't risk Keane checking the trip record and finding the discrepancy.

I got out of the car at Thai Kitchen, then walked south three blocks to the Aloha Motel. I went to the door of room 212, knocked three times, paused, and then knocked twice more. After a moment, I heard a woman's voice from within.

"Fowler?"

"It's me," I said. "Let me in."

The door opened, and I stepped inside. I was met by a tall, thin blond woman wearing a sleeveless T-shirt, Lycra shorts, and gym shoes. I smiled as I saw her.

"Hey, Blake," she said, smiling back at me.

"Hey, Gwen."

THREE

Gwen's hair was pulled back in a ponytail and her pale skin glistened with sweat. The furniture in the motel room had all been pushed to the edges of the room, with the two chairs on top of the small table in the corner, and a small square mat was in the center of the room. Gwen had never been a huge fitness devotee, but her three years in hiding had changed her. She wasn't going to let something like being imprisoned in a motel room keep her from staying in shape. *Imprisoned* was maybe the wrong word; she did leave on occasion, but only at night and in disguise. I don't know what sorts of exercises she'd been doing, but she was thinner and more muscular than she was when we'd been dating. She looked good.

"Good to see you, Blake. It's been a few days."

"Sorry," I said. "Been really busy." This was a lie, of course. I'd had very little to do over the past several days, which ironically made it harder to make excuses to get out and see Gwen.

"Any news?" she asked.

Gwen had shown up unannounced at our office three weeks ago, ending her mysterious absence of three years. She had been anxious and paranoid, as you might expect from someone who had good reason to believe her life was in danger. I'd only been able to get her to tell me the rough outline of what had happened—most of which I already knew, thanks to Keane and Selah Fiore. Gwen had insisted on keeping her reappearance secret from Keane, and I'd done my best to abide by this request—against my better judgment. I didn't entirely trust Keane, either, but I didn't think he had any reason to want harm to come to Gwen. In any case, Keane tended to figure things out no matter how secretive I was, and at some point we were likely to need his help. But Gwen insisted on keeping him out of the loop until we had a better idea of the threat she still faced.

That threat evidently had something to do with a task force Gwen had been part of, some ten years earlier. As I mentioned, Gwen had worked for the Los Angeles Department of Planning. She, along with several other city, state, and county employees, had been recruited to work for a group called the Los Angeles Future Foundation, which was nominally a nonprofit organization devoted to advancing sustainable urban growth. Gwen and the others were put on a Civil Unrest Preparedness Task Force, which was tasked with devising a plan for "long-term prioritization of city services in the event of a large-scale civil unrest and a complete breakdown of the government at the federal and state levels." What Gwen didn't realize at the time was that this wasn't a hypothetical exercise: LAFF had somehow known the Collapse was coming. But by the time Gwen realized LAFF wasn't who she thought they were, it was too late to get out.

So Gwen and the others—mostly mid-level city and county employees—had done their job, developing a plan to deal with a case of widespread civil unrest in Southern California. It became evident during the development of this plan, however, that the government simply didn't have the resources to deal with the sort of large-scale riots, demonstrations, and general chaos that LAFF was expecting, no matter how much advance warning they had. The solution was to cede a large section of the city to the chaos. The primary architect of this "Disincorporated Zone," I had recently discovered, was the man I knew as Erasmus Keane. He and Gwen had worked on LAFF's task force together—although he hadn't gone by the name Erasmus Keane then.

When the Collapse happened, the LAPD and National Guard were instructed to protect and fortify "vital areas" of the city, while leaving a conglomeration of poorer areas completely undefended, as the task force's plan recommended. A vast swath of the city, including South Los Angeles, Compton, and Huntington Park, became essentially a free-range prison. Temporary police barriers became concrete walls topped with razor wire, and any pretense of equality under the law evaporated. If you had the misfortune to live in the DZ post-Collapse, you were automatically suspect. The breakdown of the freeway system made it easy to control movements in and out of the DZ; checkpoints were set up with the ostensible purpose of identifying terrorists and other criminals and to stem the flow of illegal drugs and weapons. The drugs were usually coming out of the DZ; the weapons were going in.

It took almost a decade for the legal formalities to catch up to the harsh reality of the situation: the majority of the residents of the DZ at the time of the Collapse were undocumented immigrants, and the legal status of tens of thousands of others was thrown into question by the loss of records during the Collapse and subsequent years of near-anarchy while the state and federal governments were re-constituted. In many areas of the country the legacy of the Collapse was little more than a temporary lapse in government services, with local governments and ad hoc civilian organizations picking up the slack. But in the DZ, the Collapse was near-total. Income taxes went unpaid, vehicles went unregistered, children were born without birth certificates. Criminal enterprises burgeoned. By some estimates, over 90 percent of economic activity in the DZ was off the books. By the time anyone started to get a handle on the scope of the problem, there was neither the will nor the means to re-incorporate the DZ into American society. Los Angeles had given birth to a third-world country within its borders, and nobody seemed to know what to do about it. There was a lot of blame to go around, and plenty of people in the city government lost their jobs, but the task force—and LAFF's involvement in the Collapse—remained secret, and eventually things went more or less back to normal. It was around that time that Gwen disappeared.

I learned later that everyone on the task force had either been murdered or had vanished under suspicious circumstances. There had been such a surge in violent crime in the years immediately after the Collapse that no one had even noticed the pattern. Nobody, that is, except for Gwen Thorson. After a few of her former colleagues disappeared, Gwen had gone into hiding in the DZ. She'd been there until just over three weeks ago, when instability in the DZ began to cause her to fear for her safety. She wasn't safe in L.A. proper, either, but hiding in the DZ was apparently no longer an option, for reasons I didn't quite understand.

I knew more about LAFF and the Collapse than just about anybody, but I still had a lot of nagging questions—the most pressing of these being: who had targeted the members of the Civil Unrest Preparedness Task Force for assassination? If LAFF had wanted them dead, they would have killed them as soon as the task force disbanded, not waited six years. I also hadn't figured out how Gwen had managed to disappear so quickly, and so thoroughly that even Erasmus Keane couldn't find her. She must have had help, but so far I hadn't been able to get her to admit to anything.

"Keane and I met a client this morning," I said. "Selah Fiore."

"You're working for Selah Fiore?" asked Gwen, unable to hide her surprise.

"Looks that way," I said. "Not my choice. She tricked me into agreeing to meet her."

"Tricked you how?"

"She said she had information about you."

"And did she?" Gwen asked.

I let the question hang in the air for a moment. "You sound worried."

Gwen shrugged, trying to appear nonchalant. "Just curious."

"Come on, Gwen. It's been three weeks. Either you trust me or you don't. I don't like the idea that Selah Fiore might know more than I do about what you've been doing for the past three years. That was a very uncomfortable meeting."

"Gosh, Blake, was it?" Gwen said. "I've been hiding in the DZ, looking over my shoulder for the past three years, but clearly you're the real victim here."

"Damn it, Gwen," I said. "I'm trying to help you here. I'm already running around behind Keane's back trying to keep him from finding out about you—"

"You didn't tell him, did you?"

"Of course not," I said. "I promised I wouldn't. Although I don't know how you expect to figure out who was behind the murders of the task force members when you spend all day cooped up in a motel room, and I'm spending half my time covering my tracks from the most brilliant detective in Los Angeles."

"I never asked you to help me look into the task-force murders."

"Then what are you doing here? Why did you come to me?"

"Going to you was a mistake. I appreciate your attempts to help, Blake, but you're never going to figure out who killed those people. I've been trying for three years."

"How much investigating could you do from your hideout in the DZ? Keane and I have resources—"

"Forget it, Blake. You're just putting yourself in danger. Get on with your life. I'll be fine."

"Here in the Aloha Motel."

"I don't plan to stay here forever. Once the DZ cools down—"

"Have you been watching the news, Gwen? The DZ is worse than ever. Almost as bad as right after the Collapse. Gerard Canaan was just on TV yesterday, talking about how they were going to have to send the National Guard in."

"Gerard Canaan the oil guy?"

"He's out of the oil business," I said. "He seems to have adopted the DZ as his personal cause. Wants to try to turn it around, reintegrate it into Los Angeles."

"That's just what the DZ needs," said Gwen. "Another martyr yearning for redemption."

I shrugged. "The point is, Canaan's a smart guy. If he thinks the DZ is going to implode, I'd take him seriously."

Gerard Canaan was an oilman from Bakersfield who had gradually built his company, Elysium Oil, into one of the largest energy firms in the world. Then the Wahhabi coup in Saudi Arabia caught him off guard and he lost almost everything. Over the past few years, though, he'd made something of a name for himself as an investor in Southern California real estate. Lately he'd been spearheading a push to get the city, county, state, and federal governments to rebuild the

DZ, but government officials were wary of taking on big projects in the wake of the Collapse. There was also suspicion that certain powerful individuals—Selah Fiore among them—had a vested interest in keeping the DZ lawless. Meanwhile the DZ continued to deteriorate.

"The National Guard isn't going to take over the DZ," said Gwen. "The government doesn't want to take responsibility for that shithole."

"Well, if they do, you'll have no place to hide anymore. And if they don't, the DZ's going to remain a war zone for the foreseeable future. Either way, you can't go back there."

"I'll figure something out."

"For Christ's sake, Gwen. If you tell me what's going on, maybe I can help you. Does Selah know something? I know she was involved with LAFF. Did you work out some kind of deal with her?"

Gwen let out a long sigh. "If I tell you, it doesn't leave this room."

"Of course not. Come on."

Gwen nodded slowly, staring out the gauzy curtain of the motel window. "Yes," she said at last. "I had an arrangement with Selah."

"What sort of arrangement?"

"I told you how I was recruited by LAFF, right?"

"Yeah, they wanted you to be part of some Civil Preparedness Task Force. To develop a plan for the city to deal with the Collapse."

"Yes, although of course we didn't know about the Collapse at the time. We just thought we were working on a sort of worst-case-scenario handbook. I know it seems sinister in retrospect, but at the time it was just another project. And to be honest, it was a lot of fun. These were people who spent forty hours a week banging their heads against government bureaucracy, and they were finally given free rein to create something."

"You never told me any of this when we were dating," I said.

"I was under a strict nondisclosure agreement, as I said. I wasn't even allowed to discuss who was in these meetings with other people in my department."

"And that didn't strike you as strange?" I asked.

"It did, actually," she said. "But it was also exciting. I think they were counting on that. Counting on us to be so enthralled by the idea of being on this elite team that we wouldn't ask too many questions. Two members of the task force were dismissed early on for talking about task force business outside our meetings. Not long after that, they both lost their jobs as well. It was hinted to the remaining task force members that those two had said too much. We took the hint."

"Okay," I said. "Go on."

"The intelligence we were given gradually got more specific," she said. "Occasionally documents marked 'classified' found their way into our meetings. Documents from various federal agencies. Housing and Urban Development. The Department of Energy. The Justice Department. Even the CIA and NSA. There was no way we were authorized to look at this stuff. Eventually, I think we all realized it was a trap, but it was too late. We had knowingly consumed and passed on to each other top secret information. We could all have been thrown in federal prison for life."

"So you did what they asked."

"We had no choice," Gwen replied. "We developed a plan, like they asked. I did look into LAFF a bit on my own, but I came up with nothing. It was a privately funded organization that didn't disclose its donors. It had almost no legal footprint, just a few vaguely worded consulting contracts with various government agencies. The people we thought were LAFF employees were just lawyers on retainer. We never talked to anyone who had ever met an actual LAFF employee. The whole organization was just a shadow."

"You could have gone to the police. The FBI."

"Sure," said Gwen. "I could have walked into the local FBI office with a stack of classified documents, but I had no guarantee anyone else on the task force would back me up. LAFF would set me up as the fall guy and disband the task force. And even if the feds believed me, then what? I'd never met anyone who worked for LAFF. Just a few lawyers whose real names I didn't know. Those lawyers would scatter like cockroaches as soon as the FBI got involved."

"But you could have stopped it. Stopped Maelstrom."

"Maybe," said Gwen. "But at that point I wasn't sure stopping it was desirable."

"Why not?" I asked. "Thousands of people died, Gwen."

"In the Collapse," Gwen said. "The Collapse was going to happen either way. All we did is cauterize the wound. The result was . . . unpleasant, but it would have been worse without Maelstrom."

I shook my head. "I don't understand. If LAFF is so insidious and powerful, why did they need you in the first place? Evidently they had access to all sorts of sensitive information. Why couldn't they just design this post-Collapse survival plan themselves?"

"You're not listening, Blake," said Gwen. "There is no 'themselves.' There are no LAFF employees. They don't do anything. They're a virtual organization that exists only on paper. They hire consulting firms to hire lawyers to put together semi-official groups like our task force. They found the people capable of doing the job they needed done and manipulated them into doing it, completely in secret. And at the same time, they hide in plain sight. Hell, LAFF has a public Web site. You can read all about the wonderful work they're doing to help plan a sustainable future for Los Angeles."

"All right," I said. "So you come up with this emergency response plan. The Collapse happens right on schedule. The plan gets implemented, and the DZ is created just as you envisioned. Then what?"

Gwen shrugged. "Then we went back to work. Most of us did, anyway. A few got laid off; one woman quit because she got sick of getting IOUs from the city instead of a paycheck. But the rest of us went back to our normal lives—as much as we could during the Collapse, anyway."

"That's it? You just went back to work?"

"Pretty much," said Gwen. "Until about six years later, when people who'd been involved in the task force started dying under mysterious circumstances."

"So you decided to disappear," I said. "You could have told me."

"Not without risking your life as well," she replied. "I didn't know who was killing the task force members or why, so the less you knew, the better."

"I could have protected you," I protested. "This is what I do. I—"

"Not against these people, Blake. I couldn't risk it. In any case, there was no time. I had one chance to get out and I took it."

"What chance?"

"I'd saved some documents from Maelstrom. I was supposed to have handed them all over at the end of the project, but I copied some that I thought might give me some leverage. I was right."

"What were they?" I asked.

"Projections having to do with using the media to manipulate public opinion about the DZ. They weren't labeled as such, but it was pretty clear from the contents that the projections had come from someone inside Selah Fiore's organization, Flagship Media. And I was convinced that Selah Fiore would have been in on something like that. I didn't have enough evidence to prove anything, though, so I did the next best thing."

"You bluffed."

"Right," said Gwen. "I called up Selah and told her I had some documents linking her to a certain high-profile non-profit organization. She agreed to meet me. I told her that the documents would remain in my possession, hidden from public view, as long as I was alive. We came to an agreement."

"Selah helped you disappear?"

"Yes. Gave me an alternate identity in the DZ, under the protection of a certain warlord I believe you know."

"Mag-Lev."

Gwen nodded.

Mag-Lev was the most powerful warlord in the DZ, and as luck would have it, Keane and I had recently had a run-in with him as well: he's the guy who blew up our car. I suppose it wasn't really luck, though: Mag-Lev owed his position to Selah's influence as well. So it made sense that when Selah needed to help Gwen disappear, she asked for Mag-Lev's help.

"Dangerous getting in bed with Mag-Lev," I said.

"No more dangerous than Selah Fiore," Gwen replied. "At first Selah suggested I hide out in one of the LAFF safe houses."

"LAFF had safe houses?"

"Yeah. I don't think they ever used them for anything, but the idea was that if a LAFF agent was stuck in the DZ while riots or fighting was going on, they could get to one of these safe houses and lay low for a few days."

"But whoever was knocking off the Maelstrom people might have known about the safe houses."

"Right," said Gwen. "Which was why I told Selah no. That's when she approached Mag-Lev."

"How did you know Selah wasn't behind the task-force murders?"

"I didn't," said Gwen. "I took a chance. I was at her mercy. If Selah had wanted to have me killed any time over the past three years, she could have done it. She knew exactly where I was. I was living under the identity of Kathryn Buchanan in an apartment in Willowbrook."

"But something happened a few weeks ago to make you think you weren't safe there anymore."

"I told you: the DZ has been more on edge than usual. Lots of gang shootings, turf battles, and the like. The DZ has always been a rough place, but it's downright terrifying these days."

"There's more to it than that."

"Yes," Gwen said. "Things have been strained lately between Selah and Mag-Lev. If they had a falling out, things were going to go very badly for me."

I nodded. "It's good you got out when you did. If Selah had known where you were when Keane and I uncovered her cloning operation, she'd have used you against us."

"So here I am," said Gwen. "Three years later, and I still don't know who was trying to kill me or why. Or if they still want me dead. I don't even know for sure somebody *did* intend to kill me."

"It's a safe bet," I said, "considering what happened to the other task force members. Except for Keane, of course."

"Yeah," said Gwen. "It's funny how Keane managed to get out alive."

"You said yourself Erasmus Keane isn't his real name. He changed his identity so he wouldn't be found."

"Changed his identity and then proceeded to become a

local celebrity private investigator. It's almost like he doesn't believe he's in any real danger."

"You don't seriously think Keane was behind the murders of the task-force members."

"Behind them? Probably not. But he may have been in on them. I don't trust him, Blake. I never have."

I had to admit, she had a point. And the truth was, I didn't fully trust Erasmus Keane, either. He'd lied to me for three years, pretending he had no idea what had happened to Gwen, when he knew about Gwen's involvement with LAFF all along. Even his name was a lie; he had never told me his real name. That said, it was a lie to which he was fully committed. Whoever he once was, he was now 100 percent dedicated to the character he was playing. So in a weird way, I did trust him: I trusted him to be Erasmus Keane.

"So what did Selah hire you to do?" Gwen asked.

I gave Gwen a rundown of our meeting with Selah.

"Interesting," Gwen said. "And you definitely got the impression that she only wanted one of these coins? Any one of them, but only one?"

I regarded Gwen curiously. "That's what she said. Why, do you know something about these coins?"

Gwen shrugged. "I remember hearing about the auction at the time. I can't imagine why anybody would hire Erasmus Keane to find one. They're just novelty items, aren't they?"

"Keane is researching them now. Hopefully he doesn't find one too quickly. A few days' work at triple our normal rate would get us close to current on our lease."

"There are easier ways to make money," Gwen said. "Speaking as someone who got sucked into doing business with Selah Fiore some time ago, I'd suggest running as fast as you can in the opposite direction."

"I'll take it under advisement," I said. "Sorry, Gwen. Gotta go."

"Thanks for stopping by, Blake."

I left and hurried back to the restaurant. On the way, my comm chirped, signaling I'd received a text message. I stopped to look at the display. The sender was identified as "Lila." The message read, simply:

welcome to the game

FOUR

Being late for dinner with April, I didn't have time to ruminate on the meaning of this message. Most likely it was a mistake; I didn't know anybody named Lila. I ran the rest of the way back to the restaurant. Fortunately, April was running a few minutes late, so I had time to splash water on my face in the bathroom and cool off a bit. I exited the bathroom to see April sitting in a corner booth.

I joined her, and we ordered: pad thai for her, butter chicken curry for me. April had gotten in the habit of paying when we went out; thanks to our disastrous last case and general lack of business lately, I'd been putting everything on credit for some time. While we ate, I gave April a summary of the day's events thus far. I'd already told her about Gwen. Gwen would kill me if she knew, but I trusted April and valued her counsel about these things. Besides, if something happened to me, I wanted there to be at least one other person who knew about Gwen.

"So you're working for the woman who tried to kill us," said April. "That's an interesting choice."

"It wasn't my idea," I said.

"Is that supposed to make me feel better? If all your friends went to work for a narcissistic megalomaniac—"

"Can we not have this discussion right now?" I said. "I get it. I'm responsible for my actions."

"I didn't say it was a bad idea," April replied. "Selah must be pretty desperate to get her hands on one of these coins if she hired you. Any idea why she wants it?"

"Not a clue," I said.

"And you still haven't told Keane about Gwen?"

"Can't," I said. "I promised Gwen I wouldn't."

"You told me."

"That's different," I said. "She doesn't know about you."

"You mean she doesn't even know I exist? Did you leave out my heroic turn when you told her about our escape from Selah?"

"Did you have a heroic turn?" I asked, furrowing my brow. "Mostly I remember you getting kidnapped a lot."

"See if I help you again."

"You'll help me," I said. "You find me irresistible. Also, your job is incredibly boring, so you look forward to the distraction."

"One of those statements is true," April said. "I don't like you keeping secrets from Keane."

"Keeping secrets from Keane!" I exclaimed. "You know he lied to me for three years about Gwen, right?"

"Yes, but that's Keane," April said. "Lying is his idiom."

"I don't have any idea what that means."

"Look," said April. "I once dated a guy who would stop talking to me when he got upset. I mean, not full-on silent treatment, but he would just sort of shut down, answering questions with a simple yes or no, and when I pressed him on it, he'd deny anything was wrong. It was maddening. I tried everything I could think of to get him to communicate with me, but nothing worked. Finally I had the brilliant idea of using his own tactic against him. So I shut down and stopped talking to him. You know what happened?"

"You broke up?"

"Nope. We just stopped talking. As far as I know, we're still dating, although I haven't talked to him for six years."

"This is a fantastic story," I said.

"The point is, it was stupid of me to try to beat him at his own game. Silence isn't my idiom."

"I'm not going to argue with you on that one," I said. "But Keane and I aren't dating."

"No," she said, "but the dynamic is the same. Keane lies because he's Keane. You knew who he was when you started working for him."

"So what's my idiom?" I asked.

"That's for you to figure out," said April.

I rolled my eyes. April had a tendency to lapse into self-help book truisms at times.

My comm chirped. It was Keane. I answered.

"Where are you?" Keane asked.

"Dinner with April, remember?"

"Get back here. We need to talk to an expert about these coins." He ended the call.

"You need a ride?" April asked.

"Yeah."

"If you want, you can borrow my car. Just drop me off at my condo."

"Do you mind?"

"Of course not," said April. "I just need the car back in time to get to my boring job tomorrow."

"It's a good thing you find me irresistible."

"Don't push it."

While I was talking with Gwen and April, Keane had done some digging on the iota coins. Evidently he'd been unable to find a single coin on sale online at any price, although two had sold recently at more than double the asking price—to the same anonymous buyer. He had been unable to find any information on the original buyers of the other coins, not even a list of attendees at the auction hosted by the Free Currency Initiative in 2032. Keane prided himself on his encyclopedic knowledge in just about every field, but after running into several dead ends, he decided it was time to talk to an expert. His "expert" in this case turned out to be a man named Kwang-hyok Kim, the owner of a pawnshop in Koreatown. Among other things, Kim dealt in collectible coins, and Keane thought he might have some insight into the value of the physical iotas.

Koreatown was on the other side of the DZ, so once again we had a long drive ahead of us. It didn't help that we got stuck behind a caravan of military vehicles on Mission for twenty minutes. This was happening more and more often; the rumor was that a private paramilitary firm called Green River was building a big training facility in the desert south of Riverside, so they were constantly transporting supplies and personnel from the city. Paramilitary organizations were a growth industry; after the coup in Saudi Arabia, the U.S. military had scaled back their military presence in the Middle East, leaving a vacuum to be filled by nongovernmental organizations. So it made sense they'd built a training facility in the Southern California desert; the climate was similar to the Arabian Peninsula's, at least in the summer. I'd spent a few summers in Saudi Arabia, and I didn't miss it.

While we were stuck in traffic, Keane told me what he had found out about the coins—which wasn't much.

"Just to clarify," I said, "these coins aren't actually worth anything, right?"

"Officially they had no cash value, in either dollars or iotas," said Keane. "But of course they were limited-edition coins made especially for a high-profile event, so they are of some value to collectors."

"But how much could a coin like that possibly be worth, even to a collector?" I asked. "They're only eight years old. Even if it was made of solid gold, it wouldn't be worth more than a few hundred New Dollars."

Keane nodded. "Whatever value that coin has, it derives from an attribute other than its composition or numismatic interest."

"Like what?" I asked.

"Difficult to say," Keane replied. "But I suspect that Selah's interest in the iota coin is somehow linked to the value of the iota currency."

That didn't make any sense to me. Coins had their face value and their numismatic value. How could the value of the coin be linked to the value of the currency if the coin had a face value of zero? But then, I wasn't sure I understood where the value of the virtual iotas came from, either. The more I thought about it, the less sense it made. Iotas were literally just ones and zeroes stored on a memory drive; they shouldn't have any value at all. I broke down and asked Keane to explain it.

Keane nodded. "You're talking about the bootstrapping problem," he said.

"I am?"

"Sure. Money is essentially a collective delusion, as we saw during the Collapse. Dollars were valuable only as long as people believed they were valuable. Once doubt began to nibble at the edges of the delusion, speculators began dumping dollars in favor of hard assets, and the worry became self-fulfilling. Suddenly nobody wanted dollars anymore, and the value cratered. Eventually the feds stepped in with a restructuring plan and the dollar stabilized at about five percent of its previous value, but for a while there it was flirting with its actual, real-world value."

"Nothing," I said.

"Very nearly," said Keane. "Paper money that nobody believes in is worth slightly less than toilet paper. So the question is: how did the federal government fool people into thinking this worthless paper was valuable for so long?"

"Well," I said, "originally it was backed by gold, wasn't it?"

"Originally it *was* gold," said Keane. "Or silver. Later, coins made from precious metals were replaced by bills that could be exchanged for a specified amount of gold. In effect, these bills were symbols representing something valuable—and once you can convince people to accept a symbol of something in place of the thing, you're well on your way toward generating the requisite collective delusion required for fiat currency. Nixon took us off the gold standard in 1971. After that, dollars were backed by 'the full faith and credit of the United States treasury.' The U.S. rode its reputation for another forty-seven years, but ultimately a note that isn't backed by anything is worthless. A symbol without a referent. But it's worth noting that the delusion lasted for nearly half a century. So the problem facing anyone launching a new form of currency is: how do you cultivate that delusion? It's easy enough to do if you've got a big pile of silver or gold or platinum or uranium—something that has universally recognized value. Otherwise you have to somehow convince people that other people think your money is valuable. It has to pull itself up by its own bootstraps. That's the bootstrapping problem."

We'd arrived at the pawnshop. I followed Keane inside, where a man I assumed was Kwang-hyok Kim hunched over a counter stacked high with oddities and bric-a-brac. I'm not the greatest at estimating either heights or ages, but I would guess this guy was about two feet tall and three hundred years old. I may be exaggerating slightly. In any case, he was very small and very old, and he talked incredibly fast in a language that I deduced, with my professional detective skills, was Korean.

Mr. Kim was either very happy to see Keane or very angry at him; I honestly could not tell which. He started barking at Keane the moment we stepped into the store, which was filled with the usual pawnshop goodies: chain saws, blenders, microwave ovens, jewelry, guns, leather jackets, motorcycle helmets, etc. And coins. Lots and lots of coins. I studied these while Keane spoke with Kim.

Keane responded to each of Kim's successive outbursts in measured tones, also in Korean. I knew Keane spoke Spanish; apparently he also spoke Korean. I wondered how many other languages he spoke. There was a lot I didn't know about Keane.

Eventually Kim calmed down to the point where Keane was able to ask him about the iota. At least that's what I assumed was happening; the only word I was able to make out was *iota*. Kim shook his head and shouted out another indecipherable string of syllables. When he'd finished, Keane spoke again.

Kim nodded and grumbled something in reply. Then he disappeared into a back room, returning after a moment with a very large book. He slapped the book down on the counter and opened it to a page somewhere near the middle. He tapped his finger on the page, and I came up next to Keane to see what he was pointing at.

It was a silver-colored coin, pictured front and back. On the back was an engraving of an insect, perhaps a dragonfly. Below the insect was a very small number 3. On the front was a symbol that looked like a backward J. Underneath the symbol were the words "Not One Iota."

"Clever," I said.

Keane nodded. "This is not a pipe," he said.

"Huh?" I replied

"*The Treachery of Images*," Keane muttered. "René Magritte. The symbol is not the thing."

I didn't ask. Looking back at the book, I saw that below the picture was a paragraph of text:

(Not One) Iota Coin. Minted 2033. Mint: Unknown. Composition: Titanium alloy. Limited edition, nine known to be in existence. Produced as part of a publicity campaign to promote the iota virtual currency. Pictured is coin with serial number 3. Current market value: $N400

I frowned as I read the last part. "Four hundred New Dollars?" I asked. "Selah hired us to find a coin worth four hundred New Dollars?"

Keane asked Kim another question, and Kim rattled off another flurry of syllables.

"Says the price has spiked recently," Keane said. "He had one in the store last week. Serial number 2. Somebody bought it."

They had another brief exchange.

"Says the guy paid six hundred. Wishes he'd held out for more. Last week, two others—serial numbers 1 and 8—sold on eBay for eight hundred each. This morning he heard a dealer in Santa Barbara got a thousand for the one pictured in the book. Serial number 3."

"A thousand New Dollars," I said. "Selah Fiore probably has that in her couch cushions."

"You're missing the point, Fowler," Keane said.

"Which is?"

Keane said something to Kim, and Kim barked something back at him. Keane replied in a stern but conciliatory tone.

Kim sighed and grabbed a pen and paper. He jotted something down and handed it to Keane. Keane bowed slightly to Kim and then walked out of the store. I followed. Kim yelled something at me as I walked out. I just smiled and waved.

"What's with that guy?" I asked, as I caught up to him on the sidewalk.

"Mr. Kim? He was one of my first clients. Hired me to find his wife. He's still upset about it."

"You never found her?"

"No, I did," Keane said. "He can't stand her. Only hired me because her family was haranguing him. She was perfectly happy shacking up with a car salesman across town. Now they're stuck with each other. Some cases are better left unsolved."

"So it would seem," I said. "Inside, you said I was missing the point about the coins. What did you mean?"

"The point," said Keane, "is that demand for those coins is increasing. Actual prices are a lagging indicator of demand. There is no way to know at this point just how great the demand is. Maybe one of those coins is worth killing over."

"How is that possible?" I asked.

"That I don't know."

My comm was chiming. The display read "Selah Fiore."

"What is it, Selah?" I asked.

"Mr. Fowler?" I heard Selah say. "There has been a development in the case."

"What kind of development?" I asked.

"I can't tell you over the comm. I need you and Keane to come to my house right away."

"Look, Selah," I said, "we're not going to—"

The call terminated.

FIVE

I tried calling Selah back, but there was no answer.

"Now what?" I asked.

"We go to Selah's house."

"That seems like a bad idea."

"You're only saying that because you think taking this case was a bad idea."

"Correct."

"Too bad. We're committed now. Drive."

I sighed but pulled away from the curb and headed toward Selah's house. Selah lived near the top of a ridge in the Hollywood Hills. It would have been a ten-minute ride by aircar, but we didn't have that option. The sun was already setting; we wouldn't get there until well after dark. I called April on the way to let her know I'd need her car a bit longer.

The drive ended up taking almost an hour. I parked in the driveway and Keane and I walked to the front door. It was ajar. From inside, I heard a woman's voice speaking in agitated tones, but I couldn't make out what she was saying.

I held my finger to my lips and drew my gun. Pushing the door open, I stepped quietly inside, finding myself in a large foyer. Selah Fiore was standing across the room with her hands on her hips.

"Excuse me," Selah said. "What do you think you're doing?"

"The door was open," I said. "Are you all right?"

"You can't come in here," Selah said. "Get out."

"For fuck's sake, Selah," I said. "We just drove an hour to get here. I rang the—"

"Fowler," said Keane behind me. "That's not Selah."

"What do you mean?" I said. "Of course it's . . ." But I saw now that this Selah was not the exhausted, hollowed out woman I'd seen in the dressing room, but the version I'd seen on the soundstage. It was Selah the way she'd appeared three weeks earlier, when she was still healthy. She seemed to be regarding me with fear.

"The hologram," I said. "But why . . . ?"

"I said get out!" Selah shouted. "Get away from me! You can't—" She broke off and then turned to her right, as if facing someone Keane and I couldn't see. "No, please!" she cried. "I'm not well. What do you want?" Selah's form jerked backward, and suddenly she was sitting in an invisible chair. Her eyes darted back and forth, as if two people were standing over her. "I don't know!" she cried after a moment. "No! That whole operation was shut down. He should know that. Please . . . no. No!" Her head turned to the side and her arms moved tightly against her sides, as if she were being tied to the chair. Her head jerked back and she winced. "Please," she said. "This is a misunderstanding. Just call—"

With that, the projection disappeared. I moved across the room, my gun at the ready. Was Selah in the house some-where, trying to use the hologram to call for help? As I passed the spot where the hologram had been, I heard Selah's voice behind me. "Excuse me," she said. "What do you think you're doing?"

I spun around to see the hologram once again. Selah was now facing away from me, repeating her lines from a moment earlier. "You can't come in here," she appeared to be saying to Keane, who was regarding the projection with interest. "Get out!"

"It's a recording," I said. "Stuck on a loop."

"Yes," said Keane. "Curious."

I made my way down the hall until I came to the open door of a study. Behind me, Selah continued to plead with invisible intruders.

"I said get out! Get away from me! You can't—"

Peering inside the study, I saw the body of Selah Fiore, duct taped to a chair, her head hanging limply on her chest.

"Keane!" I said. "Help!" I ran to Selah, holstering my gun. I felt her neck: no pulse. She didn't appear to be breathing, either. The Selah in the foyer continued to protest. "No, please! I'm not well. What do you want?"

Keane came into the room and rushed to my side.

"Forget it," I said. "She's dead."

"Still warm," he said, feeling her neck.

"Look," I said, pointing to her neck. "Syringe mark."

Keane nodded.

"I'm going to check the rest of the house," I said. "Stay here."

I went through the house, gun drawn, but it seemed to be empty. Eventually I reached a pair of French doors looking out on a covered patio. Lying on the pressed concrete floor, in a pool of blood, was a large man in khaki pants and a green polo shirt. An HK automatic rifle lay next to him.

I exited through the doors and crouched down next to the man. He had a bullet hole in his forehead, and his eyes were open and fixed in place. A few feet away, lying in the fetal position in a corner, was another man, similarly dressed and armed. He was pretty clearly dead as well. Abrasions on his neck indicated he'd been strangled with some kind of cord.

If I had to guess, I'd have said the first guy was shot in place from somewhere on the ridge overlooking the back of

Selah's house. The second guard was killed later and dragged out here with his comrade—quietly enough that Selah had been surprised when she finally laid eyes on the assassin. These guys—assuming there was more than one—were pros.

I went back into the house and found Keane studying the hologram, which was going through its script for the umpteenth time:

I said get out! Get away from me! You can't . . . No, please! I'm not well.

"The projector control is on Selah's desk," Keane said. "It's locked."

What do you want?

"Meaning what?" I asked, coming up next to him and holstering my gun.

"Meaning that someone seems to have intentionally set her little speech up to repeat. Selah must have set it up to greet visitors, but her killers programmed it to endlessly repeat the last few seconds before she was subdued."

"To lure us into the house," I said. "We see an open door, hear Selah's voice, and go inside. But why? There's no one here."

I don't know!

"Security cameras," Keane said, glancing at the ceiling. "Somebody wanted to record us walking into Selah's house."

No! That whole operation was shut down. He should know that. Please . . . no. No!

"To frame us for her murder."

Please, this is a misunderstanding. Just call—

"Perhaps," said Keane.

"Then who called us?"

"Could have been Selah," Keane said. "She hasn't been dead long."

"She didn't sound like she was under duress."

Keane shrugged. "She's an actress. But maybe it was a sim, or someone using a voice modulator."

"Using Selah's comm."

Excuse me. What do you think you're doing?

"Yes."

"Well, whoever did this, they're professionals," I said. "Took out two trained bodyguards before Selah even knew they were here. Maybe somebody else who wants those coins?"

You can't come in here. Get out.

"Could be," said Keane. "Seems like a bit of an overreaction, though, considering our progress on the case so far. What interests me, though, is how they killed her."

"Poison?" I asked, thinking of the syringe mark.

I don't know!

"I don't think so," said Keane. "No signs of poisoning. Eyes are bloodshot. I think she was asphyxiated."

No! That whole operation was shut down. He should know that. Please . . . no. No!

"Then why the syringe?"

"Interrogation," said Keane. "They were trying to get her to tell them something. And they were at it awhile."

Please, this is a misunderstanding. Just call—

"How do you know that?"

"Selah's office window faces west. Come here and look at the hologram."

The form of Selah reappeared in front of us and began its spiel again. Keane and I walked around to view it from Selah's right side. Something had looked a little off about the projection, and now that I really looked, I saw what it was: Selah had a slight orange glow on her right cheek.

"Sunlight," I said.

Keane nodded. "Late afternoon. The sun set about an hour ago. Selah's been dead not much longer than that. They had her in that chair, alive, for at least two hours. Presumably they got what they wanted, suffocated her, and then faked that call to us. The question is, what 'operation' was she talking about?"

"The cloning program, maybe," I said.

"Or Maelstrom," Keane replied.

My heart sank. What if Selah had told the killers about Gwen? *Don't panic*, I told myself. Selah didn't know where Gwen was. Did she?

"Should we call the police?" I asked.

Keane shook his head. "Whoever set up that hologram probably hacked the surveillance system, too. If they intend to frame us for Selah's murder, they'll doctor the recording to make it look like we killed her."

"That's a pretty big assumption."

"And if they don't, then the recording will exonerate us. Either way, there's no reason to involve the police, unless you think they're going to be of some help to us in solving this case."

"Good point," I said. "We should get out of here."

"Agreed."

Selah was still pleading with her killers when we left.

The road back into the city from Selah's was a tortuous series of switchbacks in the Hollywood Hills. Ordinarily I would have enjoyed the drive in April's Mustang, but all I could think about was Gwen. If the people who killed Selah were the same people who had eliminated the task force members, then it made sense that they would have interrogated her to find out where Gwen was. The only question was whether Selah actually knew where Gwen was. It seemed unlikely, but it was hard to assess the situation objectively in my present state. I managed to send Gwen a quick text message before getting in the car, but she didn't reply. She had an anonymous comm, but I tried not to contact her unless absolutely necessary, in case Keane went through our records and got suspicious.

I dropped Keane off at the office and then called April to tell her what was going on. Well, I didn't have time to tell her everything, but I figured she had a right to know where her car was, at the very least. I told her I was going to check on Gwen, and then I'd bring her car back.

"You're coming from your office?" she asked.

"Yeah. Just dropped off Keane."

"Pick me up on the way. I'm at La Pirata." La Pirata was a bar on Alhambra, near downtown.

"What are you doing at La Pirata?"

"I'm drinking, Blake. It's a bar. People go to bars sometimes."

"I don't think that's going to work," I said.

"Come on, Blake. I was going to get a ride with the friend who brought me here, but she left with some creep. If you pick me up, I don't have to get a cab."

"Not a good idea," I said. "I'll just be a half hour or so."

"If I stay here another half hour, I'm going to end up leaving with some creep, too. Is that what you want?"

I was pretty sure this was an idle threat, but she did sound pretty drunk.

"Look," she said, "you don't have to worry about your girlfriend seeing me. I'll just nap in the backseat. I won't make a peep."

"Fine," I said. "Two minutes. Be out front."

Two minutes later, I pulled up to the curb in front of La Pirata, just as April emerged onto the sidewalk. She got in the car and I pulled away from the curb.

"You all right, Blake?" she asked.

"I will be, once I make sure Gwen is safe."

"Did something happen?"

I wasn't sure how much to tell April at this point. Probably better to err on the side of discretion. "I messaged her earlier and there was no response. I just want to make sure she's all right."

April nodded soberly and didn't press the issue.

Ten minutes later, we pulled into the parking lot of the motel. I parked several units down from Gwen's and got out. "Stay here," I said to April. "If I don't come back, call Keane."

"If you don't come back?" April said. "Fowler, I thought you said—"

I slammed the door and walked briskly to Gwen's door. I knocked, but there was no reply. The room was dark. I stepped back and gave the door a solid kick with the base of my shoe. It gave.

I drew my gun and reached in to turn on the light. The room appeared to be empty. I went inside.

Gwen's personal belongings lay strewn about the room, but she wasn't there. I was beginning to think I had overreacted. I holstered my gun.

"Left in a hurry," said a voice behind me.

I spun around. "Keane," I said, seeing him standing in the doorway. "What the hell are you doing here?"

"Wondering how long Gwen has been back," he said, walking into the room. He made a circuit of the room, glancing this way and that. "By the looks of things, about three weeks. But she left today, a few hours ago. Expects to be back in a day or two."

"How do you know all that?"

Keane sighed. "Pizza coupon on the dresser expired two weeks ago. Travel-size toothpaste tube in the bathroom is almost empty. Dust in the corners indicates the room hasn't been thoroughly cleaned for a while. All of that suggests that Gwen's stay at this motel began about three weeks ago, when

Selah told you about Gwen, you stopped asking me about her, and you generally started acting weird. Additionally, her luggage is here, but her purse is not. Makeup bag on the bed is open, as if she took a few items and left the rest. Coke can on the dresser was cold a couple hours ago, judging from the ring of water at its base, but is now warm, judging from the lack of condensation on the can. Dresser drawer is partially open and the contents are in disarray. 'DO NOT DISTURB' sign was on the door, although the maid isn't likely to come by until tomorrow morning. So: She has been here three weeks, left between one and three hours ago, and plans to return tomorrow, or the next day at the latest."

"He's right," said a woman's voice behind me. April. "She took just enough stuff to last her for a day or two."

"Damn it, April," I said. "You were supposed to stay in the car."

"You kicked the door in, Blake. You didn't expect me to come after you? Hi, Keane. Did you know all along, or did you just find out?"

"I suspected," said Keane. "Figured it was none of my business."

"And yet," I said, "here you are."

"Now we're on a case," Keane said. "And you're distracted. That makes it my business. April, start packing."

"Excuse me?" said April from the doorway.

"We need to get out of here," Keane explained impatiently. "Somebody will have heard the racket Fowler made kicking in that door. The police will be here soon. They'll confiscate Gwen's belongings. We have a better chance of figuring out where she's gone if we have her stuff."

"Why do I have to do it?" April asked.

"Because women pack better than men. It's science. Fowler, get the car. I took a cab here, so you're giving me a ride back to the office."

I decided it was best not to argue under the circumstances. I took the keys from April and went to the car. By the time I'd backed it up to Gwen's room, April was nearly done packing. She'd left the stuff in the kitchen, but seemed to have gotten just about everything else in the room into Gwen's two suitcases. She zipped them up and I threw them in the trunk of the Mustang. April got into the passenger's seat and Keane sat in the back. As I pulled out of the parking lot, I saw a man standing next to the bashed-in door to Gwen's room, yelling and shaking his fist at me.

SIX

"Why didn't you tell me, Fowler?" asked Keane. He didn't sound so much upset as curious.

He, April, and I were sitting around a table in what passed for a conference room on the first floor of our building. Gwen's suitcases were lying open on the table, with the contents strewn across the table and several chairs. Thus far we hadn't found any clues to where Gwen might have gone.

"She asked me not to."

Keane nodded. "Because she doesn't trust me. Can't blame her."

April remained silent, sipping at a cup of coffee. She was trying to sober up before driving back to her condo.

"I assume you saw her earlier today?" Keane asked.

"Why do you assume that?" I asked. It didn't surprise me that Keane had suspected, but I was hoping to figure out where I'd slipped up in case I needed to lie to him in the future.

"When you meet April for dinner, it's always at seven. You left a half hour early. Also, something caused Gwen to leave today, after staying put for three weeks."

"You think she left because of me?" I asked.

"Seems likely," said Keane. "What did you say to her?"

I had to think. I'd been so focused on keeping Gwen safe from whoever had killed Selah that it hadn't occurred to me that she might have left because of something I said. "I told her about our case. About Selah hiring us to find an iota coin."

"How did Gwen react?"

I shrugged. "She seemed aware that physical iota coins exist. That's about it."

"No surprise? Fear? Uncertainty?"

"Not that I could sense. But she's been in hiding for three years, Keane. I'm not sure how good I am at reading her anymore."

"Any idea where she'd have gone?"

"Not unless she went back to her place in the DZ. But that would be suicidal."

Keane nodded.

"So you don't think her leaving has anything to do with . . . other events?" I asked.

"You mean like Selah's murder?" Keane replied.

April swallowed hard, almost spitting her coffee all over Gwen's unmentionables. "Her *what*?" she gasped.

I glared at Keane. I hadn't intended to involve April in this, but Keane evidently had other ideas. Probably trying to get back at me for lying to him. "When we got to Selah's place, she was dead," I said. "Somebody broke in and killed her."

"Over the iota coins?" April asked.

"We don't know," I said.

"Well, you'd better find out," April said. "If Gwen's disappearance has something to do with the iota coins, that's the only way you're going to find her."

"We have no leads," I said.

"Not entirely true," said Keane. "Before we went to see Mr. Kim, I did some digging on the group that organized the iota auction, the Free Currency Initiative. They had some big names backing them." Keane tapped something on his comm screen and my comm chirped. I looked at the display to see that he had sent me a list of the FCI board members. There were nine names; at least five were familiar to me. One in particular jumped out.

"Gerard Canaan was pushing iotas?" I asked. "I guess it makes sense, after losing as much as he did in dollars." The majority of Canaan's fortune had been stock in Elysium Oil. When the Wahhabis turned Saudi Arabia into the Arabian Caliphate, that stock lost over 97 percent of its value. I'd have gone into a different business, too.

"Hmm," said Keane. "Several other big names on there as well. Considerable overlap with the Los Angeles Future Foundation."

"You think FCI was part of LAFF?"

"Hard to say what the relationship was, exactly. They definitely had some shared interests. Interestingly, though, Selah Fiore seemed to have no connection to FCI."

"Maybe she got left out," I said. "And getting her hands on one of these coins was her way back in."

"You mean like a Spectre ring?" said April. "A secret totem to get into the club?"

"I have no idea," I admitted. It sounded kind of stupid when April said it out loud.

"There's no reason to think any of the FCI members have one of the auctioned coins," Keane said. "Quite the opposite, in fact. If they had intended to keep the coins close, they wouldn't have held a public auction for them."

"Maybe we can get an interview with Gerard Canaan. It's worth a try, I guess."

"I'd like to know more before we talk to someone like Canaan."

"That's a Catch-22," I said. "All we've got is the list of FCI board members. How can we gather more information before we talk to someone on the list?"

"No, I also managed to come up with another list. There seems to have been a prohibition against unofficial photography at the auction, but earlier today I ran a search algorithm for public social media postings that occurred in the Los Angeles area while the event was going on, filtering for certain keywords. I came up with a list of seventeen likely attendees, and identified six more people by running image-recognition software on photographs against a public database. That gives us a list of twenty-three likely attendees of the auction. I've arranged them in order by how likely they are to have attended."

My comm chirped again. Keane had sent me the list. Keane's algorithm had assembled a small dossier on each individual, including age, comm ID, address, and a photo in most cases.

"So now what?" April asked, as I scrolled through the dossiers. "Start calling everybody on that list?"

"It's what we've got," said Keane.

"Hang on," I said, tapping my display. "This guy, Declan Colvin. Some kind of TV producer. Gwen used to date a guy named Declan."

"You think it's the same guy?" asked April.

"Could be," I said. "She used to get invited to lots of events with Hollywood big shots because of her job. Says here he's dead, though. Motorcycle accident in 2038."

"Foul play?" said April.

"Not as far as I can tell," I said. Keane's dossier included a link to a news item on Colvin's accident. "If he had one of those coins, though, he doesn't have it anymore."

"Maybe he gave it to Gwen," Keane said.

"That seems like a stretch," I said. April nodded.

"It fits, though," said Keane. "Colvin is at the auction. Maybe Gwen is there with him. He buys one of the coins, gives it to her to impress her. She breaks up with the guy, never thinks about the coin again. She goes into hiding, takes the coin with her. Then she leaves the DZ in a hurry, leaving the coin wherever it is. Fowler tells her Selah Fiore is desperate to get her hands on this coin, and suddenly Gwen disappears again."

"Gwen told me Selah helped her disappear the first time," I said. "Mag-Lev's been protecting her."

"I figured as much," said Keane.

"You didn't tell me that," I said.

"And you didn't tell me Gwen had reappeared," said Keane, meeting my glare. "This is what happens when you withhold information."

He had a point there. "So now what?"

"Do you know where Gwen was staying in the DZ?"

"No, but I know the name she was using. Kathryn Buchanan."

"Was she at one of the LAFF safe houses?"

"No," I said. "She said Selah suggested that option, but Gwen refused. She was at some apartment where Mag-Lev set her up."

"Smart," said Keane. "Okay, I'll message some of my DZ contacts tonight. Maybe we'll have an address tomorrow."

"You really think she went back to the DZ?" I asked. "That place is like a war zone these days. She left because it was too dangerous."

"She'd go back for one of those coins, though, if she knew how badly Selah wants them. If she had a deal with Selah for Mag-Lev to protect her, and Selah and Mag-Lev have had a falling out, then she's in trouble. She needs more leverage."

"Except that Selah is dead."

"Gwen doesn't know that. Did you tell her Selah was sick?"

"No," I admitted.

"So Gwen still believes Selah can be manipulated. And you told her Selah is desperate to get her hands on one of these coins. If Gwen did have one of those coins stashed in the DZ, that's where she went."

"Why wouldn't she have just told me?" I asked.

"Maybe she doesn't trust you, either," said Keane.

I awoke the next morning to the sound of my comm chirping. Looking at the display, I saw I had another message from "Lila." It read:

who do you trust?

I wrote back:

Who is this?

After I showered and got dressed, I checked my comm again and saw no reply. Probably an ex-client or someone else Keane and I had pissed off trying to get a rise out of me. I didn't have time to deal with it.

I went upstairs to Keane's office to see if he'd had any luck finding an address for Kathryn Buchanan. I still wasn't convinced Gwen had one of the coins, but if there was any chance she had gone back into the DZ, I had to go after her. As luck would have it, one of Keane's contacts had gotten back to him: There was a Kathryn Buchanan who matched Gwen's description living in an apartment building in an area known as Willowbrook, in the southwest quadrant of the DZ.

I had ended up driving April home a little before midnight so Keane and I could keep her car for a bit longer, but there was no way she'd let us take her car into the DZ. It took nearly an hour for us to find a driver willing to take us to Gwen's address. Getting to the DZ was no problem, but drivers hate going through the checkpoints, and most car companies don't have the proper insurance for the DZ. The driver pulled up around 10 A.M. in an ancient Buick that smelled like stale cigarette smoke. Keane and I got in the back. Half an hour later, we were at the DZ checkpoint. The checkpoint took almost another hour; due to the increased violence of late, the LAPD goons manning the border were being more thorough—and belligerent—than usual. But we made it through without incident, and twenty minutes later we pulled up in front of the address Keane had been given.

The building was a three-story, gray-blue stucco block that looked like something the Soviets would have built to house their troops in Cuba during the Cold War. It was nestled among several similar buildings, all of which were in considerable disrepair. Graffiti covered the lower parts of the walls and the windows on the first floor were boarded up or latticed. In front of the buildings, where there once had presumably been lawn, there was dry ground with a sparse covering of weeds boxed in by a chain-link fence topped with razor wire. And this was actually a pretty nice neighborhood for the DZ.

I'd gotten pretty good at picking locks since going to work for Keane; I managed to get the padlock on the gate open in about ten seconds. Keane and I went through the gate and I closed it behind us, leaving the lock open in case we needed to make a quick escape. We walked briskly to the front door of the building, unlocked it, and took the stairs to the third floor. Gwen's apartment, number thirty-nine, was at the end of the hall. As we exited the stairway I saw a tall, skinny man sitting in the hall, his back against the left wall, legs splayed out in front of him. He wore dirty jeans and a pink Hello Kitty T-shirt. He had a three-day beard and his hair was long and greasy. I had my gun drawn, but he didn't even glance at it. I gave him a nod as I walked past.

"You guys friends of Kathryn's?" the disheveled man asked, as I approached apartment thirty-nine.

"Just watering her plants," Keane said. I knocked on the door.

There was no answer. The man stared at us dumbly. After a moment, he got slowly to his feet. He walked to a nearby door, opened it, and disappeared inside, closing the door behind him.

I knocked again, but still there was no answer. I got out my lock pick and started to work on the door. This one took me almost thirty seconds. I opened the door, holding my gun out before me. The apartment seemed to be empty. I went inside, Keane following. He closed and locked the door behind us.

Making a quick survey of the apartment, I determined that it was vacant. Gwen's apartment was clean and surprisingly well-furnished. She'd always had good taste, but I was surprised she'd even been able to find furniture of this quality in the DZ. Maybe it had been part of her deal with Selah.

I holstered my gun. "Looks like she's already been here," I said. On the counter was a half a bowl of what looked like canned chicken soup. It was room temperature, but it didn't look like it had been there more than a few hours.

"She left here in a hurry, too," said Keane.

"Possibly against her will," I said.

"Yes," said Keane. "We should look for the coin."

"I'm more concerned about Gwen than the coin."

"The coin is the key to finding Gwen."

I wasn't so sure about that, but I supposed we might as well take a look around while we were here. We might find a clue as to where Gwen had gone.

"Well, if you were Gwen, where would you hide a novelty coin?"

"It may not be hidden," said Keane. "If she had any idea of the coin's value, she'd have taken it with her."

Keane started with the kitchen drawers; I went into the bedroom. I went through all of Gwen's dresser drawers and her nightstand but found no coin. I went back into the kitchen to see how Keane was doing. He was crouched on the floor, looking through cabinets, his back to the entry door. As I entered the room, I saw the door handle turn.

"Keane!" I hissed, drawing my gun. "Door!"

Keane got to his feet and turned around as the door opened. A large man, wearing the colors of the Tortuga gang, entered the room. Behind him were two more men, similarly garbed. The Tortugas worked for Mag-Lev. The guy in front held a Glock pistol; the two behind him had AR-15s.

"Looking for someone?" said the large man, striding into the kitchen. He seemed unconcerned that I was pointing a 9mm SIG Sauer at him.

"Just trying to find some popcorn," Keane said. "My partner and I were about to start a Selah Fiore movie marathon. You guys are welcome to join us if you like."

"Show's over," said the large man. "You're coming with us."

I glanced at Keane and he gave me a curt nod. Shooting our way out of this situation wasn't going to work; I might be able to take out one or two of them before they got a shot off, but Keane was unarmed and we didn't know if there were more Tortugas downstairs. Besides, it was pretty clear we had found who had taken Gwen. If we wanted to see her, our best bet was to cooperate.

I moved to holster my gun, and the large man shook his head. I sighed but handed it over. One of the other guys frisked me and Keane and took my Beretta as well. Then we were prodded downstairs, brought outside, and shoved into the backseat of an old Lincoln SUV. The big guy drove while one of the others held a gun on us.

Fifteen minutes later, we were standing in a luxuriously appointed office that contrasted starkly with its location in a dilapidated old building in the worst part of the city. Two armed men stood against the walls, watching us. Behind a large desk was a man Keane and I had met before: Mag-Lev, the most powerful warlord in the DZ. Mag-Lev was an ugly, mean-looking man with a clean-shaved head. He sat with his elbows on the desk, his chin resting on his fists, studying us impassively like a wolf regarding its prey. The left side of his face was disfigured by a horrible burn scar, and his left eyelid drooped over a dead, bloodshot eye.

Mag-Lev certainly looked the part of the DZ warlord, but the fact was, Mag-Lev was a fraud. He'd been a little-known sitcom actor named Giles Marbury before Selah Fiore had plucked him out of obscurity and made him into the terrifying figure known as Mag-Lev. That said, he'd taken to the part with gusto, and I wasn't certain he was entirely sane. If he was holding Gwen, she was in real danger—and so were Keane and I, come to think of it.

"Good to see you again, gentlemen," said Mag-Lev. "Care to explain why you were sniffing around one of my apartment complexes?"

"Got lost," said Keane. "We heard John Wayne's grave was around there somewhere."

"Funny," said Mag-Lev. "What's your interest in Kathryn Buchanan?"

Interesting. Mag-Lev had been protecting Gwen for three years and he didn't even know her real name. I guess that's what happens when you get promoted to a position way beyond your level of experience. Mag-Lev was charismatic and ruthless, but he wasn't particularly bright.

"I don't know who that is," said Keane.

"Don't play dumb, Keane. It doesn't suit you. Kathryn Buchanan has been under my protection for the past three years. Three weeks ago, she disappeared. Yesterday, she came back. And now here you are."

"Then you do have her?" I asked.

"Oh, so you do know who I'm talking about," said Mag-Lev. "Yes, Kathryn is staying with me."

"Against her will," I said.

Mag-Lev shrugged. "The situation in the DZ has changed. I'm keeping her here for her own protection."

"And to use her as leverage against Selah Fiore," Keane said.

"Selah needed a reminder of our agreement," said Mag-Lev.

"So that's it," I said. "You and Selah have a falling out. The other warlords start getting ideas about moving in on your territory. You know Selah wants Kathryn kept safe, so you get the idea to use her against Selah, but by the time this occurs to you, she's already gone. Lucky for you, she came back."

"I had people watching her apartment," said Mag-Lev. "Why does Selah want her? She's stopped returning my calls."

"She's probably just busy," I said. "Doing . . . movie stuff."

"Whatever Selah's paying you, I'll double it," said Mag-Lev.

I suddenly realized that Mag-Lev thought Selah had hired us to find Gwen. No doubt Keane had already picked up on this.

"I doubt you have that kind of money," said Keane. "But I'll tell you what. We'll go to Selah, tell her that you have Kathryn, and that she's safe and unharmed. She is unharmed, yes?"

"She's fine," said Mag-Lev.

"We'll need confirmation of that," said Keane.

Mag-Lev nodded to one of the men at the door, who exited the room.

"Assuming Kathryn has not been harmed, we will explain the situation to Selah. I'm sure we can come to a mutually satisfactory agreement. You'll retain control of the DZ, and Kathryn will be returned safely to Selah."

"You think you can get Selah to agree to that?" Mag-Lev asked skeptically.

"Based on my understanding of Selah's interests, it shouldn't be a problem."

The door to the room opened again, and Gwen stumbled in. She didn't look good. Her hair was tangled and her jeans were scuffed and torn at the knees, as if she'd been thrown to the ground. Her right eye was nearly swollen shut and her lower lip was swollen and bleeding. The gunman walked in behind her, his rifle pointed at her back.

"Gwe—" I started, forgetting myself.

"Jesus Christ!" Keane shouted, drowning me out. "You said she was unharmed."

"I said she's fine," said Mag-Lev. "And she is fine."

It took a momentous effort of will to keep from jumping over Mag-Lev's desk and beating the shit out of him—or getting shot to death in the process, which was the likelier outcome.

"Kathryn, are you all right?" Keane asked.

Gwen nodded, glancing from Keane to me.

"She was a bit reluctant to come with my men," said Mag-Lev. "But I assure you she's safer here than out there."

"Selah won't be happy to see her like this," Keane said. "Get her cleaned up. Get her some clean clothes and ice for those bruises. I'm going to tell Selah you haven't harmed her and hope she doesn't go ballistic when she sees her."

"You heard him," said Mag-Lev to the gunman. The man opened the door and motioned for Gwen to leave. Gwen looked at me desperately.

"It'll be okay, Kathryn," I said. "We're going to talk to Selah. We'll get you out of here."

Gwen nodded and left the room, the gunman following her.

"Good," said Mag-Lev. "We'll get Kathryn cleaned up and you talk to Selah. You've got twenty-four hours. Either Selah gets behind my efforts to stomp out these rival gangs or I deliver Kathryn to her in a bag."

SEVEN

Mag-Lev's men dropped us off back at our office. They even gave me my gun back. Not surprisingly, Mag-Lev's thugs were waved through the checkpoint with barely a glance from the LAPD. Ironically, Tortuga lieutenants were the exact sort of people these checkpoints were supposed to keep from getting out, but of course things never worked like that in real life. Exceptions were made for the powerful, and the ordinary people got bent over.

At present, Keane and I sat at our conference room, finishing up lunch and plotting our next steps. "So," I said, around a mouthful of reheated lasagna, "how are we going to convince Selah Fiore to support Mag-Lev's efforts to take back the DZ when she's . . . you know, dead."

"We're not," said Keane.

"Then what are we going to do?"

"Go back and get that coin."

"We can't just—" My comm chirped. The display read "Selah Fiore."

"What the hell . . . ?" I muttered, stopping to answer it. "This is Fowler."

"Mr. Fowler?" said a voice that sounded uncannily like Selah Fiore. "We need to talk."

"Cute," I said. "This isn't the sort of trick you can play more than once. Whoever you are, you need to get some new material." I put the call on speaker.

"I apologize for the deception," said the voice. "It's very important that we meet."

Keane watched me quizzically from across the table.

"I'm hanging up now."

"The police have found the body," the voice said. "And the surveillance footage. It doesn't look good for you and Mr. Keane. I can help you."

"I'm sure you can," I said. "As you're the one who created the problem."

"Please, Mr. Fowler. I can explain everything. Meet me at Bolero in Hollywood in half an hour. Reservation will be under the name Hearst." The call ended.

"Our mystery caller again," Keane said.

"Yeah," I said. "Must be someone using a voice modulator. Whoever it is, they know about Selah's murder. She wants us to meet her at that Brazilian restaurant, Bolero." I'd once tried to make a reservation for me and Gwen at Bolero. They had a six-month waiting list.

"Smart," Keane replied. "Public place, high profile."

"Says she'll be under the name Hearst. Like William Randolph, I suppose."

"Or Patty," Keane said.

"How do we know she won't have the cops waiting for us?"

"We don't," said Keane. "Call her back. Tell her to meet us at the northeast corner of San Pedro and Sixth in ten minutes."

"We can't get to San Pedro and Sixth in ten minutes."

"We don't need to," said Keane.

I shrugged and hit the callback button. After some time, the person with Selah's voice answered. "I hope you're on your way, Mr. Fowler," she said.

"Change of plans, Ms. Hearst," I said. "Meet us at the northeast corner of San Pedro and Sixth in ten minutes."

"I prefer not to be seen on the street," said the voice.

"Your choice," I said. "We're not going to Bolero." I hung up and turned to Keane. "Now what?"

"Call a cab. Have them wait at the northeast corner of San Julian and Sixth. Then call April."

"Got it," I said, realizing what Keane had in mind. I sent the coordinates to the cab app on my comm. Then I called April.

"Hey there," she said. "What's up?"

"I need a small favor from you."

"What else is new?"

"You can see Sixth Street from your office, right?"

"Part of it, sure."

"Good. In about seven minutes, a woman is going to be walking down Sixth Street from San Pedro to San Julian. At least I assume it will be a woman. She'll be on the north side of the street."

"Tell her it'll be more like ten minutes," said Keane. "And she'll be carrying a bouquet of red roses."

I shot Keane a puzzled glance, but didn't ask. "Keane says—"

"Yeah, I got it. I'm looking out the window now. I can stay here until your mystery woman shows up. What does she look like?"

"That's what you're going to tell me," I said. "Call me when you see her."

"Okay, chief," she said. "Over and out."

I honestly don't know why April puts up with this shit.

"All right," I said. "Now what?"

"Now," Keane said, getting up from the table, "we take April's car to Grand Park."

I got up and we walked to the street, where I had left April's car. We got in and I headed west toward downtown.

Keane said, "At four fourteen exactly, call our mystery woman back. Tell her to go east on Sixth until she gets to a flower shop. There's one a few doors down from the corner. Have her buy a dozen red roses, then walk back toward San Pedro. Keep her on the line until she gets there."

I nodded and kept driving toward Grand Park. Something had been bothering me about the iotas, and I figured now was as good a time as any to ask Keane about it.

"Earlier you mentioned the bootstrapping problem," I said. "But you never explained how iotas got around it."

Keane nodded. "The intrinsic value of a virtual currency derives from the algorithm on which it's based," he replied. "A virtual currency like iotas or XKredits is based on an algorithm that creates artificial scarcity. The algorithm presents a series of puzzles, and individuals can use computers to solve those problems in exchange for more units of the currency. This operation is called 'mining.' Every time a puzzle is solved, the next puzzle becomes slightly more difficult. For example the very first puzzle might have be 'Guess a number between one and ninety-nine.' The next puzzle would be something like, 'guess a number between one and one hundred.' And so on, with each puzzle a little bit tougher than the last. Even assuming endless increases in available computing power, eventually mining becomes too processor-intensive to be worthwhile. So while there's theoretically no limit to the number of XKredits or iotas that could be in circulation, in practice there's a clear point of diminishing returns.

"In addition to the value imparted by this artificial scarcity, a virtual currency like XKredits or iotas has some inherent advantages over physical currency. Because of the decentralized, nonphysical nature of the system, it's possible to execute payments with zero transaction cost—no credit card fees or bank fees. Also, these payments are theoretically untraceable. Ironically, virtual currencies get much of their value from the actions of the governments trying to suppress them: by making certain financial transactions illegal, they increase the incentive for buyers and sellers to use untraceable currencies.

"Despite these advantages, as you pointed out, virtual currencies still aren't actually based on anything. They don't represent anything in the real world—no pile of gold or silver. So in the end, their value derives purely from speculation. People mining or buying the currency in order to sell them at a profit later on."

"The greater fool theory," I said. "Even if you were a fool to buy XKredits at a certain price, you can always find a greater fool to sell them to for even more in the future."

"Exactly," said Keane. "A market based purely on speculation is going to be extremely unstable, and unlikely to tempt large institutional investors, who want stability. That's why XKredits remain a curiosity, with less than one percent of the global currency market. Even after the Collapse, more people use dollars—old dollars, that is—than XKredits."

"So how did iotas do it?" I asked.

Keane smiled. "The creators had a big pile of gold."

"Bullshit," I said.

"Not literal gold, obviously," Keane said. "Virtual gold. As well as silver, platinum, dwarven gems, magic swords, and spaceships. And real estate, of course. Lots of real estate. Entire planets."

"You're talking about video games," I said.

"Massively multiplayer games, yes," said Keane. "There are now roughly two billion habitual players worldwide, spending an average of five hours per day playing online games. While these people are playing those games, the game world is their reality, and the law of supply and demand applies just as much inside the game as outside. Prior to the invention of iotas, each game had its own proprietary currency, and these currencies had the same weakness as any state-backed fiat currency. For one, in order to transfer wealth from one game to another, players had to rely on third-party services engineered to get around the mercantile-style controls put in place by the game manufacturers. The transaction costs were high, and the player risked being sanctioned by the game's administrators for violating the rules. The more serious problem with proprietary currencies didn't surface, however, until the bankruptcy of Carthage Interactive. They'd bet big on an interstellar trading game called *Equus*, but it turned out to be a big money loser. They pulled the plug on the game without any notice. Analysts estimated that nearly two billion dollars' worth of virtual property simply disappeared."

"Make-believe stuff," I said.

"You underestimate how much of the world is composed of make-believe stuff," said Keane. "Money isn't the only collective delusion around. In any case, many players, who had been watching Carthage's financials, saw the end coming, but there wasn't much they could do about it. It was impossible to cash out of the game, because the money used to buy all this make-believe stuff existed only in the game. So when Carthage pulled the plug, the money disappeared along with the rest of the universe."

"And the iota was supposed to fix that problem."

"The iota system was an open-source algorithm developed by a group of volunteer developers to allow both in-game and inter-game financial transactions. It shortly became the default standard for gaming currencies. Players liked it because they could leverage their wealth creation in one game to overcome obstacles in another game. Developers liked it because it offered a prebuilt interface for in-game financial transactions, so it was one less thing they needed to build. There was some resistance at first from the big game companies, who wanted to maintain control over their own development infrastructure, but iotas soon became the standard in independently developed games, and competitive pressure eventually forced the big names in the industry to adopt the iota infrastructure as well.

"At this point, there was nothing preventing iotas from being used for other sorts of transactions. Everyone knew iotas could be used in games, so they had objective value, even though the objects iotas could be traded for were entirely virtual at this point. Soon game retailing sites began allowing game licenses themselves to be purchased with iotas. And from there, it was a short leap to accepting iotas for electronic devices and other physical goods. Iotas became, almost entirely by accident, an alternative form of real-world currency. At this point, the feds would ordinarily have taken an interest, but the spike in iota usage occurred shortly after the Collapse, when the federal government was having a hard time just keeping the lights on in D.C. Geeks buying headsets and joysticks with pretend money was not a priority."

"And then the Free Currency Initiative came along to give the iota a shot in the arm," I said.

"Right," said Keane. "A few weeks into the iota boom, when the dollar was bottoming out, the Free Currency Initiative was formed. These guys were smart. They knew iotas were on the verge of going mainstream, but they also realized the feds were eventually going to get a handle on the dollar situation. When that happened, they were going to come down hard on iotas and anything else that threatened their fiat currency. So the FCI made a big play, trying to inject enough iotas into the economy so that by the time the feds got their act together, it would be too late to stop them. The government could outlaw iotas, but only at the expense of pissing off a lot of constituents and, more importantly, campaign donors. And because iotas were untraceable, even if they outlawed them, the black market would live on."

"And the celebrity auction was part of that play," I said.

"The auction and all the prep work leading up to it," Keane replied. "Getting nonprofits and corporations on board. It was a clever bit of business."

I nodded. I still didn't understand who was behind all this maneuvering or why, but I'm not sure I had the head for understanding monetary theory.

At four fourteen I called the mystery woman.

"I'm not there yet," said the voice. "Give me five more minutes."

I glanced at Keane, who scowled.

"You've got two," I said. "Don't hang up until you're at Sixth and San Pedro."

She said something that I didn't catch.

"What was that?" I asked.

"Told my driver to run the lights," she said.

"This is your personal driver or a cab?"

"Neither," said the woman. "I've been given a sort of . . . personal escort."

"All right," I said, not sure what to make of this.

"Keep her talking," said Keane.

"What the hell am I supposed to say to her?" I asked, muting my comm.

"Doesn't matter," said Keane. "I just want to make sure she's not giving anyone instructions."

I sighed and unmuted the comm. "So," I said. "I'm a big fan of yours. I've probably seen *Road to Tomorrow* twenty times."

The voice laughed. "That was a very long time ago, Mr. Fowler. Were you even alive when that movie came out?"

"I watched it when I was in basic training. First movie of yours I ever saw. Is it true you had chopped onions in your pockets for the crying scenes?"

"You understand I'm not actually Selah Fiore, right?" she said. "Also, it was garlic, not onions. Selah thought she was being clever, raiding craft services for onions. But she was a silly kid, sheltered. She didn't know what onions looked like. It did work, though, more or less. She said the smell lasted for days."

"I would imagine so," I said. I'd remembered the garlic story from an anniversary retrospective of Conan O'Brien's show a few years back. Whoever was playing the role of Selah had done her research. "I think I've seen every movie Selah ever made," I said. "Even that god-awful thing where she was a mermaid in that kid's swimming pool. Pretty sure I watched it with Japanese subtitles."

"A bootleg, no doubt," said the voice. "I don't believe it was ever released in the States. Anyway, I . . ." The voice trailed off.

"You what?" I asked.

She was quiet for a moment.

"Ms. Hearst?"

"I'm coming up to the corner."

"Okay," I said. "Have the driver let you out. Tell him to drive to . . ." I glanced at Keane, who shrugged. "Tell him to drive to Knott's Berry Farm," I said. Why not? I thought. Drivers never get to have any fun in these scenarios.

I heard her giving muffled instructions to the driver, then a door opening.

"I'm here," she said. "Where are you?"

"Go east on Sixth. There's a flower shop a few doors down. Buy a dozen red roses. You know what roses look like, right?"

"I have a vague idea," she said.

"I wasn't sure, after the onion thing. If you walk out of that store with gardenias, this whole plan goes to hell."

"What a shame that would be," said the voice. "All right, I'm walking into the store."

There was some noise on the line, and then I heard her asking someone for a dozen red roses. More noise and muffled talking.

"What's going on?" I asked.

"I'm buying roses, Mr. Fowler. As per your request. Please be patient." The line was silent for a moment. "All right, exiting the store."

"Good. Walk east back toward San Pedro. Let me know when you're there."

After a few seconds of silence, she came back on the line. "I'm here. Where are you?"

"Keep walking until you get to San Julian."

"I tire of these games, Mr. Fowler. You'd better be at the corner when I get there."

"You'll see me soon enough," I replied. My comm chirped, indicating there was another call waiting. "I'll be right back," I said. "When you get to San Julian, stop and wait for further instruction." I switched to the other call. "April, what have you got?"

"I see your mystery woman. I borrowed a pair of binoculars from the pervert in the next office. Mystery woman has a nice figure. Wearing a gray skirt with a royal blue blouse. Can't get a good look at her face; she's wearing a hat."

"And she has the roses?"

"A bouquet of red flowers, yes. Could be tulips for all I know, but she's got flowers."

"Is she alone?"

"As far as I can tell. There's nobody else on that side of the street except a couple of panhandlers."

"Okay," I said. "Let me know when she gets to the corner."

"She's almost there now. Who is this woman?"

"I honestly have no idea," I said.

"Well, she's at the corner."

"Do you see a cab nearby?"

"Hmm. Yes, just around the corner, on San Julian."

"Okay, hold on." I switched back to the mystery woman. "Ms. Hearst?"

"Still here, Mr. Fowler."

"There should be a cab parked around the corner."

There was a pause. "I see it."

"Get in the cab. Alone."

"You mean without the roses?"

"You can keep the roses."

"You really know how to make a girl swoon, Mr. Fowler."

I switched back to April. "She should be getting in the cab," I said.

"She is," April replied.

"Is she still alone?"

"Yes. She just closed the door."

I muted April. "Now what?"

"Get on First Street heading east," said Keane. "And toss the call to me."

"Gladly," I said, and sent the call to Keane's comm. I started the car and pulled onto the street.

"Ms. Hearst?" Keane said. "This is Erasmus Keane. Tell the cabdriver to head west on Sixth." There was a pause. "Good. Now I need you to listen very closely. Your cabdriver should have a license number displayed on the dashboard. Do you see it? Okay, I want you to look at the last digit on the license number. Do not read it aloud. Just look at it. Do you have it? Good. Again, without saying it aloud, add three to that number. Got it? Okay, now multiply that number by five. Yes, it's for a very good reason, Ms. Hearst. Trust me. Do you have it? Okay, good. Finally, subtract four from that number. Do not say the number aloud; just remember it. Where are you now? Excellent. Tell the driver to turn right on Hill Street. Call me back at this number when you're coming up to First Street." He ended the call.

"What was that about?" I asked.

"Just giving her something to do," said Keane. "Cab rides are boring."

I had turned onto First Street, and was now heading east toward Grand Park. I switched my comm back to April. "Hey, sorry about that," I said. "I think we're done with you for now."

"Such a gentleman," said April. "You're not going to tell me why we're stalking this poor woman?"

"Later," I said. "Thanks a lot, April."

"Fine," she said, and ended the call.

After a moment, Keane said, "Odd that they would make the coins out of titanium, isn't it?"

"I suppose," I replied. "Don't they make jewelry out of titanium?"

"Yes," said Keane. "It's hypoallergenic and corrosive-resistant, as are several other metals, including silver and gold. Unlike those metals, however, titanium is nearly indestructible. Highest strength-to-weight ratio of any metal. Melting point just over three thousand degrees Fahrenheit. Extremely difficult to work with. Kim said it's very rare for coins to be made from any sort of titanium alloy."

"So why did they do it?"

"As yet unclear," said Keane. "What did you make of the mayfly?"

"Is that what that was?" I asked. "I thought it was a dragonfly."

Keane shook his head. *"Leptophlebia nebulosa,* in the order *ephemeroptera."*

"Like Ephemeral," I said.

"From the Greek *ephemeros*, meaning 'lasting only one day.' The mayfly is a common symbol for ephemerality or something short-lived. Strange thing to put on an indestructible coin, don't you think?"

"The whole thing is strange," I said. "A physical coin that symbolizes a virtual currency while claiming not to symbolize it?"

"Yes," said Keane. "Somebody put some thought into this. It's more than a simple marketing gimmick, that much is certain." He stared intently into space for some time. I shrugged.

A few minutes later, Keane's comm chirped.

"Erasmus Keane," he said. Then, after a brief pause, he continued, "Okay, tell the driver to go straight at the light. Let me know when it turns green. Beautiful day, isn't it? Los Angeles the day after a good hard rain is the best. Washes away all the dust and—Okay, good. Have him drop you off at the Grand Park Metro station. Should be just ahead on your right. Tell me when you're there. Excellent. Get out of the car. You still have that number in your head? Excellent. Here's what you're going to do. Go down into the Metro station. Let me know when you're inside. This is fun, isn't it? Like being in a spy novel. No? Well, I suppose it's a matter of perspective. Okay, good. Now look at the display showing the train arrival times. Do you see it? Good. You're going to number the trains, starting at the top. So the first train is number one, the second is number two, the third is number three, and so forth. Pick the train number corresponding to the number I had you remember earlier. Yes, I'm getting to that. Look at only the last digit of the train number for the train corresponding to your number. Do you have it? Good. Multiply that number by three. Don't tell me. Do you have it? Okay, now add ten to that number. Good. Yes, we're almost done. Stick with me. Triple that number. Do you have it? Good. Finally add the last digit from the train number to your total. Do you have it? Excellent. Do not say the number or anything else, except to indicate that you understand these instructions. If the number you ended up with is even, you're going to exit the station to the north. If the number is odd, you're going to exit to the south. Please exit now, disposing of the roses in a trash can on the way out. While you are walking, I would like you to sing 'Que Sera, Sera.' It's okay if you don't know all the words, just do the best you can. Yes, it's important. Yes, I'm being serious. Very nice. You have a wonderful voice, Ms. Hearst. Let me know when you're outside. Very good, thank you. Okay, now, if the last digit of your number is greater than five, I want you to turn left. Otherwise, turn right. Understand? Excellent. Keep walking and singing until I give you further instructions." He muted the call.

"What the hell was all that?" I asked. "You've got the Metro train schedule memorized?"

"Just be at the corner of Temple and Broadway, heading south, in four minutes," Keane said.

"Temple and Broadway?" I said. "You realize you're having me drive literally right past the courthouse? City Hall is one block away."

"We're hiding in plain sight," said Keane. "Have some gum." He had pulled a pack of chewing gum from his pocket and was proffering me a piece.

"No thanks," I said. I turned left on Grand, which would take us to Temple.

"I'm not asking," said Keane. "Take the gum."

I took the gum, unwrapped it, and popped it in my mouth. It was best to choose your battles with Keane. "Seriously," I said around the gum. "How on Earth are we going to have any idea where our mystery woman is going to end up?"

Keane sighed. "You really don't get it?" he asked. "I had

such high hopes for you, Fowler." Keane had pulled a notepad from his pocket and was scribbling on it with a pen.

I frowned, trying to make sense of Keane's instructions. Even if he had the train schedule memorized, there was no way he could know the cabbie's license number. The only explanation was that it was a trick, a sort of mental sleight of hand. "You rigged the question so the answer is the same, regardless of the inputs," I said.

"Ha!" Keane exclaimed. "There may be hope for you yet! The value of the cabbie's license number was immaterial. The algorithm I had her apply to it would produce a number with a one in the ones column regardless of the number she started with. The result was that she was looking at the first train on the display."

"And you knew the number of the first train?"

"Hey? No, I don't even know how many trains would be listed. That's why I went with the first one. It didn't matter what number she picked, because the second algorithm would predictably yield a multiple of ten. An even number, meaning she would go north, and a zero in the ones column, meaning she would turn right. I just needed the appearance of randomness, so that anybody listening in would be suitably confused. Someone with a basic understanding of algebra could figure it out in a few minutes, but by then she'll be long gone. Good, she's still singing. She really does have a lovely voice. *The future's not ours to see, que sera, sera.* Slow down, we're early."

We had turned onto Temple and were coming up on Broadway.

I took my foot off the accelerator, coasting as slowly as I could without attracting undue attention. We hit the light green and kept going. The park was coming up on our right.

"Pull over here," Keane said. "I'll take the wheel. Mystery woman should be coming down that path. Rendezvous with her and bring her back here. I'll go around the block and be back here in five minutes exactly."

"Roger that," I said, stopping the car.

"Tossing the call back to you," he said, flicking his finger on his comm display. Suddenly I heard Selah Fiore—or an exceptionally good facsimile thereof—singing "Que Sera, Sera" in my ear. "And take this," he said. He tore off the sheet from his notepad and handed it to me. I glanced at it and nodded.

"You know what to do?" he asked.

"I think I can manage." I hopped out and Keane slid over into the driver's seat. "See you in five."

EIGHT

Keane drove off, and I headed down the sidewalk. Ahead of me were a series of wide steps leading up to a raised plaza. I hurried up them so I'd be able to see mystery woman coming. For all Keane's brilliance, he couldn't have picked a much worse place to rendezvous with her, from a tactical perspective. There were cops all over the place and very little cover. Much of Grand Park is really more of a wide-open plaza crisscrossed by wide concrete paths than an actual park. It was bordered by several government buildings, so cops, lawyers, and various other species of parasite could often be seen cutting through the park on the way to the scene of their next crime. Ordinarily the cops would be a stabilizing influence, but being wanted for murder made their presence an unwanted complication. I made it to the plaza only to find there was another set of steps a hundred feet or so ahead. Mystery woman would be coming down those steps in less than a minute, and she'd have a much better vantage point on me than I'd have on her.

I turned off the path, my sudden interest in a commemorative plaque coinciding with the advance of two uniformed LAPD monkeys coming down the steps. I crouched down so as to take in every detail regarding Ira and Evelyn Klein, who had made this plaza possible through a generous grant. While reflecting on the beneficence of the Kleins, I pulled a pen from my jacket pocket and lay Keane's note on the top of the plaque. Keane had written:

Stamp on your comm and place it and your earphone in this trash can.

Below this I scribbled:

Then head south.

When the cops had passed, I glanced up to see a shapely woman in a gray skirt and blue blouse coming down the steps. She wore a wide-brimmed beach hat, and I caught only a glimpse of her face as she came down. She looked like Selah Fiore, but it was hard to tell from this distance. I turned away from her, walked to the nearest trash can, and spat my gum out into my hand. Then I stuck Keane's note to the side of the can and walked back down the steps I'd just come up. I was now hidden from mystery woman's line of sight. I turned right down the sidewalk, picked up my pace, and unmuted my comm.

"Ms. Hearst?" I said.

The singing in my ear stopped. "Mr. Fowler," said mystery woman. "I'm about to call a cab and head home. I've had enough of your—"

"You're not going to call a cab," I said. "If you didn't want very badly to talk to me and Keane, you wouldn't have put up with his nonsense so far. Here's what you're going to do. About thirty feet ahead of you, on your right, is a trash can." I was guessing at this point, assuming that mystery woman had continued walking at an average pace since coming down the steps. "Do you see it?"

"Yes."

"Walk to that trash can. There's a note stuck to the side. Follow the instructions on the note."

I muted my comm and turned right, climbing another set of steps that ran parallel to the ones I had just come down. I was back in mystery woman's line of sight, but hopefully she was preoccupied trying to decipher Keane's handwriting.

"Is this really necessary?" the voice asked.

I unmuted my comm again. "Afraid so," I said, crossing the path without glancing in mystery woman's direction. I heard the woman sigh, and then the line went dead. I continued walking for another fifty feet and then turned and crouched down, finding another fascinating plaque. Glancing up, I saw mystery woman heading south down the path, perpendicular to the path I had just taken. I ducked back down, remaining hidden until I was certain she had passed. I glanced up to confirm her location, then quickly scanned the area for any signs of surveillance. Seeing nothing out of the ordinary, I stood up and cut across the lawn toward the sidewalk behind her.

"Don't look back," I said in a clear but casual tone, as I stepped onto the sidewalk. "Just keep walking."

She gave no sign of having heard me.

When I was about ten feet behind her, I slowed to match her pace. "See that bench on the right? You're going to sit there, right in the middle."

She again did not react, but after a few more paces veered to the right toward the bench. As she sat, she turned to look at me, but I wasn't where she expected. I'd ducked around behind the bench, timing my approach perfectly with the turn of her head as she sat down. Bugs Bunny would have been proud.

Before she could rotate her torso to look behind the bench, I put my left hand on her shoulder, pinning her in place. I took another look around to make sure no one was making a beeline toward me or otherwise showing untoward interest. "I apologize, Ms. Hearst," I said. "I need to check you for weapons and tracking devices."

"Do what you must," she said, irritated but resigned. I still couldn't see her face, thanks to her hat.

"Spread your arms across the back of the bench," I said. She did.

Her arms were bare—and flawless. There was literally not a mark on them. No inoculation scars, no freckles, no wrinkles, no liver spots. Medical science had progressed a lot over the past few decades, but there was no way this woman was near sixty. Those arms looked like they'd just rolled off the perfect-arm assembly line that morning.

After a moment of distraction, I ran my left hand down her left side to her hips, down to her knees, and then did the right side. What I could see of her legs looked just as good as the arms. Her body was soft, supple and—from what I could tell—completely natural. No girdle to smooth the lines or artificial padding to round out curves. I'm a professional, but I will admit to forgetting a couple of times exactly what I was looking for.

"About done?" she asked.

I grunted something vaguely affirmative and checked my comm. Keane would be at the corner in one minute. Really I should have checked under mystery woman's skirt as well, but that would undoubtedly have drawn some looks—not to mention protests from mystery woman. I got the sense that whatever her interests were in wanting to talk to us, she wasn't going to put up with much more. In any case, there was no time.

"Get up," I said. "Walk back the way you came, then turn right at the trash can where you dumped your comm. Go down the steps. A car will be waiting for you at the corner."

I stepped around the bench and walked away, returning the way I'd just come. I glanced back to see if I could get a look at mystery woman's face, but she was already walking in the other direction. My plan was to head down the flight of steps to the south, then turn left on the street and jog east to the corner where Keane had dropped me off. Mystery woman would go east first and take the flight of steps farther north. Basically, we were each tracing two sides of an elongated rectangle, meeting at the far corner. Hopefully Keane would be there as well, or mystery woman and I were going to have an awkward reunion probably culminating in an arrest.

When I got to the bottom of the steps, I turned left and jogged east, glancing at my comm display with a worried look on my face, as if I were late for an appointment at the courthouse. My worry became a whole lot more convincing as I approached the corner to see three men in LAPD uniforms chatting in exactly the spot where Keane had dropped me off. I saw April's car approaching a hundred feet or so down the street.

I now had several options, all of them terrible. I could stop in my tracks, call Keane, and tell him to pick me up farther down the road. This would nix our rendezvous with mystery woman and probably draw the attention of the cops. I could veer off toward the car and hop in, hopefully avoiding a close look from the cops but also nixing our rendezvous. Or I could just stand helplessly by while mystery woman pointed me out to the cops—which seemed to be the winner by default.

I slowed to a walk as mystery woman came down the steps ahead of me, just to the left of the cops. The good news was that they weren't paying any attention to me. The bad news was that they were all staring at mystery woman. All it would take is for her to point with her finger and every law enforcement officer in the vicinity would have his eyes on me. "There he is, officers!" she would scream. "The man who killed me!"

Except the woman coming down the stairs was, of course, not Selah Fiore. Selah Fiore was dead. This woman was, as I'd suspected, at least thirty years younger than Selah. And while her face resembled Selah's, her hair was black, not blond. She'd had it pulled back under the hat, but now the hat was off and her hair, unleashed, flowed behind her like a plume of billowing smoke. She came down the steps slowly, deliberately, just enough of a bounce in her step to let you know she knew exactly what she was doing.

Every heterosexual male in the area was looking in her direction. I say this not as a matter of empirical observation but rather out of a deep understanding of what makes men tick. My life was in mortal danger, and I couldn't stop looking at her. She smiled at the cops, walking right up to them without a glance in my direction. "Beautiful day, isn't it?" she said in Selah Fiore's voice.

The survival part of my brain managed to wrestle the procreation part to the floor as I realized that mystery woman was stalling for time so I could get away. I tore my eyes from the scene and forced myself to put one foot in front of the other until I was at April's car. Keane was double-parked, but so far traffic had flowed around him without much fuss. The first driver to get behind him and lay on the horn was going to break mystery woman's spell, though, and draw the attention of the cops.

I got in the backseat, leaving the door open.

"What's happening?" said Keane, who was also staring at mystery woman.

"What's happening is that you picked the worst place in Los Angeles for a secret rendezvous," I said.

Keane shrugged. "I had a lot to work out."

"Tell me about it," I said.

Mystery woman was now pointing back up the steps, and one of the cops was nodding. A moment later, the three of them ran up the steps toward the plaza. Mystery woman walked to the car and got in, closing the door behind her.

Keane pulled away from the curb. "What did you tell them?" he asked.

"Timmy is trapped in a well," she said. "What difference does it make?"

"None, I suppose," said Keane. "Welcome aboard, Ms. Hearst. Sorry for the cloak-and-dagger routine."

"You were right to be concerned," she said. "The cops would have been waiting for you at Bolero. My name's not Hearst, by the way. It's Fiore. Olivia Fiore."

NINE

I couldn't stop staring at her. The resemblance to Selah was clear as soon as I'd seen her face, but now that I looked at her close up, it was uncanny. Except for the hair and somewhat lighter skin tone, she looked exactly like the simulacrum of thirty-year-old Selah I'd seen the previous day, only younger.

"Are you Selah's daughter?" I asked.

"I am," she said.

"I didn't realize Selah had any children."

"She doesn't," said Keane from the driver's seat. He was taking us south down Broadway, in the general direction of our office. I hoped he wasn't planning on taking Olivia there. You never know with Keane.

"My mother kept my existence a secret," Olivia said. "Wanted me to have a normal life. I grew up in Belgium."

I shook my head. What was it with Selah Fiore and Belgium? Her secret genetics institute had supposedly been located in Belgium, too. If Olivia's backstory was as fake as that of the Tannhauser Institute, she'd probably never been out of Southern California.

"Of course you did," said Keane, who clearly shared my skepticism. "Why did you call us?"

"Which time?"

"Start with the first one."

"You know the answer to that," said Olivia. "To frame you for my mother's murder."

"Why?"

"To get you out of the way. To keep you from looking into the iota coins."

"Who killed your mother?" I asked.

"I don't know," Olivia said.

At that moment, my comm chirped. I glanced at the display. I'd received yet another message from "Lila." It read:

she is lying

I glanced at Keane, who seemed to be intent on the road. As far as I could tell, there was no one else who could hear our conversation. Did "Lila" have a bug in April's car? I wrote back:

We should meet.

To Olivia, I said, "Bullshit. You were helping to cover it up."

"I didn't have any choice," Olivia replied. "I'm being blackmailed."

"By whom?"

"I don't know. After class yesterday I got a call from a lawyer. He said my mother was dead, and that there were some discrepancies with her estate. I was told not to talk to anybody, not even the police. He said to come to Los Angeles at once."

"You flew from Belgium to Los Angeles last night?"

"What?" asked Olivia. "No, I grew up in Belgium. I live in San Luis Obispo now. I'm in the engineering program at

Cal Poly. Anyway, I met this lawyer at a diner in Hollywood."

My comm chirped:

not yet

"This lawyer have a name?" I asked.

"Tad Curtis," she said. "I looked him up before meeting him. Works for some huge firm downtown. Mr. Curtis tells me all about some insane genetic engineering program my mother was running, says that the feds are sniffing around and that if they find out what she was up to, I could lose everything."

"Your inheritance, you mean," I said.

Olivia shook her head. "I didn't stand to inherit anything. All I ever got from my mother was a trust fund. Basically a bribe to keep me quiet. She didn't want anyone to know about me; thought it hurt her cold-bitch reputation or something. I didn't care; I barely knew my mother. I was raised by nannies and then sent to boarding school overseas. The trust fund wasn't much, but it gave me enough to live on and pay for school. I'm a year and a half away from graduation. If that money dries up now, I've got a lot of student loans and no way to pay them back."

I could hardly believe what I was hearing. "You tried to frame us for murder because they threatened your goddamned trust fund?"

"There's more to it than that," she said. "Mr. Curtis told me my mother had been killed because she tried to back out of a business deal with several other very rich people in Los Angeles. He called it LAFF."

"The Los Angeles Future Foundation," I said.

She nodded. "They're pretty shady, I guess. They wouldn't

let her out of the deal, so my mother decided to go to the feds. It was her only way out. But LAFF found out she'd betrayed them and had her killed. According to Mr. Curtis, the guy who warned LAFF was named Erasmus Keane. He said Keane was some kind of criminal mastermind who knew about the Collapse in advance. I wouldn't have believed it, but he showed me documents. They made Keane look pretty bad. He says Keane was worried that LAFF was going to kill him next, so he was going to turn state's witness. But if he did that, all my mother's dirty laundry would get aired and her estate would be locked up in probate forever."

"And all you had to do to fix things was make a phone call," I said. "Get me and Keane to Selah's house."

"That was Mr. Curtis's idea. He coached me so I could pretend to be my mother."

"You must know that framing us was not the primary purpose of that call," said Keane, glancing in the rearview mirror. "If this Mr. Curtis had that information about Gwen, he could have just used a voice modulator and made the call himself."

Olivia nodded slowly. "They were setting me up," she said. "Putting me in a compromised position. Now they can control me by threatening to release the recording of that call. If I had been thinking clearly, I would have realized it at the time, but I was so stressed, and Mr. Curtis made it sound like it was urgent, that I make the call right that moment. He was very persuasive, I'm afraid."

"Well, you're in bed with the devil now," I said. "Why did you help us? You could have told those cops at the park I was a suspect in your mother's murder. Why didn't you?"

"Because I know you didn't kill her, for one. And once I had a chance to think about Mr. Curtis's story, I realized it was pretty far-fetched. I did some research on Mr. Keane, and well . . . he didn't sound like the kind of guy who would work for LAFF. For one thing, you guys live in a shitty building on the edge of the DZ. If Keane had some pull with a group of billionaires, I'd expect you to live in a nicer neighborhood."

"You were going to let the cops nab us at Bolero," I said.

"All I did is ask to meet you," Olivia said.

"But you knew it was a trap."

"I suspected. Mr. Curtis told me to try to persuade you to back off. I was to give you assurances that the security footage from my mother's house would be destroyed. But he had no reason to think you would believe it."

"Why did you call me, then? The second time, I mean?"

"He has me over a barrel, as I said. And frankly it's only a matter of time before the police catch you anyway, so I figured there was little harm in accelerating things."

"Mr. Curtis was with you when you called?"

"He was."

"So he agreed to let you rendezvous with us, without the cops?"

"He had people following me," she said. "He told me to follow your instructions and he'd keep an eye on me. Apparently he underestimated you."

"If he'd really wanted to follow you, he'd have planted some kind of tracking device."

"There was no time," she said. "I don't think he really expected you to say no to the Bolero meet. Figured you'd be desperate."

"Any idea who this Tad Curtis really works for?" Keane asked.

"I assumed he worked for these LAFF people," said Olivia. "Wouldn't you?"

"Perhaps," said Keane. "The bigger question, though, is: What does this person or persons want leverage over you for? What are they trying to make do, other than get me and Fowler locked up? Do you know something of value to them?"

"I doubt it," said Olivia. "Like I said, I had almost no contact with my mother. I didn't know anything about her finances or illegal secret projects. I'm just a college student."

"Well," I said, "clearly there's something that—" I broke off as Keane answered his comm in Korean. He spoke a few quick sentences and then ended the call.

"That was Mr. Kim," he said. "Says someone was just in the store with an iota coin. Serial number seven. Said he heard the price had spiked."

"What did Kim tell him?"

"Said he'd give him two thousand New Dollars on the spot, and he might have a buyer willing to pay a lot more. Guy said he'd be back."

"Shit," I said. "Kim let him leave?"

Keane nodded. "My mistake. Didn't give him clear instructions. Never imagined somebody would walk in off the street with one of the coins."

"Did he get the guy's name?"

"Eric Brassey."

"Comm ID?"

"Didn't leave one."

"We need to find this guy," I said, looking him up on my comm. "There's an Eric Brassey in Burbank. No comm ID, but there's an address in Burbank. Keane, pull over."

Keane nodded and pulled to the curb. For all his genius, Keane was a lousy driver, and we needed to get to Burbank fast. If whoever was after these coins knew Eric Brassey had one, he was in serious danger.

"You need to get out," I said to Olivia.

"What?" asked Olivia. "Here? You can't leave me here!" She had a point. We were getting close to the DZ; this was a pretty sketchy neighborhood. No place for a pretty young woman alone with no gun and no comm.

"Fine," I said. "We'll drop you off later."

Keane got out and switched places. I pulled the car away from the curb and made a quick U-turn, heading back north toward Burbank. Ten years ago, we could at least have hopped on the freeway, but most of the freeways in and around Los Angeles were now automotive graveyards, thanks to post-Collapse chaos. The upside was that there were roughly twenty thousand fewer automobiles clogging up L.A.'s surface streets, so traffic wasn't actually much worse than it had been at the peak of L.A.'s population boom.

It took us nearly half an hour to get to the address, and I was so intent on my driving that I completely forgot about dropping off Olivia. The house was a respectable two-story gray stucco affair in an upscale neighborhood. A Cadillac aircar with Nevada plates was parked just down the street from the driveway. I pulled up behind it and threw the car into park.

"Rental car," said Keane, looking up the plate on his comm.

I nodded. I had a feeling somebody had already found Eric Brassey.

"Wait here," I said. My instruction was actually meant for Keane, but Olivia nodded as well.

I grabbed my SIG Sauer from the glove box and got out of the car. Putting my hand on one of the side jets of the Cadillac, I found that it was still hot. Holding the gun low, I made my way briskly up the driveway, reaching the door just in time to hear three muffled gunshots from inside. I tried the door: it was unlocked. I opened it and glanced inside. The living room was empty, and I heard no more noise from inside. I went in.

To my right was an open dining area, and beyond that a kitchen. Other than a few couches and chairs, there was no cover to speak of and no walls to hide behind. Straight ahead of me was a sliding glass door leading to a patio area. Along the right wall were windows looking out on the front lawn.

Bringing the gun to shoulder level, I crept along the wall through the living room, stopping to listen when I got to a doorway. Hearing nothing, I peeked around the corner: formal dining room, unoccupied. In the middle of the left-hand wall was another doorway that led to a hall. I walked across the room and peeked down the hall. I saw no activity. At the end of the hall was the foot of a staircase leading up to the second floor. I heard footsteps coming down. Raising my gun, I rounded the corner to see two men, armed with semiautomatics, coming toward me.

"Stop right there and drop your—" I started, but it was pretty clear they had no intention of following my instructions. Unsure who these men were, I erred on the side of caution: rather than firing, I dived out of the way. They demonstrated no such compunction. Gunshots rang out and the drywall at the end of the hall exploded into pieces as bullets tore into it.

I ran down the hall, trying to find some cover before the two men reached the bottom of the stairs. Whoever these guys were, I was now fairly certain they weren't cops. They wore black combat gear but no insignia I could see, and even the LAPD generally weren't this eager to fill random strangers with lead. Judging from the shots I'd heard earlier, they'd already killed at least one person, and they intended for me to be next.

I ducked into an open doorway on the right, which turned out to be a bathroom. The door jamb splintered as more gunshots sounded. The men were using suppressors, but in a narrow hallway, gunshots are still loud. So-called "silencers" don't make that *thwip*ping sound you hear in movies. They just sound like quieter gunshots. Mine were going to be a lot louder.

I shifted my gun to my left hand, wrapped my arm around

the doorway, and fired five shots blind. Then I pulled back, sank into a crouch, and leaned into the hall again. As I did so, more bullets tore into the door jamb, just over my head. One man was firing from the landing of the steps; the other was about fifteen feet away and moving toward me, hugging the wall to his right. Clever. Trying to pin me down so his partner could sneak up and take me out. I saw surprise on the face of the nearer man; he leveled his gun at me, but I was quicker. Unfortunately, my first shot was wide, and the recoil caused me to miss the next three as well. I guess I wasn't as good with my left hand as I'd remembered. The guy in the hall got off three shots, but he was startled and aiming too high; the bullets *thwack*ed into the drywall over my head. The guy at the stairs was holding his fire, undoubtedly worried about taking out his teammate. My last three shots hit the approaching man square in the chest. He grunted and stumbled backward, catching his balance against the wall. I was using armor-piercing rounds, but these new nanofiber vests are nearly impenetrable. I'd slowed him down, but it was going to take a headshot to stop him.

The bad news was that I was out of bullets, and these guys knew it: the catch had slid back, indicating the chamber was empty. I had another magazine in my jacket, but it was going to take a few seconds to get it loaded. A few seconds, it turned out, that I didn't have. Just as I smacked the magazine home, the man I'd shot came around the corner, his gun pointed directly at my right eye. I jerked my head to the left out of pure instinct. The gun went off as I whacked my head against the open door; I felt the bullet zip past my ear. Momentarily dazed, I brought my gun up and fired randomly, hitting him three times in the abdomen. It didn't even faze him. He took aim at my head again, and this time there was nowhere for me to go. Off-balance and disoriented, I made a split-second choice: I could either grab his gun hand to redirect it, or I could aim for his head and hope I could get a shot off before he did. I picked door number two.

I heard a muffled gunshot, and at first I was convinced I'd been killed. But then I saw the brain matter splattered across the wall in front of me and realized I'd blown a hole in the top of his head. He slumped to the ground, dead.

As he did so, his left arm fell limp to the ground and his hand opened. A silver coin rolled across the floor toward the kitchen. I nearly grabbed it before it rolled away, but I was too slow. I drew back into the bathroom as bullets tore into the hardwood floor in front of me. I was still plotting my next move when I heard footsteps thumping down the hall toward me.

This time I decided discretion was the better part of valor. I stepped back from the doorway into the shower, holding my gun at shoulder height. The guy didn't bother to stop; he ran right past the bathroom, stepping over his fallen comrade's corpse. I got off three shots as he passed, and I'm pretty sure at least one hit, but he didn't stop.

I ran forward into the hall, pivoting left and firing again. My aim was high this time; the man had reached down to snag the coin, which was still rolling toward the kitchen. He grabbed it with his left hand and then spun around, firing wildly in my direction. I fell back into the bathroom. When I glanced out again, the man was nowhere in sight.

I moved swiftly down the hall and peered around the corner to the left. The man had just reached the front door. I had a clean headshot, but I couldn't bring myself to do it. It's one thing to blow somebody's head off to save your life; it's quite another to execute somebody as they're running away. I shot him five times in the torso, but it barely slowed him down. He threw the door open and ran outside. By the time I got to the door, he was already to the Cadillac. I thought about taking out the tires, but then what? The guy would be stranded and desperate, and he was still wearing body armor. Meanwhile, Keane and Olivia were cowering in April's car a few yards away, and I had exactly three bullets left. No, it was time to let this fish go. Whatever the significance of that coin, it wasn't worth risking all three of our lives over. I watched as the guy got in his car and drove away.

Keane got out of the car and ran over to me, Olivia following close behind.

"Why'd you let him go?" Keane snapped, predictably.

"No choice," I said.

Keane shook his head disapprovingly but didn't argue.

"We need to get out of here," I said. "Neighbors must have heard those shots." The LAPD's response time was lousy since they'd cut their ranks by half after the Collapse, but in nice neighborhoods like this, there was still a reasonable chance a cruiser would show up within ten minutes of a report of gunshots.

"I have to look inside," said Keane, brushing past me and stomping up the driveway.

"Damn it, Keane," I said. "There's no time!"

But there was no stopping him. He was already halfway to the house.

"Stay here," I said to Olivia, and ran after him.

I followed Keane through the house to the scene of the carnage. "Nice shot," he said, examining the hole below the man's chin. A starburst of powder burns emanated from the wound. Keane riffled through the man's pockets, but found nothing of interest. Spare magazines, a locked comm, mini-flashlight, a few other mundane items. He carried no wallet of any form of ID. These guys seemed to be professionals.

"Where's Eric Brassey?" Keane said.

It took me a second to remember that was the name of the

guy who lived here, the one who had gone to see Mr. Kim about the iota coin. "Upstairs, I think."

Keane went down the hall and bounded up the stairs. I sighed. If we were going to get caught, I might as well try to gather some more data. I went through the dead guy's pockets again, to make sure Keane didn't miss anything. His face was clean-shaven, his hair cropped short. No visible tattoos or piercings—except the one under his chin, obviously. There was a hairline scar running down his left cheek to his neck, and the hair on his right hand seemed to have been permanently burned off. Chemical burns, I thought. The kind you see on military veterans. This guy looked to be in his late thirties, definitely old enough to have seen some action. I checked his hands. Uniformly rough, but no pronounced calluses, like someone who did a lot of physical work of varying kinds. Rolling up his sleeves, I found a small tattoo on his shoulder: a banner with the number 99 on it.

My comm chirped again. Another message from "Lila." It read:

disappointing :(maybe you are not ready for this game

I was about to tell "Lila" how I felt about her game when a woman's voice just over my right shoulder nearly gave me a heart attack.

"What's that?" she said.

"Jesus, Olivia," I said. "I told you to wait outside."

"I didn't. What does the tattoo mean?"

"Probably nothing," I said, standing up. I knew exactly what it meant, but we'd showed enough of our cards to Olivia—or whoever she was. I wasn't convinced her meeting with us wasn't part of some ruse on the part of LAFF, and I'm sure Keane suspected the same. At any moment, she could decide our relationship wasn't working out and call the cops on us. We needed to ditch her ASAP. "Keane!" I yelled. "We're leaving!"

Once again I heard sirens in the distance, and was relieved to hear Keane bounding back down the stairs a moment later. "Go," I said to Olivia, pointing to the door. I didn't particularly want her with us, but I wasn't about to leave her here so she could spill her story to the cops. Thankfully, she went without resistance. We went outside and got back in the car. Keane, following close behind, got in the backseat next to Olivia. I pulled away from the curb. I hadn't gone fifty feet before I saw the red and blue flashers of an aircar approaching from the distance. All we could do at this point was hope we hadn't been seen leaving the house; panicking and hitting the gas would only draw attention. We couldn't outrun an aircar. Once they spotted us, they'd get a fix on our location and track us until we ran out of gas.

Fortunately, the flashing lights began to fade in the distance; the aircar seemed to be landing in front of Eric Brassey's house. We breathed a collective sigh of relief. Olivia seemed to be as relieved as Keane and I, although if she was half as good an actress as her mother, I'd never know if she was faking.

"What did you find out about Brassey?" I asked.

"Hey?" Keane replied. I don't know where he picked up this verbal tic; every time he did it, I wanted to punch him in the face. I'd once dated an Australian girl who used to reply "Hey?" to questions she didn't understand, but with her it was adorable. Keane not so much.

"Eric Brassey. The guy whose house we were just in."

"Oh," said Keane. "He's dead."

"Anything else?"

Keane thought for a moment. "He had a lot of coins."

I sighed and made a right turn onto San Fernando, which would take us back toward our office. My comm chirped: April.

"Hey, April," I said. "Sorry to cut you off earlier. Things have been—"

"Forget it, Blake. We've got bigger problems. The police were just here."

"At your office? What did they want?"

"They were asking about you and Keane." Her voice went quiet. "They think you killed Selah."

I sighed. So Keane was right again. We'd been set up. "What did you tell them?"

"That I haven't seen you since dinner yesterday. So try not to contradict me when they catch you."

"Thanks, April."

"Good luck, Blake."

I ended the call. "We can't go back to the office," I said. "Cops are looking for us."

At some point, we were going to have to deal with the cops, but not while Gwen was still being held by Mag-Lev.

"Find us a hotel," Keane said. "Someplace that will let us pay in cash. Or iotas."

"I've only got forty bucks on me," I said. "And I don't think we have much more than that in our iota account." I'd been using my credit account for most of our expenses over the past few weeks, but if the cops were looking for us, there'd be a watch on that account.

"I've got some money," said Olivia from the backseat. "I'll get us a room."

"You are not part of the investigative team," I said.

"I've got nowhere to go," said Olivia. "If LAFF or whoever it was that killed my mother finds me, I'm dead. And you guys are broke."

I sighed. She was right. We were stuck with her.

TEN

Olivia got us a pair of adjoining rooms at a motel downtown. I didn't trust her, and I didn't like having to rely on her generosity, but we didn't have much choice. It was getting late, I was exhausted, and we needed a place to lay low while we plotted our next move.

While Olivia took a shower, Keane and I took advantage of her absence to discuss the case. I was sitting on my bed; Keane was in a chair next to a tiny desk.

"What do you make of Olivia?" I asked.

"Clone," said Keane. He didn't elaborate.

I nodded, having come to the same conclusion. We'd been talking around the possibility since we first found Selah's body, and by now the evidence was overwhelming. Part of Selah Fiore's plan for immortality had been creating genetically engineered clones of human beings. As far as we knew, she'd only cloned a few people as test subjects, but it made sense that she would have made at least one of herself, as a fail-safe in case something happened to her. Selah Fiore turns up dead, and lo and behold, her long-lost daughter appears to take on the mantle of Flagship Media. Good insurance policy for Selah, who was nothing if not a shrewd businesswoman. Hair and complexion aside, Olivia was a dead ringer for her mother. And she didn't talk like a twenty-year-old college student. She talked like Selah Fiore.

"Do you think she knows?" I asked.

"She suspects, at the very least," replied Keane. "Presumably Selah would have programmed Olivia with most of her own memories, as well as the bogus backstory about Belgium and Cal Poly. I wouldn't be at all surprised if there's an Olivia Fiore enrolled at Cal Poly, in fact. Selah was thorough. The question is how far she was willing to go with the ruse."

"You mean whether she thought it was necessary for the clone to believe the backstory," I said.

"Precisely. As Twain said, 'If you tell the truth, you don't have to remember anything.' If she believed the story herself, she'd be able to pass a multiphasic lie detector—which might very well be necessary, if she wants to take over Selah's empire."

"She acts like she has no interest in her mother's—that is, in Selah's—money."

"Yes," said Keane. "'Acts' being the key word. The problem with Selah going the self-deluding route is that, well, she's Selah."

"Meaning that she's too much of a narcissist to screw with her own memories?"

"That, and also that she's too smart not to figure it out. Unless she erases everything she knows about the cloning program, she's going to know all the signs of implanted memories. So she's stuck in a paradox."

"The only way the clone can be fooled into thinking she's not Selah is for Selah to have altered her memories to the point where she's not Selah. Thus defeating the purpose of cloning herself."

"Very good, Fowler."

I shook my head. The existential issues were beyond me. I was more curious in the logistics anyway. "So how would that work, exactly? There's another secret cloning facility somewhere? They've got Olivia in a box, and when Selah dies, somebody breaks the glass and lets her out?"

"It wouldn't have to be an actual cloning facility, just somewhere they can keep her in suspension. But yes, some event would presumably trigger an alert telling the technicians in the facility to revive her. Maybe Selah had to enter a code every twenty-four hours to prevent the alarm from being triggered. Or, more likely, she had an implant to monitor her heartbeat or brainwaves. Activity stops for a certain amount of time and *voilà*, Olivia wakes up in a house in San Luis Obispo, fresh as a daisy."

"But if Olivia is Selah's insurance policy, it's got a fatal flaw. Literally. The clones age too fast."

Keane nodded. "Unless Selah found a way around that problem, which seems unlikely."

"I wonder if there are more of them," I said. "Like if this one dies, another one takes its place." It had occurred to me that perhaps "Lila" was yet another clone of Selah, orchestrating all of this from some secret hiding place.

"Doubtful," said Keane. "The estranged-daughter story would only work once, if that."

"How long does she have?" I asked.

"Hard to say," Keane replied. "Selah's other clones aged at close to twenty times their normal rate. If this one's aging anywhere near that fast, she will start showing her age within a few months. But that's the least of her problems. Odds are she'll die of some kind of cancer or degenerative disease within a year. Her cells are multiplying way too fast for her body to stay healthy for long."

"So what's the point? Why let loose a clone of herself if it's only going to die a painful death in a few months?"

"That's an excellent question," said Keane. "Based on what Selah said about the coins, my guess would be that her intention was to secure her legacy. But we shouldn't assume Olivia's motivations are identical to Selah's. Even if they have the same memories, they are in different circumstances. We also don't know whether Olivia is acting alone."

"You think her cooperating with us is a ruse?" I asked. "That she's still taking orders from this Tad Curtis guy?"

"Or whoever Tad Curtis is working for, assuming Tad Curtis even exists," Keane replied. "She could be plying us for information."

"How would this mysterious mastermind know about the clone? Selah presumably kept it a secret."

"Not necessarily," said Keane. "She may have hinted that she had a fail-safe to discourage attempts to kill her."

"But she would have kept the details secret. How would our mastermind know where she was?"

"Come on, Fowler," Keane said with a frown. "Surely you've figured that out."

I thought for a moment. "Selah told him," I said. "That's what her killers were trying to get out of her before they executed her." In my mind, Selah's killers had been after Gwen, but of course they didn't care about Gwen. They didn't even know she had one of the coins.

"So our mastermind needs to get Selah out of the way for some reason," I said. "But he knows she's got this insurance policy, in case something happens to her. So he has his thugs interrogate her until she tells them where the clone is. They go there and . . . um, abduct her, I guess? Tell her to cooperate or else?"

"Or maybe Olivia's story is something like the truth," said Keane. "Maybe they really did trick her into calling you. She's definitely too smart to be as naïve as she's pretending to be, though. We have to assume she's using us. That fact does not preclude us using her, however."

"Use her for what?" I asked. "Other than temporary lodging, I mean?"

"Not sure yet," said Keane. "We're tragically short on clues, despite the day's endeavors."

"There is one thing," I said. "The guy I killed had a tattoo. A banner on his arm with the number 99 on it."

Keane frowned. "And does this mean something to you?"

"Yeah," I said. "I've seen it a few times before, on guys who worked for a private security company called Petoskey."

"What does the 99 mean?"

"It refers to the Battle of Jeddah," I said. "Also known as the Massacre at Jeddah. I wasn't there, but I knew some guys who were. November of '24. American forces were dug in, waiting for an attack. Supporting us was a company of guys from a private firm called Petoskey. Mercenaries, mostly ex-Marines and the like. Good guys, most of them. We ribbed them for being our cleaning crew; they tended to get assigned to the shittiest details, security for low-level diplomats, crowd control, stuff like that. At the end of the day, though, we were all on the same side. Anyway, the Americans are hunkered down, waiting for these insurgents to attack. Word comes down from the brass that Jeddah's a lost cause. The insurgents have a dirty bomb—like the one those end-times assholes used in Santa Monica in '22, but a lot bigger. A non-nuclear device that has a core of something radioactive, like plutonium. These guys are true believers, Jihadists in the worst sense of the word. They're going to set this thing off in downtown Jeddah and seed the place with enough radioactive dust to make it uninhabitable for the next thousand years. We had the manpower to defend the city against a frontal assault, but there's no way to defend a city that size from every goat farmer with a pickup. So we got out. Let them have the city."

"I don't recall a dirty bomb exploding in Jeddah," said Keane.

"It didn't," I replied. "That was bad intel. An informant misheard something. But the Allied commanders in Jeddah were panicking, trying to get all our guys out of this city before it turned into the Chernobyl of the Gulf. They did get out in time; commandeered every vehicle they could lay their hands on—airplanes, boats, buses, whatever they could find. Only problem was, in the confusion nobody told the Petoskey guys."

"You're saying the Petoskey contractors got left behind."

"It was the middle of the night when our guys got the order. And like I said, it was chaos. The officers were trying to be secretive about it, because we'd made some kind of deal with the regional security forces, and they weren't going to be happy about the Americans pulling out. Frankly, it's a miracle none of our guys got left behind. Some of the Petoskey guys figured it out, but what could they do? There were no vehicles, no way to get out. You can't just walk out of Jeddah. You've got the Gulf on one side and desert on the other. And the desert was full of guys whose hobbies were molesting goats and decapitation. A few of the Petoskey guys might have been able to hop on a transport or bus, but then they'd be leaving their buddies behind. So they stayed—all three hundred and forty of them. Care to guess how many survived the invasion?"

"Ninety-nine," said Keane.

"You got it," I replied. "Less than one out of three got out alive, and most of those were badly wounded. I've seen that tattoo a couple times before. Other Petoskey guys who made it out of Jeddah. They are, generally speaking, not a group of guys you want to fuck with. Survivors. Mean as hell, with a huge chip on their shoulders."

"Do you think the guy who got away was a Ninety-niner as well?" asked Keane.

"No idea," I said. "Could be. I wouldn't be surprised if the guys who killed Selah were Petoskey, either. They definitely had some kind of special ops training."

"Petoskey doesn't seem to exist anymore," Keane said, looking at his comm display.

"They lost their contract with the army in '25. Political bullshit meant to scapegoat the Petoskey guys for their own slaughter. Anyway, Petoskey folded not long after that."

"This is interesting," said Keane, his face still buried in his comm. "Petoskey's assets were bought by a company that was later merged into Green River."

"Green River?" I said. "I keep seeing their trucks all over town. Supposedly they're building some kind of training facility out in the desert. They provide security for a lot of companies in the Middle East."

"Yes," said Keane. "Including Saudi Arabia."

"Well, not anymore," I said. Saudi Arabia didn't technically exist these days. Since the Wahhabi coup, it was officially known as the Arabian Caliphate.

"Right," said Keane. "Green River had a contract to provide security for Gerard Canaan's company, Elysium Oil. That didn't go so well for them, though. They underestimated the strength of the Wahhabi forces and lost control of most of Elysium's facilities. The new government nationalized everything and Elysium's stock tanked."

"I'm not seeing what any of this has to do with the iota coins."

"Nor I," said Keane. "But this is the second connection we've found to Gerard Canaan. He was also on the board of the Free Currency Initiative."

"It makes sense he'd get into iotas. He lost his shirt on a

physical commodity; maybe he figured he'd fare better with a virtual one. But you're saying you think he sent those guys to get the coin from Eric Brassey as well."

"It's a working theory," said Keane. "It coincides with the idea that the value of the physical iotas is somehow linked to the value of the iota currency."

"How?"

"Hard to say," said Keane. "We need more data. This Green River connection interests me. Something isn't right there. What have you heard about this training facility they're building? I'm not finding anything online."

"It's supposed to be a secret," I said, "but you can't do something on that scale without people noticing. Rumor is the facility is supposed to be somewhere south of Riverside, near the old air force base."

"Hmm," said Keane. He spun around in his chair and tapped a series of keys on his notebook. While he did whatever he was doing, I lay back and closed my eyes. I was on the verge of sleep when he spoke again.

"Strange," he said. "I'm scanning the satellite imagery for that area, but not seeing anything that looks like a training base. Frankly, I'm not seeing anything that looks like anything. If there's a building here, it was built by Wile E. Coyote to trap the Road Runner."

"Maybe look in a wider area?" I asked.

"I'm going to try running a differential on satellite imagery from a couple years ago. If something large was built in that area recently, this should pick it up."

While Keane was doing this, Olivia walked in, wearing nothing but a towel. I had to remind myself that behind that pretty face was the mind of a megalomaniacal narcissist. It didn't stop me from looking, though.

"What are you gentlemen up to?" Olivia asked, sitting down on the bed next to me.

I found myself unable to speak.

"Looking for the Road Runner," Keane said. After a moment, his brow furrowed.

"Find something?" I managed to ask.

"Hmm," said Keane. "Building. Looks like a warehouse, though. Not a training facility. Wouldn't you expect a military training facility to have . . . I don't know, an obstacle course or something? An athletic track, at least? There's nothing here but a big square building. Not even a parking lot."

"Maybe there's parking under the building?" I suggested.

"What are you looking for?" Oliva asked. "Did you say something about a training facility? Maybe I can help."

We ignored her.

"I'm not seeing any other candidates," said Keane. "It's either this building or . . . hello."

"What?" Olivia and I said together.

"This property is owned by a real estate holding company. Care to guess what company is leasing it?"

"ACME?" I suggested.

"Empathix."

"Selah's company?"

"That's the one," said Keane. "I think we found our training facility."

"But they don't do military training. They develop holograms and sim . . . oh." It made perfect sense, now that I thought about it: With the sort of virtual reality training simulations Empathix employed, the trainees wouldn't need tracks or obstacle courses. Just a building and some VR goggles.

"What are you two talking about?" asked Olivia. "What's Empathix?"

"Olivia," said Keane, "what do you want?"

"What do you mean?"

"I mean, what do you want? Why are you here?"

"The same as you," said Olivia. "To figure out who Tad Curtis is working for. Who killed my mother."

"Good," said Keane. "We need you to do something."

"What?"

"Get us into that Empathix facility."

ELEVEN

The next morning, Keane and I were sitting in the lobby of the Empathix building, a big steel box in the desert just outside Riverside. Keane had done some digging and found a comm ID for a guy named Sam Chaudry, who was evidently in charge of some kind of augmented-reality project called Minotaur. Sam's current address was listed. Keane had guessed, based on Chaudry's résumé, that he was in charge of the Riverside facility. Olivia had called him, pretending to be Selah, and had managed to get us an appointment for 8 A.M. I was half-expecting to be met by armed Green River mercenaries—or worse, the police—but promptly at eight a small man in a suit and tie walked into the lobby, smiling nervously. Evidently Olivia had impressed upon him that we were very important investors who needed to be given a tour of the facility.

"You must be Mr. Barnes and Mr. Hewitt," said the man. "I'm Sam Chaudry. Selah Fiore told me you were coming."

"Hi, Sam," said Keane, shaking his hand enthusiastically. "Jack Barnes. Selah's told us a great deal about your Minotaur program, and we decided it was time to come see for ourselves."

"I was actually very surprised to hear from Ms. Fiore,"

said Sam. "She's never been to this facility. I wasn't sure she was even aware of Minotaur."

"Oh, she's aware, all right," said Keane. "She's very impressed with your progress. Didn't she say that, Mr. Hewitt?"

"Yes," I said. "That's what she said. Very impressed. With Minotaur."

"Well, that's great to hear," said Sam. "I know she's a very busy woman. So, did you want the full tour of the facility, or just get right down to business?"

"Let me ask you something, Sam," said Keane. "If I were to characterize this building as a big steel box in the desert with some fancy equipment inside it, would that be accurate?"

"Er," said Sam. "I suppose so."

"Good!" exclaimed Keane. "Then let's skip the box and go right to the fancy equipment. Minotaur is what we came to see, Sam. Let's get to it."

"Very good," said Sam. "Follow me, gentlemen."

We followed Sam down the hall to the elevator, then got off at the second floor and went down another hall to a small control room that was separated from a much larger room by a thick sheet of Plexiglas. Sam opened a cabinet and pulled out a helmet with a large visor. He set this on the desk behind him and then opened a sliding door to retrieve a fairly convincing mock-up of an M4-A4 carbine, the current standard-issue weapon for the U.S. Army.

"So," Sam said, "which one of you wants to be the guinea pig?"

"I'll do it," I said, taking the mock gun from him.

"Fine," Sam said. He reached into the closet and pulled out something that looked very much like the vests worn by the men who had broken into Eric Brassey's house. I handed the gun to Keane while Sam helped me into the vest. He then handed me a pair of leather gloves. "This way, gentlemen," he said, walking past me with the helmet. He opened a door that led to the larger room and we followed him inside. The floor of the room was made of something slightly spongy, like a gym mat. Red circles, about an inch thick and maybe ten feet in diameter, covered the surface of the floor in a staggered pattern. In the middle of each circle were two small platforms in the shape of footprints.

"If you would, Mr. Hewitt," Sam said.

I stepped into a circle, placing my feet carefully onto the footprints. As soon as I had done so, a padded metal ring, about three feet in diameter, descended from the ceiling and stopped just above waist level. Looking behind me, I saw that it was suspended by a single robotic arm.

"What's this for?" I asked. "In case I—"

Suddenly a series of small belts, articulated like earthworms, shot out of the floor, wrapping tightly around my boots. I instinctively tried to lift my right foot, and yelped as I realized I was pinned. I fell forward, catching myself on the padded ring.

"Sorry," said Sam. "I'd have warned you, but it's sort of a rite of passage here. Everybody does it."

"I'm not sure what the point of this simulation is if I can't move my feet," I said.

"We'll get to that," said Sam. "Mr. Barnes, could you hold the gloves for a moment?"

Keane took the gloves, studying them with interest. Sam handed me the helmet.

I put on the helmet and managed with some difficulty to get the chin strap fastened.

"Good," said Sam. "Now the gloves."

Keane handed me the gloves. As I put them on, Sam explained, "All of this gear—the vest, the gloves, the gun—are approximate versions of the real thing. Except for the helmet. The helmet is a production-model Minotaur combat helmet. This is exactly the same helmet worn by soldiers in the field.

The line between augmented reality and artificial reality is a very fine one, as you'll see." He handed me the gun. "You know how to use one of these, Mr. Hewitt?"

"I have some idea," I said.

"Excellent," said Sam. "I could try to explain to you how this works, but it's easier just to show you. When you're ready, go ahead and put the visor down. Mr. Barnes, this way, please."

Sam led Keane back to the control room. I flipped the visor down and found myself staring at a wall. The same wall I'd been looking at before I put down the visor.

"Is something supposed to be happening?" I shouted.

"Patience, Mr. Hewitt," Sam said in my ear. "And there's no need to shout. There's a mic built into the helmet."

"All right."

"Now, I have several scenarios to choose from: jungle recon, desert stronghold assault, urban pacification—"

"Urban pacification," Keane and I said together.

"Very good," said Sam. "Give me a moment, Mr. Hewitt."

I waited a few seconds. "I'm still not—" I began. Suddenly I was standing on a city sidewalk. It was the middle of the day; the sun was almost directly overhead. The street was deserted, and most of the stores on both sides of the street were closed and locked up. Several were boarded up. The street signs on the corner said FLORENCE and COMPTON.

I was inside the DZ.

"This is amazing!" I exclaimed. I had gone several steps down the street before realizing my feet were still strapped to the pads on the floor. How the hell was I walking? I stopped, looked down, and raised one of my feet. Nothing seemed amiss.

"We can see what you're seeing, Mr. Hewitt," said Sam in my ear. "If you're wondering how you're able to walk, your feet are attached to articulated pneumatic joints that allow your legs a full range of motion. The pads sense when you lift or push down with your foot and respond accordingly. When you step forward, the arm slides backward, giving the illusion of forward motion. I don't recommend trying to run yet, as your brain may have difficulty equating the passing of objects with the lack of actual forward motion. You get used to it, but it can cause a sense of vertigo in newbies."

I nodded, now looking at the gun in my hands. What had clearly been a model of an M4-A4 now looked very much like the real thing. It was incredible. The simulation somehow recognized the model and rendered it as the real thing, so convincingly that I would have sworn it was a real gun. Next I looked at my hands and arms. The visor had transformed my street clothes into a combat uniform and boots, but other than that it rendered my body exactly as it actually looked. Opening and closing my hand in front of the visor, I found myself wondering if I was actually looking at my hand or if I was looking at an extremely realistic simulation of my hand. What was the difference? How would I know?

"Don't get all solipsistic on us, Hewitt," said Keane in my ear. "Some of us would actually like to look at things other than your navel."

"Sorry," I said. I'd forgotten Sam and Keane were seeing everything I was seeing. The technology was essentially the same as that which Selah's director had used to insert thirty-year-old Selah into a scene in place of an android. Empathix had developed both.

"He'll wake up soon enough," said Sam.

"What's that supposed to mean?" I said, suddenly on edge. I scanned the street for signs of movement.

"Just that it's a combat simulation," said Sam. "Not a standing-and-looking-at-your-hands simulation."

"Want to give me a clue as to what my objective is?" I said. "Who are the bad guys in this scenario?"

"Whoever's shooting at you," said Sam. "Try not to get killed."

"Fantastic," I said. I had gotten to the corner, and I peered around and scanned the intersection. Still I saw no one. "Are there any people in this—" As I said it, I heard gunfire from somewhere to my right. Higher than street level. Somebody in one of the windows down the street. I moved backward to take cover in a doorway.

"Who's this guy shooting at?" I said.

"You tell us," said Sam.

I was about to swear at him and explain that generally soldiers did not get dropped into a hostile environment, alone, with no idea who they were supposed to be fighting, when a shattering window behind me answered my question. I peeked out from around the corner and saw movement in a third-story window kitty-corner to me, second building down the street, third window from the right. If that was the shooter, he was too far away for me to take out with an M4-A4 and no scope. I left my doorway and ran down the street, intending to take cover behind an abandoned car, but came to a halt after a few steps, a wave of disorientation flooding over me. I saw what Sam meant about running. My legs moved and the scenery moved past me, but the actual sensation of motion was a bit off.

"The pads tip forward slightly as you run," said Sam, "giving the illusion of momentum. But it's very difficult to fool the vestibular system. As I said, you'll get used to it. Just take it slow."

"Take it slow," I muttered. Easy to say when you're not being shot at. It took an active effort to remind myself that this was a simulation. The only hint was the vertigo I got from running. I decided to walk the rest of the way to the car. Bad idea.

Something hit me in the chest, just below my left collarbone, and a split second later I heard a gunshot. It felt like getting hit with a ball-peen hammer. A red outline of a human figure briefly flashed in the upper right of my field of vision, a radiating red circle showing where I'd been hit.

"Holy shit," I said. "He's using live ammo." It was a stupid thing to say, of course. There was no "he," there was no gun, and there was no ammo. The vest was rigged.

"Pneumatic percussive vest," said Sam in my ear. "The interior is fabric composed of alternating cells filled with gases that react explosively with each other. When you get hit, the Minotaur system signals the vest, which sends a current to the appropriate area, opening microscopic gates between the cells. The cells momentarily expand to twenty times their previous size. I'm told it feels very much like getting shot."

I could confirm that. At least, it felt like getting shot in a bulletproof vest. Having a bullet actually tear through your flesh was a whole different level of unpleasantness. "What if I get shot somewhere the vest doesn't cover?" I asked. Recovering from the shock of being shot, I ducked down and took cover behind the car.

"We have full percussive suits," said Sam. "But the manufacturer is still working some bugs out. The system will alert you if you get shot somewhere else; you just won't feel it. All this stuff is designed by another company. We just do the software."

"You do the training as well," I heard Keane say.

"We work closely with our clients to develop training programs," Sam said. "The training itself is generally conducted by their personnel, but of course they have to understand the software to train their guys. It also helps to have them on-site because it's an iterative process. We learn about user-experience problems firsthand that our own testers wouldn't spot. Sending a software tester into an urban combat simulation and sending a trained soldier into the same simulation can have quite different outcomes, as you might imagine."

Looking through the window of the abandoned car, I saw movement. I stood up and took aim, resting my elbow on the roof of the car. It would be tough to hit anything at this distance, but I could give the guy a good scare. I let go a burst of rounds at the window. The faux M4-A4 was loud, and it recoiled just like the real thing. I could swear I smelled the acrid, slightly metallic scent of gun smoke.

I didn't stick around to make sure, though. As soon as the last round of the burst exited the barrel, I was on my feet, running down the street. I did my best to ignore the vertigo and slid to a halt behind another car. Something in the back of my mind registered amazement at the uncannily realistic simulation of dusty concrete skidding under my boots. How the hell did you program something like that?

The survival part of my brain, however, had already directed my body to take aim at the window again. I took deep, slow breaths, trying to steady myself. I had a clear shot at the window, and was now close enough to hit it if I took careful aim. After a few seconds, I saw movement again, but held my fire until I had a clear view of the shooter's head and torso. I squeezed the trigger, letting loose another burst. The shooter disappeared from view.

"Well done, Mr. Hewitt!" Sam exclaimed in my ear. "Shall we make things a little more interesting?"

"Why not?" I said, feeling cocky from my success. My confidence wavered as a dozen or more men poured around a corner two blocks down, taking up positions in doorways and behind vehicles. They all carried rifles of some kind, and many of them wore Kevlar vests. They didn't wear uniforms, per se, but they bore the colors of the Tortuga gang. The Tortugas were the most vicious and powerful gang in the DZ.

"You said interesting, not suicidal," I said, taking cover behind the car.

"No need to fear, Mr. Hewitt," said Sam. "The cavalry has arrived." An overhead sketch of the street appeared at the top of my field of vision. It was just bare lines indicating the outlines of buildings, cars, and other objects, so I could see through it. In the middle was a small blue dot that I took to be me. At the top of the display were a dozen red dots representing the Tortugas. Advancing from the bottom were six green dots with names under them. I instinctively looked behind me, and saw several men in combat gear approaching. I had a brief moment of panic before realizing these guys were on my side.

"You're the squad leader, Mr. Hewitt," Sam said. "The men will follow your commands."

"How's the AI?"

"Try insulting Sergeant Chao's sister and find out."

I located Chao by his label over to my left. He was about five eight, but his arms were like tree trunks. I decided to stay on Chao's good side for now.

"Hey, Chao," I said. "Any idea what the fuck we're doing here?"

"Securing this street, sir," Chao replied. "We're supposed to rendezvous with Bravo Company at Gage and Compton at twelve hundred thirty hours."

The time display on the lower left read 1219. That gave us eleven minutes to take these guys out. As the worst-case scenario was getting a few bruises on my chest, I opted for aggressive tactics. "Chao and Baker, you're with me," I said. "We're going to cross the street and move doorway to doorway, leapfrog style. Gutierrez, Swartz, and Parker, move down this side of the street, using the cars for cover. Stay even with me; I'm going to be moving fast. Suppressing fire only until we get to Sixty-Eighth Street. Gutierrez, when your crew reaches that downed utility pole, spread out and take cover. Be quick about it. We don't want to give these yahoos time to think. Once you're in position, lay down as much cover as you can, and Chao, Baker, and I will advance like the badass motherfuckers we are. When we reach the barber shop, reload and advance. Keep shooting until these guys are grease stains on the pavement or we've chased them past Gage Avenue. And then shoot some more. Just don't advance beyond Gage, and watch for friendly fire. Let's move!"

I darted across the street, trying to focus on the building in front of me to suppress the motion sickness. The Minotaur display told me Chao and Baker were right behind me, and Gutierrez and the others were moving down the left side of the street. I fired a volley roughly in the direction of the Tortugas and then sprinted down the street to the next doorway. "Chao, go!" I said. Chao darted past me, followed by Baker. To my left and in front of me, I heard more bursts of fire.

"Hey, Sam," I said, fighting nausea. "How the hell do I reload?" I'd been watching my ammo count, in the lower right-hand corner of the display, steadily dropping.

"Pull the cartridge out and slap it back in," said Sam. "Your ammo supply is theoretically unlimited."

Well, that was a pleasant departure from reality. I took a moment to remove the cartridge and slap it back into place. The ammo count went back to 30. Very nice. I ran after my squadmates. We reached another doorway, and this time Baker went first. I came up behind him while Chao reloaded. Chao ran after Baker, and I followed. In this way, we advanced a hundred feet or so down the road, occasionally taking advantage of parked cars when they offered better cover than the doorways. The Tortugas began shooting at us shortly after we began to advance, but we were only now getting in the range where they had a chance of hitting us.

"Keep moving!" I shouted, as Chao and Baker began to lag. We were now close enough that a lucky shot could hit one of us, and the worst thing my guys could do at this point was slow down. If one of them held cover for too long, one of the Tortugas might anticipate where he was going to go next, get a bead on that location, and take him out as soon as he moved. Two doorways later, I pointed to a burned-out husk of an SUV. My squadmates nodded, and the three of us made a run for it. On my heads-up display I saw the other three mercs moving up on my left. I glanced over to see them hunkering down behind the utility pole. I motioned at them to spread out, and they did so. Gutierrez was at the end of the pole closest to me, Parker was at the splintered base of the pole on the sidewalk, and Swartz was right in the middle. It occurred to me, as I watched the small, lithe figure of Captain Swartz taking aim over the pole, that she was a woman. Sure enough, when I focused on her dot on the display, a dossier popped up identifying her as Rebecca Swartz. There was even a photo. She was cute. I wondered, with a name like that, whether she was ex-IDF. Then it occurred to me that she was a computer program, and I that I really needed a fucking vacation. I looked back at the overhead display and the dossier disappeared.

"Everybody reload," I said. "I want that suppressing fire in five seconds."

I popped the cartridge out and back in, bringing the little number in the corner back to 30. I counted to three and then motioned for Chao and Baker to advance from around the right side of the SUV. They nodded and began to move. I leaned around the left side of the chassis, let loose a burst, and then ran out into the middle of the street, zigzagging as I closed the distance between me and the Tortugas. I stopped, brought my rifle to my shoulder, took aim, and fired.

If—God forbid—you're ever in a situation like this, don't do what I did. You will most likely die. In fact, I fully expected to. I did it partly because I wanted to see how my "team" would react and partly because, while the Minotaur system was fascinating, I wasn't getting any closer to keeping me and Keane out of prison by playing video games. It was time to end this, one way or another.

So I just stood there in the middle of the street, taking aim at the first guy I saw. These guys were hiding behind cars and construction sawhorses; they had either expected to intimidate us with sheer numbers or hadn't expected us to advance this rapidly, because they sure weren't trying very hard to hide. I took out the first guy right through the sawhorse he was hiding behind, and then moved on to the guy on his left, who had his rifle propped on top of a Volkswagen coupe. He hadn't noticed me yet; he was firing single shots in the direction of Chao and Baker, who were behind me and to my right. I shot him in the head and he slumped to the ground. Another guy, wearing a Kevlar vest, was crouched on the sidewalk ahead and to the left, firing toward my guys hunkered down behind the utility pole. I shot him in the thigh and he fell to the pavement, screaming.

Figuring I had pushed my luck about as far as it would go, I broke into a sprint directly toward the gap between the Volkswagen and the sawhorse. There was another burned-out car on the left side of the road fifty feet or so behind the rough line that the Tortugas were firing from; if I could make it to the other side of that wreckage, it would be all over. While Chao, Baker, and the others kept the gangbangers busy, I could take potshots at them from behind. Again, this was a terrible idea from a tactical perspective. I was needlessly endangering my life for a quick, dramatic finish. But I had to admit, it was kind of fun.

I ran past the Tortugas and kept going. I didn't bother to zigzag this time, guessing that my best chance was to get behind the car before the Tortugas realized what I was doing. I was almost there when I felt two quick raps in my back, just below the shoulder blades. I winced but kept going. I figured the system would let me know if I was dead. I hoped there wasn't some kind of death simulation mode programmed into the vests to keep people from doing the kind of thing I was doing—like maybe all the gas chambers would explode at once, knocking all the air out of my lungs.

So far, though, nothing like that had happened. I made it to the other side of the car and spun around. To my glee, I saw that two of the Tortugas had attempted to follow me. Bad idea. They were caught in the open, and their flak jackets didn't help them. I got one in the neck and the other in the femoral artery. I reloaded and took stock of the situation. Chao and Baker had taken out two more guys to my right, and the other three members of my squad were now advancing down the street. The Tortugas were in full-panic mode. Those that weren't dead or injured were trying to make it to the opening of an alley to the west, where they could escape to another street.

"Let 'em go," I said. "Our objective was to clear this street. They're somebody else's problem now." As soon as I finished talking, I bent over to puke. The vertigo had finally gotten the better of me. "Sorry, Sam," I said, looking at the puddle of vomit on the sidewalk in front of me, which I knew was actually a puddle of vomit on the floor of the simulation room.

"No worries, Mr. Hewitt. It happens all the time."

"So is that it?" I asked. "We cleared the street. Do I get a set of steak knives or something?"

Sam didn't respond, so I assumed I had missed something. All the Tortugas were dead or fleeing except for the guy I'd shot in the thigh, who was still lying on the sidewalk, screaming.

"Seriously, Sam," I said. "Are you really going to make me rendezvous with—Hey, Chao, stand down." Sergeant Chao had approached the screamer with his weapon raised. He now stood about three paces away, barrel still aimed at the guy's head. "Sergeant Chao," I said, "lower your weapon!"

"He's a Tortuga, sir," Chao replied. "Standing orders to eliminate."

TWELVE

I stepped between Chao and the man on the pavement, who was still screaming. "It's a violation of the rules of engagement, Chao. Stand down."

Chao didn't waver.

"God damn it, Chao, stand down! Sam, what is this? Are these guys programmed to execute prisoners?" The other members of the squad stood by, watching the confrontation unfold.

"I think we're done, Mr. Hewitt," Sam replied. "The scenario is over, so if you can just take off the helmet—"

"Don't shut it down!" I snapped. "Barnes, don't let him touch anything."

"I'm on it," Keane said. "Proceed."

"Sergeant Chao," I said. "Who ordered you to execute prisoners?"

"Sir," said Chao, "we have standing orders from Command to eliminate all gang members in the DZ. Please step aside and let me do my job."

"I'm ordering you to answer my goddamn question, Chao. Who told you to execute prisoners?"

"Sir, step aside or I will relieve you of your command."

I couldn't help laughing. "You'll relieve me of my command? You're a bucket of electrons, you pathetic fuckstick. You're not even a real person. I take this helmet off, you disappear."

"Mr. Hewitt," said Sam, "I don't recommend trying to explain—"

"Shut him the fuck up, Barnes," I said.

The other members of the squad were watching me anxiously.

"Sir," said Chao, "you're acting erratically. I'm hereby relieving you of your command on the grounds that you are mentally unfit for duty. Please hand Captain Swartz your weapon."

"Wow," I said. "This is amazing. You're all completely convinced that you're real. Look, I'm not letting you shoot this man, okay? It's not happening. So stand down." I was aware on some level just how insane this was: I was standing up to one figment of my imagination to prevent him from murdering another figment of my imagination. None of these people were real, so it made absolutely no difference if one of them got killed. But real or not, it pissed me off that these guys had been programmed to violate the rules of engagement. Actual Green River soldiers had gone through this very training and had probably been faced with this very scenario: kill the gangbanger or be relieved of your command. Fuck that. This was a matter of principle.

"Sergeant Chao," I said. "Rules of engagement countermand your orders. I'm not going to tell you again. This man is not to be killed."

"Hewitt," said Keane. "You realize these are simulations, not people? They can't learn. The next time somebody runs this simulation, they'll reappear exactly as they were, with no memory of this."

"I know," I snapped. "It just pisses me off."

"Sir," said Gutierrez, "who are you talking to?"

"My fairy godmother," I said. "Sam, shut it off."

"I told Sam to get a cup of coffee," Keane replied. "I kind of want to see where this is going."

"Seriously, Barnes," I said. "Getting shot in this thing hurts. I can already feel the bruises forming. By the time I get this helmet off—"

"Drop your weapon, sir," said Gutierrez. "You're not right in the head."

Now what? Drop my rifle and surrender? Try to get the vest off before they shot me? I wasn't kidding about the bruises; the designers of this vest had been serious about making you not want to get shot. Of course, that was only if I got hit in the chest. For a moment I considered shooting myself in the head to see if that would get me out of the simulation.

That's when Swartz shot the screaming man. Two quick shots, right in the forehead. His body went limp.

I raised my rifle and swept a burst at my squad. They were so surprised that none of them even got a shot off before diving to the pavement. I turned and ran, putting the burned-out car between me and the squad. "Any time you want to shut it down, Barnes," I yelled. Automatic weapon fire rang out, and I heard glass shattering behind me. I turned down an alley, hoping it wasn't a dead end.

Straight ahead, about fifty feet down, was a brick wall, but the alley seemed to branch off in a T to the north and the south. I sprinted to the T. When I was almost there, I heard Keane's voice in my ear: "Go right here, Hewitt."

Banking on Keane being more curious than sadistic, I went right. More gunfire from the alley, and bits of masonry exploding to my right as bullets hammered the wall. Up ahead was daylight. I shoved the nausea down and kept running.

"Go left at the street, Hewitt," said Keane.

I got to the sidewalk and turned sharply to the left. I was breathing hard and drenched with sweat. I knew on some level that I was standing in a room with my boots strapped to robotic arms, but it sure as hell felt like I was running for my life through the DZ. I wanted to ask Keane where he was sending me, but I was too out of breath to talk. I could only hope he had my best interests at heart—and I was not at all confident I wasn't better off at the mercy of the psychopathic robot squad.

"Cross the street here and go into the shoe store," said Keane.

"You've got . . . to be . . . kidding me," I gasped.

"Trust me, Hewitt," Keane said. "You'll dig this."

Seeing the sign for the shoe store just ahead and across the street, I darted across the street, threw the door open, and ran inside. The glass shattered behind me and three more ball-peen hammers pounded me along my left shoulder blade. A horrified sales clerk stood at the register, holding a pair of men's sandals.

"Box those up," I gasped. "I'll pick them up later."

"Go to the back of the store," said Keane.

I ran to the back of the store, throwing open the door to the stockroom.

"Hey!" the clerk yelled after me. "You can't go back there!"

"Look for a pair of Louis Vuitton pumps," said Keane.

"Fuck you, Barnes," I gasped.

"I'm serious, Hewitt. This is important. Louis Vuitton pumps. Size six, black."

"Unfucking . . . believable," I muttered. This had to be the most absurd ending to an urban firefight in history: squad leader shot to death by his own men while searching for a pair of goddamned Louis Vuitton pumps. I dropped my gun and gave a mighty push to a steel shelving unit filled with shoeboxes. It crashed against the wall, wedging itself between the door I'd just come through and another shelving unit. That would buy me a few seconds, at least. Hopefully the shoes I needed weren't at the bottom of that pile.

I located a shelving unit full of women's shoes right about the time my psycho robot squad started banging on the door. I followed the numbers on the boxes until I got to the size sixes, then started tearing into Louis Vuitton boxes. The black pumps were in the third one. "If you tell me to put these on," I said, "this relationship is over."

"Look in the toe of the left shoe," said Keane.

I felt inside the shoe and found something that felt like a key. I pulled it out. An honest-to-God skeleton key, just like in the movies. "How in the hell . . . ?" I asked. The psycho robot squad continued to bash against the door. Their initial efforts had only wedged the shelving unit more tightly in place, but now they were making progress through sheer brute force: one of the supports of the unit had begun to buckle, and the door had opened a few inches.

"I'll explain later," said Keane. "Go to the back of the storeroom. There's a door that should lead outside, to an alley. Put the key in the lock, turn it one full rotation to the right, and then turn the handle."

I ran to the back wall and put the key in the lock. As I turned it, I heard the sound of metal shearing behind me. In the rear cam display, I saw the shelving unit collapsing on itself. The door was open a good foot, and the slight figure of Captain Swartz was wriggling through. The lock clicked and I turned the handle and pulled. The door to the alley opened. Behind me, Swartz was leveling her rifle. I went through the door and slammed it shut behind me.

I was about to ask Keane how he knew about the key to the door leading to the alley when I realized I wasn't in an alley. I was in the middle of an old-growth redwood forest that seemed to go on forever in every direction. The door I had come through was gone. Right in front of me was a redwood tree that must have been three hundred feet high. Its trunk was a good twenty feet in diameter. A scattering of light trickled through the branches overhead. I could hear birds in the trees.

"Mr. Barnes," I said, slowly turning around to take it all in, "where the hell am I?"

"Mendocino," Keane replied. "Nice, huh? I told you it was going to be cool."

"How did you know this was here? And how did you know about the key?"

"Easter egg," Keane said. "I noticed some peculiar things in the simulation while you were vanquishing your cybernetic adversaries. That downed power pole in particular."

"What about it?"

"It had a CalComm logo on it," said Keane.

"And?"

"CalComm folded in 2032. This simulation is using old data. A very particular set of old data. One that I'm intimately familiar with."

"Project Maelstrom," I said, realizing what Keane was saying. "This isn't the DZ as it exists in reality. It's the DZ as it was imagined shortly before the Collapse."

"Not just imagined," Keane said. "Designed. It's amazingly similar to the real thing; certainly close enough for training purposes. But it's not a model derived from the DZ. It's the model the DZ was derived from."

"The model that you built."

"Correct. I've always liked Mendocino, but it's such a hassle to get up there. A lot of walking. I prefer to just teleport there instantaneously. I used to eat my lunch here."

"How big is it?"

"It's infinite in all directions," Keane replied. "The trees are generated by a fractal algorithm. You could walk for a thousand years and never see two identical trees."

"Well, consider me impressed, Mr. Barnes."

"I wish I could take credit for it," said Keane, "but most of the actual development was done by a guy named Ed Casters. He was never officially on Maelstrom, but I used him for a lot of complex modeling work."

"Where's Ed Casters now?" I asked.

"Evergreen Cemetery," replied Keane. "He died in a car accident a few days before Gwen disappeared."

"Canaan got to him," I said.

"I assume so," Keane said.

What a shame. The person who had designed this forest was clearly a genius. "It's too bad they don't have one of these in the actual DZ."

"This *is* the actual DZ," said Keane. "The platonic ideal. The one you've been to before is just a pale shadow of this one."

"If you say so," I replied. "I'm taking this stuff off."

I removed the gloves and the helmet, then started on the catches for the vest. Apparently sensing what I had in mind, the robotic arms I was standing on retracted into the floor and the straps securing my boots loosened and disappeared back into their slots, like someone slurping up spaghetti. I was left standing on the raised footprints. I picked up the gun from the floor, took a step toward the door, and was hit by a wave of vertigo.

"Easy, Mr. Hewitt," said Sam's voice over a speaker. "It can take a minute to acclimate to the real world again."

I stood still for a time, taking several deep breaths. When the worst of the vertigo had passed, I walked the rest of the way to the control room and opened the door. Keane was sitting at the desk, watching data scroll past on a monitor. Sam was standing behind him, looking displeased.

"Surprised to see you're still here, Sam," I said. "I thought maybe the violations of the Geneva convention had been too much for you."

Sam smiled weakly. "Yes," he said. "I'd forgotten that this particular squad can get a little . . . overly ambitious."

"That's one way to put it," I said. "I suppose you're going to tell me that stuff at the end was just a test, designed to see how the trainee would handle a squad going rogue? Of course, that wouldn't explain Chao's insistence that he'd received standing orders to execute gang members."

"I just write software," said Sam. "The reality of the situation—"

"The reality of the situation," said Keane, "is that Green River is training to wipe out the gangs in the DZ. Up until Chao's performance at the end there, this whole simulation could be written off as a generic urban pacification exercise, but it's pretty clear this training program has a very specific goal in mind. When is Green River moving into the DZ?"

Sam didn't reply.

"Ms. Fiore told you to give us everything we wanted, did she not?"

"Yes, but . . . I don't know anything about Green River's operations. I just helped design the training program."

"And how is the training going?" Keane asked. "I don't see a lot of Green River personnel around."

"Th-they're on a rotating schedule," Sam stammered. "Some days they—"

"Sam," said Keane, "have I done something to make you think I'm the sort of person who would accept the sort of horseshit you're shoveling?"

"Um, no?" Sam said.

"Good. When did they leave?"

"Yesterday," Sam replied.

"Much better," said Keane. "Now, here's the thing, Sam.

Selah doesn't know about Green River's plans to take over the DZ, and she is going to be very upset when she finds out. I can call her now or I can let her figure it out on her own, after the attack on the DZ starts. The second one would give you a little time to cover your tracks and possibly start looking for a new job. Which would you prefer?"

"Um, the second one."

"Excellent. Here's what you're going to do. You're going to send the source code for the Minotaur system to my comm. Don't try any stupid tricks like corrupting the file headers or infecting it with a virus. I'm a genius; I'll see right through it. In return, we don't tell Selah Fiore what kind of operation you're running here."

Sam nodded. "I'll send it," he said. "Right away."

"Good. Also, I need one more thing."

"What?" Sam asked weakly.

"There was a project Empathix worked on several years ago. An economic forecasting model. I'm not sure what you'd have called it internally; I know it as Maelstrom."

"I'm . . . familiar with it," Sam said.

"Excellent. I need you to send me everything you have on that project. The modeling algorithm, the source data, documentation, everything."

"I could get in a lot of trouble for that," said Sam. "I mean, Minotaur is bad enough. Ms. Fiore did tell me to give you whatever you asked for, but—"

"Sam," said Keane. "I didn't mention this earlier, because frankly I didn't see any need to terrify you, but you're making this difficult. Do you know what treason is?"

"Of course," said Sam, "but I didn't—"

"You did, Sam. You knowingly assisted an illegal invasion on American soil. It's a textbook case. They probably won't even give you a jury. Hell, you'll be lucky if you're allowed a lawyer. You'll get hauled before a secret military court, given a summary trial, convicted, and almost certainly sentenced to death by lethal injection. There's a good chance your family will never even know what happened to you, which is probably for the best, because you don't want your loved ones remembering you as a traitor anyway."

"They can't—"

"They absolutely can, and almost certainly will, unless you delete all evidence pointing to an invasion of the DZ. You'll have plenty of time unless I make a call to the FBI as soon as I leave this building."

Sam swallowed hard. "I'll send it to you," he said. "All of it. I promise."

"Good!" Keane exclaimed. "Mr. Hewitt, I'm hungry. Let's go get lunch."

THIRTEEN

"Well, that explains the Green River presence," I said. We were in April's car, on our way back to L.A.

Keane nodded. "Gerard Canaan is going to use them to do what the National Guard and the Army can't. Pacify the DZ."

"Do you really think Selah Fiore was out of the loop? How could she not know? Empathix is her company."

"I'm sure she knew about the plan, but I suspect it was an option of last resort, in case the chaos in the DZ got out of hand. If at all possible, Selah wants—or wanted—to maintain the status quo. She makes a hell of a lot of money from movies and TV shows filmed in the DZ, and probably from a whole lot of other off-the-books deals with Mag-Lev. Establishing order in the DZ is the last thing Selah wants. She wants just enough chaos to keep the DZ interesting and profitable."

"But then things in the DZ start deteriorating," I said. "Selah gets worried. So she and Canaan make a deal, come up with a plan to pacify the DZ so they can maintain control if things get out of hand. But Canaan doesn't share Selah's concerns about maintaining the status quo. He jumps the gun. Selah resists, so he has her killed."

"Something like that," said Keane. "But killing Selah was

a risky play. And Gerard Canaan is a patient man. It took him nearly two decades to turn a profit on Elysium Oil. Why is he so anxious to invade the DZ right now?"

"The coins," I said.

Keane nodded. "That was my thought as well. "Outside the DZ, he's got free rein to beg, borrow, steal, or kill to get the coins. But if there's one in the hands of Mag-Lev or one of the other warlords, he's powerless to get his hands on it."

"I don't think Mag-Lev has one," I said. "He didn't seem to even consider the possibility we were in the DZ for any reason other than to find Gwen. And if he knew how badly Selah and Canaan want the coins, he'd have used it as a bargaining chip with Selah. Mag-Lev is clueless."

"Agreed," said Keane. "One of the other warlords must have one. And whoever it is, he knows how badly Canaan wants it. He's counting on Canaan's impotence inside the DZ to help him get a high price for it."

"But Canaan is calling his bluff. How long do you think we have?"

"Not long," said Keane. "Days. Maybe hours."

"So what now?"

"We've got to get Gwen's coin while we still can."

"If she even has one," I said.

"We have to assume she does," Keane said. "It's the only leverage we have against Canaan. The only chance to stop the invasion and maybe save Gwen."

I sighed. Keane was right. Eventually Mag-Lev was going to find out that we'd played him: Selah was dead, so there was no way we were going to talk her into helping him in exchange for Gwen. Our only chance was to use the coin to get Canaan to put pressure on Mag-Lev.

"All right," I said. "If the cops are looking for us, though, I can't go through the front door. Find me a gap. Somewhere near Willowbrook if you can manage it."

Keane nodded and went to work on his comm.

There were only a few streets you could legally take from Los Angeles proper into the DZ. Most of the smaller streets had been blocked off, and the major arteries now had checkpoints set up that were very similar to international border crossings—except for the fact that they were manned by the LAPD rather than border patrol agents. The security checks at these checkpoints were generally perfunctory; as far as I could tell their purpose was mainly to allow the LAPD to confiscate enough drugs, guns, and money to keep the checkpoints running. That said, there was no way a guy wanted for murder was going to be able to get through one.

The east and west borders of the DZ were, for the most part, congruent with the old interstates, the 110 and the 710; the highway barriers had been topped with razor wire. The highways themselves were littered with broken-down vehicles and other hazards and had been officially declared a no-go zone by the city, meaning that the government took no responsibility for anything that happened there. The original intent of this policy had presumably been to free the government from liability in case someone broke their leg trying to get into or out of the DZ; the practical effect was that the highways were now patrolled by armed drones that would fire armor-piercing rounds into anything vaguely humanoid until it stopped moving. Judging by the number of dead raccoons and possums that lay scattered across this wasteland, the drones' parameters had been set to err on the side of mayhem.

Fortunately, Keane kept a running list of weak points in the border. The list was updated frequently based on tips from Keane's various contacts inside and outside the DZ, as the LAPD was constantly repairing severed razor wire, and various miscreants were constantly making new gaps. You were still taking your life into your hands trying to cross the border, but if you could scale a couple of walls and avoid attracting the attention of the possum-killers, you had a decent chance of making it across. Of course, if you were crossing *into* the DZ, your fun was only beginning.

I had a backpack in the trunk with several spare magazines, but I was going to need some other supplies for a trip into the DZ. As we neared downtown, I pulled into the parking lot of a hardware store, backing up against a bush so that our license plate was hidden from the street. "Wait here," I said to Keane, who was still buried in his comm display. "I'll be right back."

After scanning the area for cops, I popped the trunk and got out. Moving the backpack aside, I pulled up the trunk liner and grabbed the lug wrench from where it was nestled next to the spare tire. I checked the size; looked like 3/4". I put the wrench back down, closed the trunk, and went inside the store. I went to the nuts and bolts aisle and grabbed an L-shaped anchor bolt and a hex nut that measured 9/16" on the outside. Then I picked up a battery-powered circular saw, a package of microfiber rags, some industrial-strength epoxy, a small hammer, a pair of leather work gloves, twenty feet of nylon rope, and a roll of duct tape. On the way out, I also grabbed a small LED flashlight, three bottles of water, and four granola bars, just in case this little adventure took longer than I planned. I surrendered nearly all my remaining cash to the cute Latina manning the register, then exited, tossed my bounty in the trunk, and got back in the car.

"Get anything for me?" Keane asked.

"No," I said.

Keane sulked.

I started the car and pulled around to the back of the building and parked. I popped the trunk and got out of the car. I removed the lug wrench, the anchor bolt and nut, the epoxy and the hammer, placed them on the asphalt, and then sat down cross-legged next to my treasures. First I made sure that the nut would fit inside the lug wrench. It would, just barely. There's enough play in a 3/4" wrench that a 9/16" nut will usually fit inside—but you'll have a hell of a time getting it back out, which was precisely the idea. I coated the inside of the wrench and the outside of the nut with epoxy and then hammered the nut into the wrench. I gave it a couple minutes to harden, then twisted the anchor bolt into the nut. The end result of this was a very strong U-shaped piece of metal, with one leg of the U several inches longer than the other. I tied one end of the nylon cord to the bottom of the U, smeared epoxy along one side of the longer leg, then lay the nylon cord against the epoxied surface. Finally, I wrapped duct tape tightly around the whole business, starting with the end of the U that had the rope hanging off it and continuing past the joint between the anchor bolt and the lug wrench. This was both for structural purposes and to dampen sound. I looked up to see Keane watching me.

"Grappling hook," he said. "That's rather ingenious, Fowler. Where'd you learn to do that?"

"Right here in this parking lot," I said. "It's called improvisation." I got a certain smug satisfaction from being better at certain types of problem-solving than Keane. I began tying a series of knots in the rope, one every foot or so. "Did you find me a gap?"

"I did," said Keane. "Tossed the coordinates to your comm."

I nodded. Having finished my knot-tying, I got to my feet and shoved the makeshift grappling hook and the other supplies into the backpack, and slammed the trunk. We got back in the car, and I drove to the motel where Olivia had gotten us a room. Hopefully she was still there, and not somewhere conspiring with Gerard Canaan.

"Good luck, Fowler," Keane said, getting out of the car. He closed the door behind him and I drove away.

I pulled back onto the street, heading south along the eastern border of the DZ. Following the surface streets south and then west, I drove cautiously to avoid drawing the attention of the LAPD. The gap Keane had located was near the southern corner of the western border. I parked the car at the end of a cul-de-sac, beyond which was a concrete wall marking the border. I got out and grabbed my supplies from the trunk. I wished I had thought to take a flak jacket from the office, but it was too late for that now. I told myself I'd move faster and be more comfortable without it. At least until I was dead.

FOURTEEN

I went to the wall and turned left. According to Keane's intel, there was a gap in the razor wire about fifty yards north of 136th. It took me awhile to spot it; a good thirty-foot section of the wall's top was hidden by an overgrown clump of eucalyptus, but it was more or less where Keane's source had indicated.

After looking around to make sure I wasn't being observed, I slipped behind the eucalyptus and worked my way toward where I'd seen the gap. Hopefully I hadn't misjudged the location; it would suck to get to the top of the wall and get a face-full of razor wire. I pulled the grappling hook from the backpack and made a couple of loops of slack in the cord. It took me three tries to get the damn thing over the far edge of the wall; thanks to the proximity of the vegetation, I had to throw it almost straight up. The first time it failed to grab and the second time it nearly brained me.

The wall was only about ten feet high, so if I could have gotten a running jump I could conceivably have pulled myself up by my fingertips, but the eucalyptus made that difficult. Besides, I wanted to get a feel for the grappling hook in case the wall on the other side of the highway was higher. I'd designed the hook specifically for these highway barriers; as far as I knew they were the only walls I needed to get over. Once I'd made sure the hook was secure, I put on the gloves and the backpack, got a firm handle on the rope, then planted my feet against the wall. To be perfectly honest, I felt like a complete idiot, scaling a wall in broad daylight like Adam West in that cheesy *Batman* series from the 1960s. Fortunately the eucalyptus gave me a fair amount of cover from any potential spectators in the area.

I pulled myself so my eyes were level with the top of the wall; thankfully I was dead center inside the razor wire gap. Someone had cut the wire and cleverly coiled the loose ends into the eucalyptus stalks, so that it was virtually impossible to see the gap unless you knew where to look. Thank God for Keane's network of anonymous hooligans. I let go of the rope with my right hand and grabbed the top of the wall. I got my left hand on the wall as well and pulled my upper body onto the wall.

For a moment, I remained as still as possible, listening for the telltale buzz of a drone. I heard nothing but the low rumble of traffic and the occasional staccato gunfire from somewhere in the DZ. Below me was a paralyzed river of pre-Collapse vehicles, all peeled paint and cracked tires, receding into the afternoon haze to my left and to my right.

I pulled myself bodily onto the wall, coiled up the rope, and tossed it and the grappling hook down to the cracked asphalt shoulder below. Then I spun around and lowered myself down as far as I could before letting go. I landed in a crouch next to the grappling hook. I grabbed it and the rope, stuffed both in the backpack, and stood up.

To get into the DZ, I now had to cross ten lanes of highway and scale another wall like the one I'd just come over. The tricky part of this was that I didn't know exactly where the razor wire gap was on the far wall; Keane's intel said that it was a "short walk" to the north. Whether that meant ten feet or a quarter mile, I had no idea. I could only cross the highway and turn north, hoping that I'd see the gap when I got close.

I made my way through the abandoned vehicles toward the far wall, staying low and zigzagging north when the cars were too close together for me to squeeze through. When I got to the last row of cars before the median, I crouched in the space between a Buick sedan and a UPS truck, listening for drones. Still I heard nothing but traffic, the occasional shout, and, farther away, gunfire. I darted across the median then skidded to a stop again in a small gap between two cars in the first northbound lane.

The intuitive thing to do when you're in the no-go zone is to get out as fast as you possibly can. This is a sucker move. The problem is that if you're moving, a drone will spot you sooner than you can spot it. Given the ambient urban noise, you can only hear a drone coming from about two hundred yards away, and that's if you're quiet and listening for it. The effective range of a drone's guns is about fifty yards on full automatic or a hundred and fifty yards firing singly. The bullets will go a hell of a lot farther than that, but drones are so lightweight that the recoil tends to throw off their aim. The drones are also programmed to take ambient noise into account; basically they'll get as close as they think they can before shooting. What this means is that if you have good hearing and you can make yourself be very still and very quiet, you can usually hear the drone coming before it starts shooting.

So I forced myself to breathe slowly and did my best to block out the noise of the cars, voices, and occasional distant gunfire, listening for that telltale hum. Still I heard nothing. I crept forward through the gaps in the cars, zigzagging what I hoped was a "short walk" to the north. The cars were lined up on the shoulder here, so when I got to the last row, I was only about eight feet from the wall. Looking to the top of the wall, I scanned left and right but saw only an unbroken stretch of razor wire. Fuck.

Once again I forced myself to be still and listen. Once again I heard nothing but ambient noise. I pulled back and crept between the two rows of vehicles for another fifty feet or so. Then I peeked out again and looked for the gap. I saw what looked like a break in the razor wire about eighty feet farther north. My instinct was to run toward it, but I forced myself to stop and listen. This time I heard, amid the shouts and rumble of traffic, a constant, high-pitched whine. After a few seconds, I was able to determine the direction of the sound. It was somewhere to the south, coming my way.

I made a run for it.

The problem was this: the optics on these drones are pretty damn good; I figured it was about fifty-fifty that it had already spotted me. If that was the case, I was as good as dead if I remained on the road. I had a clear escape route planned, and I was fairly certain I could get over the wall before I was in optimal firing range. The drone would take pictures of me and forward them to the LAPD, but it wouldn't pursue me into the DZ. Even if the LAPD's facial recognition software tagged me as a wanted fugitive, there wasn't much they could do about it but wait for me to leave. The LAPD had no official authority inside the DZ. They could put a bounty on my head and hope the local warlords would turn me over, but that would take time. All I needed to do was get to Gwen's apartment, grab the iota coin, and get out. So I ran.

Unfortunately, it quickly became clear that I had misjudged the gap. That is, what I thought was a gap was just a slack point in the wire where a support was missing. If I tried to climb over that part of the wall, I'd bleed out before I'd got twenty steps into the DZ.

Okay, Fowler, I thought. Don't panic. There's got to be a

gap here somewhere. Stop, take a step back and look for it. There was no point in trying to be subtle now; the drone had certainly seen me. If it was closing at top speed, I'd be in range in about three seconds. But I saw no sign of a gap in the razor wire. It was time for evasive action.

I turned and ran back into the sea of dead cars. Hiding from a drone is difficult; if it loses track of you, it switches to infrared. Drones can see right through cars. Fortunately, shooting through cars is a little bit more difficult, so I was reasonably safe as long as I could keep a vehicle between me and the drone. That would buy me a little time, but it wasn't a long-term strategy. The only way out of this was for me to disable the drone. It would already have called its fellows for backup, but I might at least buy enough time to find the gap— assuming it actually existed—and get out.

Drones aren't particularly hardy; the trouble with trying to shoot one down is that they are small and fast-moving, making them hard to hit. Well, that's part of the trouble. The other part is that by the time you get a shot off, it's probably already killed you six times over. I needed a way to lure it in close without letting it shoot me—and as I knelt on the hot asphalt, I had an idea for how to do that. It was a lousy idea, as most ideas borne of desperate circumstances are, but it was the only one that had managed to float to the surface of my not-quite-panicking brain at that moment.

I peered through the windows of the nearest car but, not finding what I was looking for, moved on to the next. This one too had nothing to offer me. Keeping my head down, I crept to a third car. The buzz of the drone was loud now; I didn't dare look, but I guessed it was only a few car lengths away. It had slowed down, knowing that I was nearby. It was probably having a little trouble pinpointing my exact location because the cars were radiating enough heat to scramble my heat signature. It couldn't see me unless I moved or it caught a glimpse of me through a window. I got on the ground and rolled under a school bus, the asphalt hot where it contacted my bare skin. Emerging on the other side, I scampered behind the bus's left front tire and scanned the area in front of me. I could hear the drone buzzing back and forth right on the other side of the bus.

Just ahead and to my right, I saw what I was looking for. Well, not exactly what I was looking for, but it would do: a badly weathered and warped four-foot-by-eight-foot sheet of OSB siding, the stuff they use for the exterior walls of cheap apartment buildings. Probably slid off the back of a pickup on its way to a construction site. I crawled toward the sheet, doing my best to keep the bus's tire between me and the drone. Then I lifted the sheet and crawled under it, the warp in the sheet making it possible to lie flat on the pavement with the sheet lightly resting on my shoulders. My head was oriented toward the bus and my gun lay flat on the pavement, with my right hand on top of it.

It was hot. Almost unbearably hot. Despite the OSB shielding the pavement from direct sunlight, I felt like I was lying on a griddle. After about three seconds, I could feel perspiration pouring down my sides, and the sweat in my eyes was making it near-impossible to see. I couldn't keep my head off the asphalt without rocking the OSB, so I forced myself to press my right cheek against the pavement. I'm not a big crier, but that brought tears to my eyes. I half-expected to hear the sizzling of bacon.

The upside to all this was that I was—I hoped—now virtually invisible to the drone. I was hidden from its conventional camera under the OSB, and the asphalt was so hot that I couldn't be much more than an indistinct blur on its infrared cam. The trick now was to stay conscious until the drone got close enough for me to shoot it down. I must have been losing a pint of water a minute.

Evidently my hiding spot was even better than I'd hoped: I waited there for a good three minutes and it never even came around the bus. I heard its buzzing growing more distant. This was no good; it wouldn't stop looking until it found me, and any minute it was going to be joined in the search by every other drone in the area. It was time to seize the initiative.

I momentarily raised my head from the pavement and barked, "Hey!" Then I lay back down, trying to be as still as possible. After a few seconds, I caught a glimpse through my blurry vision of something coming around the back of the bus. It was extremely tempting to raise my gun and just start shooting, but my reflexes were no match for the drone's. The nanosecond it identified something potentially human in the area, it would direct its fire at me. The best I could hope for was a draw—and taking the drone with me to the great beyond was going to be little consolation.

So I waited as the drone buzzed ever closer to my hiding place. At one point it stopped and hovered for several seconds about five feet from my face. A droplet of sweat had run down my cheek and was now hanging from the tip of my nose, causing it to itch something fierce. It was all I could do not to brush it away with my thumb.

Finally I heard the drone moving away. Doing my best to blink away the sweat and tears, I gripped my gun and pulled myself into a sniper position. As I did so, the sheet of OSB tipped on my back like a lever on a fulcrum, and a corner touched the pavement with a barely audible tap. The drone pivoted to face me and I fired.

Not waiting to see if I'd hit it, I rolled out from under the OSB. I heard the sound of automatic gunfire and felt gravel hitting me in the face. I scrambled to the other side of the bus. The gunshots had stopped, and I was miraculously unhit. I heard a strange noise like a June bug ramming into a screen door and realized the drone was whacking into the side of the bus. I'd winged it. I ran around the other side of the bus to approach it from behind. By this point, its gyros had compensated for the damage and it was once again hovering in place, but it was facing the wrong direction. I wiped my eyes with the back of my sleeve, took aim, and fired. The drone shattered into pieces. The main chassis hit the ground, gave a little whine, and died. I knew how it felt.

Dizzy from the heat, I collapsed against the bus and sank to the ground. Once the gushing of blood in my ears faded, I forced myself to listen for more drones. Thankfully I heard nothing. Hopefully I had a minute or two before the next wave hit. I took several deep breaths, trying to steady my hands and ease the nausea, then opened the backpack. I guzzled down an entire bottle of water, discarded it, and drank half of another. I put the half-empty bottle back in the backpack, threw it over my shoulders, and got to my feet. Taking another moment to listen for drones, I still heard nothing, so I walked back through the cars toward the far wall. I found the gap in the razor wire another sixty feet or so down from where I'd been looking. As I tossed the grappling hook up, I heard the sound of several more drones approaching.

I was still a little shaky, so it took me longer to get to the top than last time. I spotted at least three drones, and they were almost in range. I left my grappling hook and rope on the wall and threw myself down the other side, landing hard on a patch of gravel. Ahead of me were several dilapidated apartment buildings covered with so much graffiti it was hard to tell what color they'd originally been painted. I took off running toward the opening of an alley between two of them. I was fairly certain the drones wouldn't pursue me past the wall, but there was no point in testing their programming. Once I was safely ensconced in the alley, I leaned against a wall and drank some more water. The sound of gunfire was closer and more persistent now. I heard a child wailing somewhere, and several men yelling at each other in anger. The air smelled of burning garbage and urine.

I'd made it into the DZ.

FIFTEEN

I wended my way through the urban maze that was the Disincorporated Zone. I had only two goals in mind: (1) get to Gwen's apartment as quickly as possible; and (2) don't get killed. As I was largely unfamiliar with this part of the DZ and didn't know where the lines were drawn in the current gang war, the best I could do in service of goal number two was to actively avoid the sound of gunfire. This rule of thumb served me well; by keeping to the alleys and side streets, I made it to the address Gwen had specified in less than forty minutes. Despite it being the middle of the afternoon, the streets were nearly deserted—a fact that was more disturbing than reassuring. Although I saw no active fighting, clearly the residents of this area were staying indoors as much as possible.

I made it to the gate without incident, and had no trouble getting through the padlock and the lock on the building's outer door. I moved quietly up the stairs, finding the hallway deserted. Breathing a sigh of relief, I continued down the hall to Gwen's apartment, picked the lock, and slipped inside.

I spent the next hour going through every cabinet, drawer, and cupboard in Gwen's apartment looking for the coin. I had almost given up when I finally glimpsed a silver disk at the bottom of a shoebox full of random junk that had been stuffed in the back of her bedroom closet. So Keane's suspicion was right: Gwen had gone back to the DZ for the coin, but had been intercepted by Mag-Lev's thugs before she had a chance to get it.

Holding it in my hand, I had to laugh. It felt cheap. Titanium is a lightweight metal; that's why they use it on things like airplane frames. It's incredibly strong, but it feels like tin. The iota coin was like a prize you'd get out of a cereal box. I'd have put it in a shoebox in my closet, too.

I held it between my fingers and studied it for a moment. It was identical to the one in Mr. Kim's book. On the front was the backward J symbol, which I took to be the Greek letter iota, under which appeared the inscription "Not One Iota." On the back was *Leptophlebia nebulosa*, the mayfly. The only difference between Gwen's coin and the picture was that this one bore the serial number 7. I stuffed the coin in my pocket.

By this time I was starving, and the granola bars in my backpack didn't sound very tempting. I took the backpack off and made myself two ham and cheese sandwiches, which I washed down with a Diet Coke. Once I had eaten, I became aware of how sticky and exhausted I was. I was tempted to take a nap at Gwen's place and sneak out of the DZ later on in the night, but it probably wasn't a good idea to stay in one place too long. Somebody might come looking for Gwen or the coin. So I splashed some water on my face, put the backpack on, and went to the door. I pulled it open with my left hand, holding my gun in my right. The hall was empty.

I closed and locked the door behind me and made my way down the hall. I was halfway to the stairs when a door opened just ahead of me. I raised my gun as a man emerged into the hall. It was the grungy guy I'd seen earlier, but now a pistol dangled from his hand.

"Haven't seen Kathryn for a while," said the man.

"Yeah, well," I replied, continuing toward him. "We all have our crosses to bear."

"Maybe you tell me where she is," he said.

"Maybe I don't."

He pointed his gun at me and I stopped walking. I nearly shot him at that point. In retrospect, I should have.

"Mag-Lev said to keep an eye out for her."

"Look, friend," I said. "Kathryn isn't here, as you can see. This really isn't any of Mag-Lev's business."

"Maybe you tell him that."

"You live in a world of maybes, don't you?" I said. "Look, I get it. One of Mag-Lev's guys comes by, tells you there's something in it for you if you can find out where Kathryn is. Here's the problem: Mag-Lev already has Kathryn. That's why she isn't here now. So you're wasting your time."

The guy thought for a moment. "Maybe you explain all that to Mag-Lev."

I was about to shoot him in the face just to liven up the conversation when I heard another door open behind me. I spun around to face the newcomer, a chubby Latino wearing gym shorts and a wife beater. He was pointing a gun at me as well. Dumb, Fowler. Really dumb. You should never have let yourself get boxed in like this.

So the question was: Could I take them both out before one of them shot me? I put the odds at about three to one in favor. These guys were clearly not pros; I could put two in Fatty's chest, pivot and take out Slim before either of them knew what was happening. But here's the thing: these guys weren't killers; they were just random losers hoping to make a few bucks. I didn't want to kill them if I didn't have to. I wasn't bullshitting when I'd said they were wasting their time; we could sort this out with a quick call to Mag-Lev. Also, not to put too fine a point on it, but a one-in-four chance of getting shot is still way too high. Getting shot sucks. A lot.

I raised my hands in the air, letting the SIG Sauer dangle from my index finger. "Seriously, guys," I said. "This is a misunderstanding. Kathryn's gone, and she's of no use to Mag-Lev anyway. Do you have Mag-Lev's comm ID?"

Silence.

"It's okay," I said. "I do." I don't generally have DZ warlords on speed dial, but Keane and I had recently had some dealings with Mag-Lev. "I'm going to holster my gun, all right? Just stay calm." I turned sideways so that I could see both of them, then ever-so-slowly lowered my hands to chest level, bringing them in front of me. I took the barrel with the fingers of my left hand, grabbed the bottom of the grip with my right, and then gently slid it into the holster. "Airplane goes back in the hangar," I said as I tucked it into place. "Nobody gets hurt. Now here's what I'm going to do. I'm going to tap my comm and say Mag-Lev's name to call him. I'll put him on speaker so we can all have a nice conversation together, okay?"

Neither of the men spoke, but Slim shrugged, which I took as a go-ahead.

I tapped my comm. "Call Mag-Lev," I said. Nothing happened. I tapped it again, glancing down to make sure I'd activated it properly. "Call Mag-Lev," I said again, louder this time. Still nothing. Technology was not my friend today.

I glanced at the comm display. No Signal, it read. Fantastic. I wondered if this was a momentary glitch or if the war in the DZ had escalated to the point where the communications infrastructure was being targeted. "Can't get a signal," I said.

"Been out all day," said Slim. "I'm gonna have to go talk to Froggy."

"Froggy?" I said. "Who the hell is Froggy?"

"Mag-Lev's guy. He's the one who came by here asking about Kathryn."

Great, I thought. Middle fucking management. I'd be in this hallway a week before these guys talked to anybody in Mag-Lev's organization who knew anything. I was really wishing I had shot Slim when I'd had a chance.

"C'mere," said Slim. I glanced at Fatty, to my right, who nodded. I walked toward Slim, stopping a few feet in front of him.

"Gimme your gun," Slim said.

Having committed to a peaceful resolution, I didn't see any alternative. I gently withdrew my gun from its holster and handed it to Slim, handle first.

"Open that door." He indicated the door he'd just come out of.

I sighed and turned the handle, and was immediately assaulted by the odors of marijuana and feet.

"Go in."

I went into the apartment. Most of the windows had been covered with blankets and dirty laundry and other refuse littered the floor. All things considered, I preferred Gwen's decorating style to Slim's.

Slim followed me in. "Siddown."

I moved a pizza box out of the way, removed my backpack, and sank into a couch.

"Jorge," said Slim to the fat guy in the hall, "you watch him. I'ma go talk to Froggy."

Jorge waddled into the room, pointing his gun at me. I noticed his finger was on the trigger.

"Jesus, Jorge," I said. "Trigger discipline. Don't make me come over there and show you how to use that thing."

I swear to God, Jorge turned the gun toward his face and looked right down the barrel.

Slim grabbed his hand and pointed the gun to the floor. "Leave it like this unless he gets up," Slim said. Jorge nodded. That seemed like a compromise I could live with. He put my gun on a shelf behind Jorge. "I'll be back in an hour."

Slim walked out, closing the door behind him. I smiled at Jorge. Jorge stared dumbly back at me, his gun pointed directly at his big toe. It was going to be a long hour, assuming Slim wasn't being overly optimistic. I found myself wondering how trustworthy someone named "Froggy" was likely to be. If Froggy were a stand-up guy who knew his business, I might actually be out of here in an hour. If he were some whacked-out paranoid drug addict, he might instruct Slim to shoot me in the head to appease the lizard people. There was no way to know.

I was still pondering this half an hour later, when I heard shouts and gunfire from somewhere nearby. We'd been hearing gunfire in the distance for some time, but it seemed to have gotten a lot closer. Jorge went to a window and pulled back the blanket. From the rosy glow that shone through, I deduced that the sun was setting. More automatic fire sounded somewhere below.

"What's going on, Jorge?" I asked, eyeing my gun on the shelf a few feet away.

"Shooting," said Jorge.

"No kidding," I said. "You might want to turn off the—"

There was another burst of gunfire and Jorge fell backward to the floor, covered with blood and broken glass. He'd taken at least one bullet in the face, just below his left eye, and several more to the neck and chest. Jorge never knew what hit him.

I lunged off the couch, grabbed my gun off the shelf, and crouched low to the floor, then crawled back toward the door and turned off the light. Now the room was dark except for the minimal red glow coming through the crack in the blanket over the window. The gunfire below was near constant. I went into the adjacent bedroom and pulled the blanket over the window aside slightly.

Outside it was chaos. In the thirty seconds that I scanned the street, I counted three different groups of armed men, and I honestly couldn't tell who was fighting whom. There was one group hunkered down behind a pile of broken concrete down the street to the left, another group that was firing from the several windows and doorways across the street and, although I couldn't actually see them, another group that was firing from the alley between the building I was in and the one to my right. At first I thought the two groups I could see were both targeting their fire at the group in the alley, but those two groups seemed to be trading occasional potshots at each other as well. It was unclear what they were fighting over—it was possible somebody had found out one of the iota coins was inside this building, but I doubted it. Most likely it was just a coincidence that this particular skirmish was happening right outside. More accurately, there were probably dozens of skirmishes like this going on all over the DZ, so the odds that one would happen nearby were pretty good. There didn't seem to be anyone deliberately directing fire at Gwen's building; Jorge had probably been mistaken for a sniper.

I crawled away from the window and back into the living room. It looked like I wasn't going to be getting out of here for a while, and if I was going to have to spend the night, I wasn't going to do it in Slim's nasty apartment. Still in a crouch, I opened the door to the hall and peeked out. It was empty. I stood up and ran back to Gwen's apartment. This time it only took me ten seconds to get the door unlocked. I went inside, relocked it, and threw the deadbolt. Then I spent half an hour listening to gunfire while crawling around Gwen's apartment, pushing heavy pieces of furniture up against the door. If anyone tried to get in, I wanted them to have to work for it.

When I'd finished my barrier, I crawled into the kitchen and ate some cold spaghetti and drank a quart of milk. My hunger satisfied, I crawled to the bathroom and took a quick shower, then crawled into Gwen's bedroom. I shoved the mattress off the bed, lay down on it, and fell asleep.

SIXTEEN

I awoke to the sound of gunfire. I know, I just said I'd been hearing gunfire all night. But this was different. Not the guns themselves, but the way they were being fired.

There's a difference between the sound of automatic weapons being fired by gangbangers and automatic weapons being fired by professionals, just as there's a difference between the sound of kids playing sandlot baseball and the sound of the World Series. The languid, sporadic firing broken by long intervals of silence had given way to regular, controlled, staccato bursts broken only by the few seconds it would take to reload or advance. Gone, too, were the taunts and coordinating shouts. The only vocalizations I heard now were screams and cries for help.

An army had moved into the DZ.

I crawled to the window and looked out. The new group was advancing from the south, to my right. A dozen or so men had taken up positions in the street, taking advantage of what cover they could find from doorways and parked cars as they went, but moving too quickly for anyone to get a bead on them. From their positions and the way they were directing their fire, I got the sense that the group behind the building had been vanquished: either they'd been killed or had run away. The group across the street from Gwen's building seemed on the verge of doing the same. A few guys were still taking potshots from windows, but the street out front was silent, and bodies littered the pavement. Within a few minutes, if the newcomers kept up the pace, they were going to scare off the gang down the street to my left as well.

The good news, from my point of view, would be that there would soon be fewer stray bullets flying through the air in the general vicinity. The bad news was that if these guys really were pros, they wouldn't leave an entire apartment building unsecured for long. They'd break in and go door to door, making sure there were no snipers or other threats in the building. The bad news trumped the good news, in my opinion.

I would have liked to pretend I didn't know who these people were or what they were after, but I was fairly certain I did. Gerard Canaan had sent Green River to take over the DZ. And while I'm sure there were lots of good reasons for someone to want to take over the DZ, number one in Canaan's mind was undoubtedly locating every last iota coin in existence. If they ID'd me, word would go up the chain to Canaan that I'd been found nosing around the DZ. Even assuming they knew nothing about Gwen's iota coin, Canaan would quickly figure out what I'd been looking for. They'd get the coin and I'd probably end up "collateral damage" of the invasion, dead in an alley. Keane would go to prison for Selah's murder, and April and Gwen would probably join him.

I was tempted to flush the iota down the toilet just to keep Canaan from getting it, but that negated the possibility of me using it as leverage against him. And we still didn't know why the iota coins were so valuable. For all I knew, it could hold the key to keeping all of us out of prison. I could hide it, but where? Green River was taking over the equivalent of a

small country to find it. Tearing apart an apartment building with sledgehammers and crowbars was not going to be
a problem for them.

The fighting was right in front of Gwen's building now,
and I chanced another look out the window. I got a pretty
good look at the newcomers: they were wearing full combat
gear and Minotaur helmets. A battalion of military veterans
armed with equipment like these guys had could probably
pacify the entire DZ in a few days. It made me wonder why
nobody had ever tried it before. A question more germane to
my immediate predicament, though, was: how the hell was I
going to get out of here? I had been banking on the gangbangers getting bored and moving on; these DZ skirmishes
were more like pissing matches than actual battles. One gang
would move into another gang's territory to test the other
gang's will to defend it. Depending on the outcome of the
skirmish, boundaries would be solidified or redrawn, and
then everybody would go home. The gangs didn't hold territory in a strict tactical sense; they depended on a mutual
understanding of where the lines were. This was another of
Keane's collective delusions, I suppose: the boundaries
between two gangs were where they were because everybody agreed that's where they were.

The Green River guys didn't fight like that. They moved
forward inch by inch, foot by foot, pacifying everything in
their path. You knew exactly where the line between Green
River territory and non–Green River territory was, because
it was defined by scary-looking men with guns. If I was ever
going to get out of this building, I had to do it before I was
firmly on the wrong side of that line.

The first thing to do was to identify my escape route. I
moved all the junk away from Gwen's door as quietly as
I could and then checked the hall. It was still empty. If there
was anyone else alive in this building, they were asleep or

hiding. Just as well to leave them that way. I went to Slim's and peeked out the window where Jorge had been shot. The Green River guys were all over the street in front. That meant taking the stairs was not an option: once I got to the first floor, the only way to get out of the building was by the front door.

I went down the hall to Jorge's apartment, which was on the back side of the building. This looked more promising. There was a door to a small landing, which led to a fire escape down to an alley that was bordered by an old redwood fence. They alley was dark; if there were streetlights in the area they'd broken or been shot out. If I could get down the fire escape into the alley without being seen, I could climb over that fence and follow it to the north, deeper into the DZ and away from the territory claimed by Green River. Then I could cut west toward the border. I might run into some fighting, but if I stayed low and took advantage of cover, I figured my odds were pretty good. The only problem was the group of Green River guys who seemed to have set up shop about thirty feet away from the end of the building, right below Gwen's apartment. If I climbed down the fire escape now, chances were at least one of them would see me. Mag-Lev's deadline was now less than six hours away, but as anxious as I was to get out of the DZ with the coin, I couldn't help Gwen if I was dead.

The fact was, the Green River guys didn't particularly care about me at this point. They didn't know who I was or that I had one of the precious coins they were looking for. Unfortunately, if they saw me leaving the building now, they were very definitely going to be taking an interest in me. They'd ID me and search me, and it would be all over. I just needed to give them something else to focus on for a while, so they wouldn't bother me as I was leaving. Explosions are good for that.

I went into Gwen's kitchen and verified that she had a gas oven. I retrieved an oscillating electric fan I'd seen in the bedroom, closing the door behind me. I put the fan on the kitchen counter, plugged it in, and turned it on full blast. I set my flashlight on the floor with a napkin draped over it so that it would give me just enough light to see but not enough to be obvious from outside. Looking under the sink, I found a box of thirteen-gallon trash bags. I took one of them and a twist-tie, then dug around in the junk drawer in the dark until I felt the pair of pliers I'd noticed earlier.

I pulled the stove away from the wall and felt for the nut connecting it to the gas line. Once I found it, I loosened the nut and pulled the connection apart. Putting down the pliers, I grabbed the trash bag and put the opening over the supply line. I set the timer on my comm, then wrapped the opening of the bag tightly around the gas line and secured it with the twist-tie.

While I waited for the bag to fill, I grabbed a tape measure from the aforementioned junk drawer and made a quick measurement of the room. Subtracting for cabinets, appliances and furniture gave me a volume of about 1,200 cubic feet. When I'd finished measuring, I checked my trash bag. It was nearly full. I gave it a few more seconds, then removed the bag and checked the timer. One minute and thirty-eight seconds.

Assuming the good people at the Glad Products Company were being straight with their measurements, that came to seven point five seconds per gallon, or eight gallons per minute. A gallon is zero point one three cubic feet, so I was getting a flow rate of about one cubic feet per minute.

I'd learned quite a bit about improvised explosive devices during my time in Saudi Arabia, and here's the thing about methane explosions: they're harder to pull off than you might think. You need a concentration of between 5 and 15 percent methane to get the gas to ignite. More than that, there's not enough oxygen for it to burn; less than that, the methane is too diffuse to catch fire. Additionally, even if you're in that range, you might just get a flash fire rather than an actual explosion if the mix is too rich or too lean. Ideally, you want right around 10 percent methane to get an actual supersonic, window-shattering explosion. The other problem is that methane is lighter than air, so it's going to tend to collect against the ceiling, giving you a rich mix up high and a lean mix toward the floor. Hence the fan, which would help distribute the gas more evenly. There was a small chance a spark from the fan would prematurely light the gas, but that was a risk I was going to have to take.

With a room volume of 1,200 cubic feet, I needed one hundred twenty cubic feet of methane to get to 10 percent. So at one cubic foot per minute, it was going to take nearly two hours for my bomb to be ready. An hour and a half would get me to 7.5 percent, which would probably do it, but I wouldn't want to go any lower than that—particularly since there was a pretty high margin of error with all these back-of-the-envelope estimates. For good measure, I moistened a towel and shoved it against the gap below the door that led to the rest of the apartment. I moistened another towel for the door to the hall. I could smell the gas already, but it wouldn't be dangerous to breathe for a few minutes yet. Methane isn't poisonous, but you get a high enough concentration of it and it will shove out the oxygen, and oxygen is kind of important for breathing.

The other thing I needed was a spark, and the easiest way to get a spark is electricity. I rooted around in cabinets until I found a twenty-foot extension cord under the sink. Not long enough. I set it aside. In a closet I located a vacuum cleaner.

Good. I removed it from the closet, then grabbed a sharp knife from the counter. After hacking off the cord where it connected to the vacuum housing, I stripped the ends of the leads. I then stripped the paper from the twist-tie I'd used earlier and twisted each end of the twist-tie around one of the leads, making a bridge between them. I could have just twisted the leads together and hoped for the best, but the breaker might trip before I got a spark with that method. This way the current would melt the twist-tie and then arc between the two leads. I tied the end of the cord around the handle of the oven, and picked up the rest of the cord, along with the extension cord.

I put the flashlight back in the backpack and put the backpack on. Opening the door, I made sure no one was in the hall, then exited the apartment with the coiled-up end of the vacuum cleaner cord, the extension cord, and the damp towel. I closed the door over the vacuum cleaner cord and shoved the towel against the gap.

I continued down the hall, letting out cord as I went. I made it almost to Jorge's apartment before running out of cord. Plugging the end of the vacuum plug into the extension cord gave me just enough length to get to an outlet in Jorge's living room, near the door to the fire escape. I set the male end of the cord down next to the outlet and sat in a chair where I could keep an eye on the door.

Then I waited.

SEVENTEEN

The Green River mercenaries moved more quickly than I thought they would. Hearing some activity downstairs about twenty minutes after I sat down, I went across the hall to Slim's apartment to investigate. As I expected, the Green River guys had cut the padlock to the gate and moved into the building. They'd be going door to door to check for guns and gang members. Unless they ran into some serious delays on the first two floors, they were going to be at the door to Gwen's apartment in less than an hour. All I could do was go back and sit in Jorge's apartment with the door open, listening for the sounds of men coming down the hall and hoping that I had enough time.

Well, that wasn't *all* I could do. In fact, I seriously considered plugging in the cord, hoping for a big enough flash fire to blind the guys outside for a few seconds, and making my way down the fire escape. I didn't like my odds, but at least there wouldn't be any collateral damage. That was the problem with my current plan: the Green River guys were going to be opening doors and possibly escorting people downstairs. If I waited until the mercs got to Jorge's apartment before triggering the bomb, there might very well be civilians within the blast radius. I hadn't been too worried about the neighboring apartments, because there were at least a couple of walls between Gwen's apartment and her neighbors. But if there were people in the hallway, they could conceivably be seriously injured or even killed by the blast.

I decided to take my chances. If there were civilians in the way, I just wouldn't trigger the bomb. That meant turning myself in to Green River, but I didn't see any other options. I wasn't going to kill innocent people to escape.

So I waited. And smashed the mirror in Jorge's bathroom. This action served a purpose other than venting my frustration: I wanted to be able to see the Green River guys coming down the hall. I left the door open and propped a shard of glass against the door jamb, angling it so that I could see anyone coming down the hall. About forty minutes later, I saw several men in full combat gear, bearing automatic rifles, exiting the stairwell. As expected, they went to the first door and knocked. They identified themselves as a "DZ security patrol," which I thought was a nice touch. The guy doing the talking was loud and authoritative, but not overly aggressive. When nobody answered after a minute, he backed up and his two comrades smashed in the door with a portable ram. The guy in charge and one of the ram guys went inside while the other two waited in the hall.

A couple minutes later, evidently satisfied that the apartment was empty, the men moved on to the door across the hall. One man remained behind to watch the stairwell. There were five apartments before Jorge's, including the one they had just gone into. Slim's was the second one on the left.

The occupant of the apartment across the hall from the one the Green River guys had just broken into had opened his door and was complaining loudly in a Haitian accent about his Constitutional rights being violated. I sympathized, but his argument was legally questionable—the DZ having been de facto disowned by the U.S. government—as well as highly inadvisable from a strictly pragmatic perspective. The man—a little black guy in short-sleeved cotton pajamas—was dragged into the hall, handcuffed, and escorted by one of the mercenaries downstairs. While the guy at the stairs held his post, the other two went inside the man's apartment to search it.

They finished with his apartment a few minutes later, and the man who had escorted the Haitian downstairs rejoined his fellows as they approached Slim's apartment. I had closed and relocked Slim's door, so they went through their usual routine of knocking, identifying themselves as DZ security, waiting a bit, and then bashing in the door. This time there was a bit of a commotion as they found Jorge's body, but they deduced pretty quickly that he'd been taken out by a stray bullet through the window. They finished clearing his apartment and moved on.

At this point, I picked up my mirror sliver and gently closed the door to Jorge's apartment. The Green River guys were getting close enough that they might notice me spying on them, and there was no point in accelerating things. I would just have to wait and listen for them to knock. And then what? I checked the time. It had only been an hour and eighteen minutes since I'd started the gas flowing. Unless the next two apartments took them eight minutes apiece, I was going to be below my minimum threshold. The gas would probably catch fire at this point, but it wouldn't blow out the windows or doors. It would just be a momentarily flash of light and a big *whoosh!* Just enough to put the mercenaries on edge.

Maybe if I could let them into the apartment and stall them somehow—the problem being that I'd look pretty suspicious hovering over an outlet with an extension cord. I needed some way to remotely trigger the bomb. I searched Jorge's place frantically for some kind of electric timer, but found nothing. There was a timer on the oven, of course, but that would require some tricky wiring I didn't have time for. I needed a switch with a simple on/off circuit.

A lightbulb went on over my head as I walked into the bathroom. Literally—the bathroom light was on a motion detector. I went back into the living room, unplugged the extension cord from the vacuum cord, and then grabbed a butter knife from the kitchen. I went into the bathroom, turned the light switch off, and then climbed onto the bathroom counter to unscrew the lightbulb. After dropping the lightbulb in the wastebasket, I yanked the light fixture off its brackets and used the butter knife to unscrew the leads. Then I wrapped the leads around the prongs of the extension cord. I got down from the counter, turned the switch back on, plugged a lamp into the extension cord, and walked into the bathroom. The lamp went on. Good. I walked out of the bathroom, turned the switch off, then flipped it back on, doing my best to remain motionless. The lamp stayed off. I very slowly withdrew my arm from the room. The lamp stayed off. Taking a deep breath and cringing slightly, I plugged the vacuum cord back into the extension cord. Nothing happened. I exhaled.

I went to the door and looked out the peephole. The Green River guys were going through the apartment across the way, which was apparently empty. Great. Jorge's place was next. My comm said that it had been an hour and twenty-four minutes. I needed at least six minutes more to be assured of an explosion. Somehow, I had to stall.

I was trying to imagine how I might do this when I heard a woman yelling loudly in the hall. Her voice seemed to be coming from the right, toward Gwen's apartment. One of the guys in the hall was yelling at her to get back inside, but she was refusing to comply. This was not welcome news. If my bomb went off, anyone within thirty feet of that door was going to be severely injured, if not killed. To make matters worse, she was complaining about smelling "tear gas" in her apartment. Nice going, Fowler, I thought. How long before the Green River guys smell it and figure out what you're up to? Hopefully they were too distracted to notice the vacuum cleaner cord running along the baseboard.

I slid my gun under the couch and opened the door to Jorge's apartment, startling the man standing in the doorway across the hall. At the end of the hall to my right, maybe ten feet from Gwen's door, was an elderly woman, still yelling about the "tear gas." Halfway between us, facing away, was another Green River mercenary. He was assuring the woman that they were not using tear gas, that this was just a routine security check, and that she needed to get back in her apartment.

"Sorry," I said to the guy across the way. "I heard the yelling. What's going on?" I turned around and quickly locked the door, then turned to face the man again.

"DZ security check," said the man. "Sir, you need to go back in your apartment."

"Security check?" I said. "Oh, okay. Did I hear something about tear gas?"

"See?" cried the old woman. "He smells it, too!"

The man to my right looked back at me and scowled. "Please, ma'am," he said, turning to face her again. "You need to get back in your apartment. It's not safe for you out here." I saw a gold oak leaf on the man's shoulder, similar to the army's major insignia. Most of these private security firms used an officer rank system modeled on the U.S. military. For combat positions they usually hired only elite soldiers who already had some military experience, so they didn't have enlisted men per se. They had civilian employees and officers. If these guys had been army, it would be pretty unusual to have a major doing door-to-door searches, but this Green River squad was probably all officers.

"She's crazy," said the guy across the hall. "We ain't using no tear gas."

"I thought I smelled something, too," I said. "This is an old building, you know. They've had problems with the pipes leaking."

"Well, it ain't us," the major said. "We'll get to you next, sir. Please go back inside."

The man down the hall was now attempting to physically move the old woman toward her doorway. The old bird was putting up a hell of a fight, but I was starting to worry the guy was going to lose patience and clock her.

"Please," I said, moving down the hall toward them. "Let me help."

"Sir!" the guy behind me yelled. "You need to get back inside!"

"It's not tear gas," I said, coming up on the other side of the old woman. "It's the pipes. They leak. Smell that? Natural gas. I already called. The guy is supposed to be coming out in the morning." I put my arm around the woman and helped the mercenary maneuver her toward her door. He seemed grateful for the help, and the guy behind me stopped yelling orders for a moment.

"Natural gas?" the woman asked, confused. "But then who are these soldiers?"

"Some kind of security check," I said. "Don't worry, ma'am. I'm sure it will all be over with soon." We had gotten to her door, and I turned to the major. "I've got it from here, sir," I said. "I'll make sure she stays inside."

"Who are you?" the woman asked.

"Why, Mrs. Graham!" I exclaimed, glancing at the name

on her door. "I'm Kevin. We met yesterday, remember? I just moved in."

"Oh," said Mrs. Graham. "I'm sorry, Kevin. My memory isn't what it used to be. Are you sure they're not using tear gas? It makes my sinuses hurt."

"No, ma'am," I said, with a smile at the major. "No tear gas." We escorted her into her living room.

"Ma'am," the major said, "are you going to be all right? Can I leave you with Kevin for a few minutes?"

"Oh, of course," said Mrs. Graham. "Kevin's a nice boy. He lives next door."

"Okay, ma'am," the major said, backing toward the door. "We'll be coming to your apartment in just a little while. Kevin will stay with you until then." But the guy didn't leave. He was still watching me. "What's your full name, Kevin?"

Shit.

"Mrs. Graham," I said, "why don't you go lie down in your bedroom. I'll handle this."

"I'm not sleepy," said Mrs. Graham. "And I should make coffee for the soldiers."

"You got some ID, Kevin?" asked the man.

I sighed. "Look, Conroy, is it?" I said, reading the name on the pocket of the man's fatigues. "Kevin isn't my given name. I had some trouble after I got out of the service. Nothing major, but I got mixed up with the wrong people. That's why I'm here. Trying to start over, you know?"

"What kind of trouble?" Conroy asked, with a frown.

"Your name isn't Kevin?" Mrs. Graham asked.

"Don't really want to talk about it," I said. "Mrs. Graham, please go to your bedroom."

Mrs. Graham scowled at me but didn't move. This was not going well. Conroy looked like he was about to call for help. It was time to mix things up a bit.

"Hey," I said, pretending to pick something up from the bookshelf to my right. "You ever seen one of these?" I was holding the iota coin between my thumb and forefinger.

"Jesus," said Conroy, looking at the coin. "Is that . . . ?"

"It's one of them iota coins. They only made nine of them. I wonder if they're worth anything."

"Where did that come from?" asked Mrs. Graham. "That's not—"

"Some kind of bug on the back," I said, studying the coin. "Like a dragonfly."

"Let me see that," said Conroy, taking a step toward me.

"What do you think this means?" I asked. "'Not One Iota.' That's weird, right? How can it be not one iota?"

"Give it to me," said Conroy, taking another step toward me. The barrel of his rifle was still pointed at the floor, but it was creeping upward.

"Oh well," I said. "It's all yours if you want it." I tossed the coin in an arc just over Conroy's head. He snagged it with his left hand and I punched him in the face.

While he was still stunned, I undid the catch on his side-arm holster and pulled out the gun, a Glock 9mm automatic. With my left hand, I redirected the barrel of his rifle and with my right I jammed the gun under his chin. By this time, he had steadied himself, but blood was gushing out of his nose down his chin and neck.

"Shhh," I said.

Conroy swallowed hard and gave a curt nod.

"Mrs. Graham," I said, "for this portion of the program, I strongly suggest you retire to your bedroom."

Mrs. Graham, a bewildered look on her face, nodded and walked down the hall.

"Conroy!" yelled somebody in the hall. "Where'd that guy go? We need to get into his apartment."

"Tell him you'll be right out with the key," I said quietly. "You've just got to make sure Mrs. Graham is okay."

Mrs. Graham went into her bedroom, closing the bedroom door behind her. Conroy glared at me.

"Hey, Conroy!" yelled the voice in the hall again. "What's going on?"

I pressed the gun harder against Conroy's jaw. Conroy glared at me harder.

"Give me a sec!" Conroy yelled. "Just making sure the old lady's okay. Thought she was having a heart attack or something. I've got the key, just hold on."

"Very good," I said. "Put down your rifle and close the door."

He lowered the gun to the ground, walked to the door and closed it.

"Lock it," I said.

He locked the door and turned around.

"Take off your gear," I said.

"Huh?"

"Your helmet, your vest, your boots. All of it. Down to your skivvies. Do it fast. I'll take that coin too."

Conroy grumbled, but he complied. I guessed I had about thirty seconds before the guys in the hall figured out something was wrong, and when they did, I wanted to be wearing as much bulletproof clothing as possible. It had also occurred to me that I had a better chance of getting out of the DZ alive if I looked like I worked for Green River. Fortunately Conroy and I were roughly the same size.

I moved the rifle a healthy distance away and then began stripping down as well, keeping the Glock close. When Conroy and I were both down to our skivvies, I heard a crash through the wall on my left. Conroy's pals had evidently decided not to wait for him and had moved into Jorge's apartment. Things were going to get really interesting when one of them wandered into the bathroom. I ordered Conroy to sit cross-legged on the floor with his hands on his head while I got dressed.

"What the hell is going on out here?" asked a voice to my left. Mrs. Graham had emerged from her bedroom into the hall. "Why are you naked?"

I was not, strictly speaking, naked. By this time I had Conroy's pants on and was working on the shirt. Conroy was still in his skivvies.

"Mrs. Graham," I said firmly. "It isn't safe for you out here. You need to go back to your room."

Mrs. Graham disappeared again. I put on Conroy's vest and started working on the boots. I was just getting the second one on when Mrs. Graham came into the hall again.

"Mrs. Graham," I said. "Please don't make me—" That's when I noticed she had a gun: a .357 revolver. Jesus. I should have known. It's the DZ. Everybody has guns. Conroy sat on the floor in front of me, chuckling at this development. Personally, I was more concerned with the bomb that was going to go off at any moment a few feet down the hall. We were probably relatively safe in Mrs. Graham's living room, but I'd feel a whole lot better if she would get back in her damn bedroom.

"This is *my* apartment!" snapped Mrs. Graham. "You don't get to tell me what to do, Kevin!"

"Please, Mrs. Graham," I said, taking a step toward her. "This is for your own safety. I—"

That's when she shot me. Twice, actually. Right in the chest. It hurt, but it would have been a lot worse if I hadn't been wearing Conroy's vest.

"Damn it, Mrs. Graham," I shouted. "Get back in your fucking bedroom!" I don't usually swear at old ladies, but Mrs. Graham was going to get us both killed. Suddenly wide-eyed, she backed into her bedroom and slammed the door.

Too late, I turned to see that Conroy had gotten to his feet and opened the front door.

"Conroy!" I shouted, pointing the Glock at him. "Close that door and—"

There was a flash and, for a moment, I saw Conroy engulfed in flames. Then the shock wave hit me and everything went black.

EIGHTEEN

I had a vague memory of Mrs. Graham standing over me and shouting, and then somebody carrying me downstairs. The next thing I knew, I was strapped into the backseat of a car. From the motion of the vehicle, it seemed we were airborne. My head hurt, my ears were ringing, and my hands and face felt like they were on fire. All I could smell was burning hair. The only other person in the car was the driver, who was wearing a Green River medic's uniform. Next to me on the seat were Conroy's Glock and helmet.

"Where are we going?" I asked blearily.

"Memorial Hospital," said the driver. "How you feeling?"

"Not great," I said, feeling my face. Touching my forehead made it hurt more. Also, my eyebrows were missing.

"You're lucky to be alive. Some asshole rigged a methane explosion in one of those apartments. Couple of civilians dragged you out."

"Was there an old lady?" I asked.

"Don't know about that," said the driver. "Your buddies are in the ambulance ahead of us. They'll be surprised to see you, I'll bet. They swore you were dead."

I nodded dumbly. One of the Green River guys must have seen Conroy's body and somehow not noticed me lying a few yards away in his clothes. They were definitely going to be surprised to see me.

"I don't think we've met," said the driver. "Name's Harper. I just transferred in from Johannesburg. You're Conroy, right?"

"Yeah," I said. "Look, Harper, you need to set this thing down." I saw lights below us, but couldn't make out where we were. All I knew was that I needed to get out of this car before it got to the hospital.

"We're almost there, buddy," said Harper. "You feeling okay? Lie down and take it easy. We'll be there in two minutes."

"No, you need to land," I said. "Now."

"You need to puke or something? Just try to hold on. If you puke in this car, I have to clean it up. Shit, I knew I should have waited for an ambulance."

I picked up Conroy's gun and pressed the barrel against Harper's neck. I was getting a little tired of threatening people with guns, to be honest, but I was too dazed and desperate to think of anything else. "Land," I said.

"You're not Conroy, are you?" said Harper after a moment.

"No, I am not," I admitted. "I'm just a guy having a shitty day who happens to be wearing Conroy's uniform." Admittedly, though, my day was going better than Conroy's.

"All right," Harper said. "There are no landing zones in this area, but I'll see what I can do."

"Any street will do," I replied. "Don't get cute." Technically, he was right. I could see we were in a residential neighborhood, presumably outside the DZ. You couldn't legally land an aircar in such a neighborhood. Practically speaking, you can land an aircar on just about any hundred-foot-long strip of pavement. Less, if you went full vertical, but that wasted fuel and attracted a lot of attention.

Harper set the car down on a quiet street, like a pro. I kept the gun on him as I got out, taking the helmet with me. "Thanks, Harper," I said. "Take the rest of the night off."

"Fuck you," said Harper. I shrugged and closed the door. I held the gun on the car until he took off. Then I checked my location on my comm and took off running. I didn't know what Green River's relationship was with the LAPD, but I suspected Harper called them as soon as he was in the air. I needed to get as far away from here as I could before they showed up.

According to my comm, I was just a few blocks north of the motel where I'd left Keane and Olivia. Doing my best to keep to the shadows, I jogged there and then walked to the door of room 17. I knocked and said, "Hey, it's me." After a few seconds, Keane came to the door. He was wearing a plain white T-shirt and boxer shorts.

"What the hell happened to you?" Keane asked. "You look like you got shot out of a cannon. And what's with the storm trooper getup?"

I pushed past Keane into the room and sat down on my bed, letting the helmet hit the floor.

Keane closed the door. "You have the coin?"

I reached into my pocket and held it up. Keane grabbed it out of my hands. "Looks just like the one in the book," he said. "Except for the serial number."

I started unlacing my boots. More than anything, I needed a shower. "I just risked my life half a dozen times to get that goddamn Cracker Jack box toy," I said. "Gerard Canaan's army is tearing apart the whole DZ looking for that thing. So I sure hope you can tell me more than that."

"The only thing I can figure," said Keane, examining the coin, "is that it somehow carries information."

"Like those fake coins in spy movies."

"Yes," he replied. "Except that this coin is clearly solid. So the information is somehow embedded in the coin itself."

"Embedded by whom?" I asked. "What kind of information?"

I'd finished getting undressed and went into the bathroom to turn on the shower. Keane followed.

"Whoever minted the coins, I would imagine," said Keane. "I did some digging while you were gone to see if I could determine who made them, but didn't come up with much. As far as I can tell, they were minted by a privately owned company in Hong Kong that no longer exists. Regarding the sort of information, that's another excellent question."

I got into the shower. The cold water felt good on my face. I scrubbed my scalp and felt the burnt ends of my hair breaking off. "Maybe it's imprinted inside the coin," I shouted. "Like you need an X-ray machine to see it." I turned off the shower and grabbed a towel.

"That would be a pretty good trick to pull off, even with a copper coin. Creating a void inside the coin somehow. And titanium is much harder to work with than softer metals."

"What about weight?" I asked. "Maybe each coin has a slightly different weight, and if you put all the weights together, you get a code or something." I peered into the mirror. I really did look like shit. My eyebrows were completely gone and my face, neck, and backs of my hands were bright red. Blisters had formed on my right cheek.

"Could be," said Keane. "But frankly it seems too obvious. And you certainly wouldn't be able to transmit much information that way. Let's suppose you can control the variation of the weight of the coin to one one-thousandth of a gram, which is about the weight of a grain of table salt. That's pretty fine. This coin weighs about as much as a quarter, which is five-point-six grams. Unless the person encoding this information wanted to be really obvious, they'd keep all the coins within a tenth of a gram of each other. So every coin is between, say, five-point-six-zero-zero grams and five-point-six-nine-nine grams, with a margin of error of just less than one milligram. That really only leaves the hundreds place and the thousands place to work with. Two digits. Hell, you get one digit from the serial number. Hard to see why anyone would go to all that trouble to hide a two-digit number."

I had finished drying myself off and wrapped a towel around my waist. Keane, obviously relieved, opened the bathroom door and walked out. I followed him. I sat down on the other bed. "Then what?" I asked quietly. "The balance is off? Maybe if you flip the coin, it lands funny?"

Keane shook his head. "Even if you could get it to land on the same side every time, that's one bit of information. Your varying weights idea was much more practical, and that was idiotic."

Keane tapped something into his notebook. I saw that he had brought up a magnified image of an iota coin that had sold on eBay a few days ago for $800. Two of the coins had been sold on eBay in the last week—serial numbers 1 and 8—to the same anonymous bidder. The bidder was presumably Canaan or someone working for him. Keane was comparing the coin I'd given him to the one on the screen. I lay on the bed and closed my eyes while he did this. I was almost asleep when he muttered something under his breath.

"What?" I asked.

"There's no difference," he said. "The front and the back are both exactly the same, except for the serial number."

"Isn't an image information?" I asked. "Maybe the image is the message."

"But then why are there nine different coins, with nine different serial numbers? And why is Canaan so dead set on getting every last one?"

"Could be he's afraid of somebody else getting the information. He wants to get every copy to hide them."

Keane shook his head. "If the image is the information, then the information is all over the place. It took me three seconds to find a six-hundred DPI image of the damn thing."

"Well, hell," I said. "Should we try tossing it, just to see what happens? Maybe it will do something crazy, like landing on its side."

Keane cocked his head at me, a very strange look on his face. "Landing on its side," he said.

"I wasn't serious," I said. "I'm pretty sure it's not going to land on its side."

"No," said Keane. "But what if it did?"

"Uh," I said. "Then it would be time for a trip to Vegas?"

But Keane wasn't listening. He was frantically searching the desk and surrounding areas for something. "I need a pencil, Fowler!" he cried. "Find me a pencil!"

Just then, there was a huge crash and the door to the room flew open. Two men in full Green River gear stood at the doorway with a battering ram. I looked around frantically for the Glock and realized I'd left it in the bathroom. The men stepped aside and two others, also in full combat gear, strode into the room, pointing their rifles at me and Keane. We put our hands up. My towel fell to the floor.

"Where is it?" one of the men asked.

"I don't know what you're talking about," I replied.

"The coin, smart guy. Don't think I won't shoot you. I don't give a shit."

Keane opened his hand, revealing the coin.

"Thanks," said the Green River man, taking the coin. "Now get dressed. You're coming with us."

NINETEEN

I got dressed and Keane and I were prodded into the back of a heavy-duty utility aircar. I didn't see Olivia; I'd nearly forgotten she was still in the adjoining room. Either she was blissfully unaware of our situation or she was behind it. I'd have bet heavily on the latter. Keane and I had let our guard down, and we were paying for it. Olivia had sold us out to Green River.

The aircar lifted off and headed northwest. Ten minutes later we descended to a pad behind a luxurious cliffside house in Malibu. Keane and I were escorted to a room overlooking the Pacific Ocean. Sitting in a chair, a tablet cradled on his lap, was a short, gray-haired man with a taut, expressionless face. I recognized him as Gerard Canaan.

"Gentlemen," said Canaan, glancing in our direction but not getting up. "Please have a seat."

We sat. One of the Green River guys handed the iota coin to Canaan, who nodded and clutched it against his chest as if it were a crucifix. The Green River guys left the room silently, leaving only a single bodyguard at the door.

"I trust you know who I am," said Canaan, peering at us

from under bushy gray eyebrows. "Thank you for retrieving the final iota coin."

"We don't work for you, Mr. Canaan," I said.

"No," said Canaan. "You work for Selah Fiore, who is sadly going to be unable to fulfill her contractual obligations. Being an honorable man, however, I am happy to pay you for your services rendered thus far. How does twenty thousand iotas sound?"

I had been about to tell Canaan to go fuck himself, but twenty thousand iotas was a hell of a lot of money. Dollars or iotas, that much money would bring us current on our lease and then some.

"Iotas, eh?" said Keane. "Interesting choice."

Canaan shrugged. "I do business in iotas when I can."

"I'm sure you do," said Keane. "Completely untraceable. No reporting requirements to deal with. You could have billions in iotas stashed away, and no one would know."

"I'm no longer as wealthy as I once was," said Canaan, "but I get by."

"So I see," Keane said, staring out the window at the waves crashing against the cliff far below. "Did you buy this house with iotas as well?"

Canaan scowled. "My finances aren't your concern, Mr. Keane. As for my affinity for iotas, I've been involved in the effort to mainstream iotas for years. I'm sure you know I was on the board of the Free Currency Initiative."

"And as I'm sure you're aware," Keane replied, "Fowler and I are wanted for Selah Fiore's murder."

"I can take care of that," said Canaan. "It will take me a few days, so try not to get arrested unless you want to spend that time in prison."

Keane nodded. "Also, Mag-Lev is holding a woman named Gwen Thorson against her will. I'd like her released."

"Mag-Lev doesn't report to me," said Canaan.

"No," said Keane, "but if I'm not mistaken, you're in the process of taking over the DZ, so pretty soon he's either going to be reporting to you or dead."

Canaan nodded. "I'll see what I can do."

"I want a pledge that you'll see to it that Gwen is returned to us unharmed. You'll need to act quickly."

I nodded, acutely aware that we were within two hours of Mag-Lev's deadline.

"This is in lieu of payment, then?" Canaan asked.

"This is in addition to payment."

"Fine," said Canaan, without even taking a second to think. "But I need one more thing from you."

"I know," said Keane. "That's why I'm not budging on the price."

A smile cracked Canaan's face. "Good. Then we are on the same page. I understand you need a pencil?"

"Yes," said Keane. "And paper."

"You should find both in that desk." Canaan gestured toward an oak desk in the corner of the room. As Keane walked to the desk, I realized Canaan was asking Keane to reveal the secret of the coins. And Keane apparently intended to do it, for a mere twenty thousand iotas.

Canaan got to his feet as Keane found a pencil and a sheet of paper in a drawer. Keane set the paper on the desk and held out his hand to Canaan. Canaan came closer, handing him the coin. I approached as well, curious as to what Keane intended to do.

"As much as I'd like to take credit for cracking the code," said Keane, rubbing the tip of the pencil on the edge of the coin, "it was Fowler who gave me the idea."

"I did?" I asked.

"I fell into the trap of binary thinking," said Keane. "We are conditioned to think of a coin as having two sides, but of course that's incorrect. It has three: the front, the back, and the edge. When you suggested looking at the edge of the coin, I realized that had to be the answer." As he spoke, he rubbed the lead of the pencil on the grooves on the edge of the coin. When he'd gone all the way around the coin, he set the pencil down and then pressed the edge of the coin against a paper on the desk. He rolled the coin one complete turn.

"Ha!" he cried, holding up the coin triumphantly. All I saw on the paper was a series of tiny lines.

"What is that supposed to be?" asked Canaan.

"A nonbinary binary solution," said Keane, with a grin. "Take a look." He held the coin before Canaan's eyes. "These ridges around the edge of the coin are called reeds. Some of the reeds have slight indentations in them. The difference is almost imperceptible when you look at the coin, and you can't see it at all if you're looking at a photo of the front or the back. But if you roll it on paper, the reeds with the indentation leave a gap." He set the coin on the desk and tapped the paper with his finger. "The solid lines are ones. The lines with gaps are zeros. All I've got to do is convert this to decimal." He did some furious figuring on the bottom half of the paper, finishing by writing a very long number on the bottom. He picked up the paper and handed it to Canaan, who frowned.

"What does it mean?" I asked.

"Beats me," said Keane. "I'd need the other coins to make sense of the code. Presumably if you put them all together, it means something."

Canaan nodded, seeming satisfied.

"Why do you want the code, Mr. Canaan?" Keane asked.

"Divulging that information was not part of our deal," said Canaan.

"No," said Keane, "but I think you have to agree that Fowler and I have been very understanding, considering that you stole the coin from us and forced us here at gunpoint. I'd like to think that we've earned some goodwill."

"You're already pushing it, Mr. Keane," said Canaan. "I don't *have* to give you *anything*. Fortunately for you, I'm a man of my word. I'll have the iotas transferred to you within the week."

"So that's it, then," I said. "I risk my life to get that damn coin and you just buy us off—with iotas, no less."

"If it makes you feel better, Mr. Fowler," Canaan said, "you're not the only ones being manipulated here."

"What's that supposed to mean?" I asked.

"It means that if you're smart, you'll take your twenty thousand iotas and get the hell out of this city while you still can. There are forces at work here beyond your understanding."

"We're not going anywhere," I said. "Not without Gwen."

"As you wish," said Canaan. "But understand that our deal is contingent on you not interfering with my plans in the DZ. If I get word of any meddling on your part, you forfeit your payment. All of it."

"Just make sure Gwen stays safe," I said. "We'll stay out of your way."

Canaan nodded. "I'll be in touch."

TWENTY

The Green River guys brought us back to the motel room. Olivia had paid through the week, and evidently the cops were still looking for us, so we couldn't go back to our office. Presumably now that Olivia had outed herself as an agent of Gerard Canaan, she wouldn't need her room anymore, and since the lock of our room was now broken, we moved into hers.

It was clever of Canaan to keep the threat of arrest hanging over our heads. I had no doubt, if he had the power to sic the cops on us in the first place, that he also had the power to call them off, but he wasn't going to do that until the DZ was secure and he was certain Keane was no longer a threat. Same thing with getting Gwen back. No doubt he'd do his best to abide by his promise to return her to us unharmed, but there was no way we were going to see Gwen until Canaan was satisfied his plans had been completed. So Keane and I sat in the motel room, hiding from the cops and wondering where we had gone wrong. Trusting Olivia was definitely at the top of the list.

"You think Olivia was working for Canaan all along?" I asked.

"So it would seem," Keane replied.

"What is Canaan offering her?"

"Hard to say. Selah was very concerned with her legacy. Assuming Olivia shares that concern, perhaps she and Canaan worked out a deal."

"What kind of deal? Selah was a multibillionaire. I can't see him being of much use to Olivia. He lost most of his money when Elysium folded."

"Did he?" Keane asked.

"Yes," I said. "You know this. It was all over the news. The Wahhabis seized the oil fields and took over the government, establishing the Arabian Caliphate."

"Sure," said Keane. "But what do we really know about the aftermath of that coup?"

"We know that Canaan lost fifty billion dollars. It's a matter of public record. He owned just over half of Elysium's stock, and the stock lost ninety-nine percent of its value. This is basic math, Keane."

"How much do you think he's paying Green River take over the DZ? And I'd wager the invasion itself accounts for only a fraction of the total cost. He's probably bribed half of the government employees in the state to get away with an operation like this. Plus there's the cost of holding the territory after the invasion. We're talking about billions of dollars. Or iotas, as the case may be."

"Maybe he's got one of those no-limit credit cards," I said. "Canaan's fortune was almost entirely in Elysium stock, and that stock is now worthless."

"Hmm," said Keane. "And what did that stock represent, exactly?"

"Ownership in Elysium Oil," I said, getting a little irritated at Keane's deliberate obtuseness.

"Right, but where did the value come from?"

"Oil fields."

"Wrong. The value came from contracts with the Saudis.

But legal contracts are just another form of collective delusion. A piece of paper that dictates reality, dependent on the understanding that a legal authority exists to enforce the contract. A legal authority that evaporated after the coup. The oil fields are still there; they're just under new management."

I had to stop and think about what Keane seemed to be saying. "You're not seriously suggesting Gerard Canaan made a deal with the Wahhabis."

"Why not?" Keane asked. "Think about it. Gerard Canaan, wunderkind of the fossil fuel industry. Develops new technology for pulling oil out of wells previously thought to be tapped out. Over the span of two decades, Elysium goes from a tiny Texas oil company to the third biggest oil producer in the world. They own half the oil wells in the Middle East. But then production peaks. Gerard Canaan is looking for the next big thing. He's ridden the oil wave as far as it can go. So what does he do next?"

"Apparently he makes a deal with a bunch of fundamentalist psychopaths."

Keane shrugged. "The rank-and-file Islamists are fundamentalist psychopaths. The guys at the top are politicians."

"Terrorists, you mean."

"War is the continuation of politics by other means. Terrorism is an asymmetrical form of warfare. And politics is simply a struggle over limited resources. The Wahhabis wanted the oil. Canaan gave it to them."

"And what did he get in return?"

"As you say, the Wahhabi sects have been involved with terrorist organizations for some time. Groups that use virtual currencies for most transactions, because they're untraceable. It's not inconceivable they could have hoarded a fortune in iotas. Canaan hands the oil fields over to the Wahhabis and they transfer a shitload of iotas into a secret account."

I frowned, not liking where this was going. "A lot of people died defending those oil fields, Keane. You need to understand what you're saying."

"Did they?" Keane asked. "I'm not being facetious. Sure, we saw the coup unfold on TV. But it was all secondhand reports, remember? The embedded reporters were all stuck in Beirut because of a sandstorm."

"You think Gerard Canaan orchestrated a sandstorm?"

"Of course not. But if there hadn't been a sandstorm, there would have been some other excuse. Mechanical problems with the plane, maybe. The point is, all the firsthand reports of the fighting we got were from Green River. We have to take their word for it that there was this highly coordinated attack on several dozen locations, taking Elysium completely by surprise. Pretty hard to swallow, except at the time there was no other explanation for Elysium losing control of all their assets in Saudi Arabia. Elysium's investors are pissed, but what can they do? Obviously Gerard Canaan did all he could; after all, he lost fifty billion dollars of his own money!"

"So you really think he sold them out. All of Elysium's investors."

"It's just a working hypothesis at this point," said Keane, "but it would certainly explain some things. And it dovetails nicely with your story about the Ninety-niners. These guys had every reason to want to give a big middle finger to the U.S. government and Elysium's investors, who were a key reason the U.S. was involved in the peninsula in the first place. Think about it. The political situation in Saudi Arabia at this point is bad and getting worse. There are rumors the Saudi royal family is in talks to receive asylum in London. Meanwhile, Gerard Canaan is bringing over as many mercenaries as Green River can supply in an attempt to hold on to his oilfields. The expert consensus seems to be that the Wahhabis don't have the firepower to take the oil fields, that they're going to have to make some kind of deal with Elysium. But someone in Gerard Canaan's position could easily alter that equation. So our source contacts him, anonymously at first, and lets him know what he's found. One way or another, the situation progresses. Canaan and the source come to an arrangement. Canaan lets the Wahhabis have the oil fields in exchange for an untraceable fortune in iotas, then returns to L.A., disgraced. He's reduced to shilling for a vanity project, some kind of virtual currency. At least that's how it appears. In reality he's further shoring up the value of a currency he's very heavily invested in. Selah Fiore was filthy rich, but she had nothing on Gerard Canaan."

"But we still don't know why Canaan wanted the physical iotas," I said.

"No," Keane replied with a frown.

"So the code didn't mean anything to you?"

Keane shook his head. "Just a string of numbers. I've got it memorized, but I've been going over it in my head and I haven't found anything like a pattern. It's just one piece of a puzzle. I'd have to see the other coins to make sense of it, but I suspect it's just an arbitrary code anyway."

"A code? For what?"

"Hard to say. You know, I've been thinking about those reeds."

"Reeds?"

"The ridges on the iota coin. Reeded edges were originally introduced to make the coins harder to counterfeit, and to prevent people from filing down the edges to get the metal. Those problems aren't really a concern with these coins. But what if using the reeds to communicate information was a way of hinting at a similar problem?"

"A problem with the virtual iotas, you mean. Counterfeiting, or a way to degrade their value?"

"Something along those lines," said Keane. "Ultimately

iotas are an algorithm, a set of mathematical rules that determine how they can be created and transferred. Iotas were pretty thoroughly vetted by game companies before they went mainstream, and there have been plenty of attempts to hack the algorithm since then, but no one has ever been able to find a flaw. It appears to be a perfect system."

"The algorithm is public, isn't it? If there's a flaw, it would be in the open, for everyone to see."

"Yes," said Keane. "In the sense that the solution to the Erdos discrepancy problem was in the open for everyone to see."

"The what?"

"Famous math problem first posited in the 1930s, finally solved in 2015. The point is, making a math problem public is no guarantee it will be solved. There could very well be a flaw in the iota algorithm that no one has found yet."

"A deliberate flaw, you mean. And the code in the coins is the key to finding it. But why? Why would somebody build a flaw into the system and then dare everyone to find it?"

"Well," said Keane. "I know why I would do it."

I realized I did as well. "For fun," I said.

He nodded. "Whoever is behind this is just playing with us. With all of us—Selah, Olivia, Gerard Canaan . . . the whole world, really."

"So this mysterious person, this trickster . . . he's the same person as Canaan's source?"

"I suspect so," Keane replied.

"Then the source was never in it for the money. He's just been toying with Canaan all along."

"Yes," said Keane. "He probably deliberately gave Canaan the idea he was looking to make a fortune, but once Canaan had been suckered in to betting his fortune on iotas, he dropped the pretense. For the past three years or so, the trickster's just been playing with him."

And the rest of us, I thought. I wondered if the trickster was the same person who had been messaging me as "Lila." I was tempted to tell Keane about her, but then I'd have to explain why I'd kept her messages a secret thus far. And I honestly wasn't sure I knew the answer to that question. Maybe I resented Keane always being a step ahead of me, and I savored the idea of having a source of information to which he wasn't privy. And yet, what had Lila actually told me? Not much. In fact, the context of her messages had communicated more than the words themselves: All I really knew was that she considered my involvement in this case part of a "game," and that she was watching my progress very closely. I couldn't see how that information would be helpful to Keane.

On some level, I knew I was being manipulated: Lila was counting on me to rationalize keeping her messages a secret from Keane. But somehow that knowledge didn't make me want to tell him, either. Whether we liked it or not, Keane and I were players in Lila's game, and I wasn't entirely convinced he and I were on the same side.

"Whatever game the trickster is playing," Keane said, "it goes far beyond a squabble over control of the DZ."

"What do you mean?"

"Exposing a flaw in the iota algorithm would have serious consequences for the global economy," Keane said. "Nothing on the scale of the Collapse, obviously. Iotas don't have that kind of reach. But let's say this code hidden in the coins—the key, as you called it—allows one to instantaneously create an unlimited number of iotas. Suddenly, the holder of the key is an iota trillionaire. He floods the world economy with iotas, buying Fortune 500 companies, cruise ships, skyscrapers, gold mines, whatever. It takes a little while, but eventually the market catches on. There are way too many iotas in circulation. The value tanks, people start to dump iotas. Eventually it becomes clear that the algorithm has been compromised, and the value of iotas bottoms out at zero. Civilization would recover, but that sort of disruption is not good for the economy. At the very least, we're looking at a pretty major recession."

"And the key holder becomes a trillionaire in hard assets," I said. "So you think that's Gerard Canaan's endgame. What he was after all along."

"Well, no. I think he assumed, along with everyone else, that the iota algorithm was solid. Then something happened to change his mind. Probably our trickster got bored because nobody had figured out his little puzzle, and decided to give Canaan something to worry about."

"The trickster told Canaan about the coins."

"Probably didn't tell him outright, but hinted at a flaw in the algorithm. It took until a few days ago for Canaan to find the connection to the coins. The trickster has been playing with Canaan for a while now, though. I suspect he gave Canaan his first hint a little over three years ago."

"When the Project Maelstrom people started to disappear," I said. "You think Canaan is the reason Gwen went into hiding."

"Correct. I think Canaan suspected someone in Maelstrom came across the flaw, and was taunting him with it. He didn't appreciate the joke."

"But now the game is over," I said. "Canaan won. He's got all the coins."

"So it would seem," Keane replied. "But I wouldn't underestimate our trickster. He may still have a card or two to play."

"Any idea who it might be?"

"Someone who was involved with iotas since the beginning," said Keane. "To know about the flaw, he must have been on the original development team that created the algorithm. And he apparently was involved with the Free Currency Initiative as well, since he was able to manipulate the coins."

"You don't think the coins were minted that way? With the message embedded in them?"

"I suspect not. I think the grooves were ground into them later. Titanium is tough, but with the right tools it wouldn't be difficult to do. Time-consuming, but not difficult."

"So we're looking for a meticulous software developer."

"Or mathematician," said Keane. "Someone very smart, with a twisted sense of humor. Probably abrasive and socially inept."

"Oh, thank God," I said. "I thought I was going to have to leave this room."

TWENTY-ONE

While Keane puzzled over the identity of the trickster, I did a little research of my own. Although Lila's messages didn't give me much to work with, it occurred to me that the name Lila itself might be a clue. I found an encyclopedia article that solidified the idea in my mind that Lila and the trickster were one and the same:

> Lila (Sanskrit: लीला, IAST līlā) or Leela, like many Sanskrit words, cannot be precisely translated into English, but can be loosely translated as the noun "play." The concept of Lila is common to both non-dualist and dualist philosophical schools, but has a markedly different significance in each. Within non-dualism, Lila is a way of describing all reality, including the cosmos, as the outcome of creative play by the divine absolute (Brahman). In the dualistic schools of Vaishnavism, Lila refers to the activities of God and his devotee, as well as the macrocosmic actions of the manifest universe, as seen in the Vaishnava scripture Srimad Bhagavatam, verse 3.26.4.

The article included a quote from a book called *The Tao of Physics*, which read in part:

"This creative activity of the Divine is called Lila, the play of God, and the world is seen as the stage of the divine play."

The good news was that Lila was apparently a creative, rather than a destructive, force. Whoever Lila was, she didn't think of herself as evil. But then evil people rarely do, I suppose.

I was about to break down and tell Keane what I had found when suddenly his eyes lit up. He had been staring at his notebook screen, going through the information Sam Chaudry had sent him.

"What is it?" I asked. "Did you find something?"

"I think I know who our trickster is."

"Really?" I asked. "Who?"

"Check this out." He tapped a couple of keys on this notebook and my comm chirped, indicating I'd received a message. I opened it.

"I found a list of Empathix developers who were assigned to the Maelstrom project. Notice anything funny?" he said.

I scanned the list. It contained eight names:

Aaron Clemson
Raj Kapoor
Rachel Stuil
Emma Spotnitz
Will Van Laar
Tamara Dhillon
Gabriel Wu
Miriam Reinhardt

Four males, four females. The majority of software developers were still men, but it certainly wouldn't be unusual to have a team with four women on it. Nor was it unusual to have several members of Asian descent. Wu was probably Chinese; Kapoor and Dhillon were, I believe, Indian or Pakistani. That left five with European-sounding surnames. Clemson was English. Van Laar was Dutch. Reinhardt was German.

But what was Stuil? How would you pronounce it? Like *style*? It looked vaguely Scandinavian. I gave up trying to deduce anything from the names.

"What kind of name is Stuil?" I asked.

Keane smiled. "The made-up kind," he said.

"How do you know?"

"I didn't, at first. I had the same reaction you did. All the other names have a clear ethnic origin, but not Stuil. So I looked it up online. There is no surname with that spelling."

"Okay, so you knew it was made up. But how does that get you to the trickster's identity?"

"Remember the developer I told you about, the one who designed the redwood forest?"

"Yeah," I said. "Ed Casters. You said he was dead."

"I thought he was," said Keane. "Ed was sort of an amateur mathematician. Absolutely brilliant, but had no patience for formal schooling. Made a living doing contract work as a software developer, mostly cryptography stuff, but also complex modeling with fractals. Ed Casters was a pseudonym. No one knew his real name. He always worked remotely, so no one ever saw him. Most companies won't hire someone to work on their systems without vetting them thoroughly, but Ed was so good at what he did, sometimes he was the only person to call."

"You're telling me LAFF put somebody on Maelstrom whose identity they didn't know?"

"No," said Keane. "As I said, Casters was never officially on Maelstrom. I subcontracted some work to him. Nothing sensitive, and all the work was approved by someone from LAFF. Casters was never supposed to have access to any sensitive information. Of course, he was also one of the world's leading experts in cryptography and computer security, so it wouldn't be terribly surprising if he hacked the Empathix data."

"And what makes you think Ed Casters and Rachel Stuil are the same person?"

"I'd known Ed Casters by reputation for several years before Maelstrom. The first time I worked with him, I did some digging. Didn't come up with much; he covered his tracks well. But the name struck me as odd, so I spent some time puzzling over it."

"And?"

"It's an anagram," Keane replied. "A tribute to one of Ed's favorite thinkers. A philosopher and mathematician."

I thought for a few seconds. There weren't many people known for their work in both philosophy and mathematics. Bertrand Russell and Gottfried Leibniz came to mind. And there was one other. "Descartes," I said.

"Very good, Fowler. *Cogito, ergo sum*: 'I think, therefore I am.' Complete balderdash, of course, but old Rene made a valiant effort at a purely rational system of thought. He also developed the Cartesian coordinate system, which we still use."

"And how does this get us to Rachel Stuil?"

"Once I knew Stuil was a made-up name," Keane replied, "I started looking for anagrams for Rachel Stuil. It took me a little while, but I found one. Another philosopher, considerably earlier than Descartes."

I thought for some time but came up with nothing.

"Heraclitus," said Keane.

"Oh, of course," I said, rolling my eyes. "The famed Heraclitus."

"Not as well known as Descartes, admittedly, but he made his own contribution to Western Civilization. And the contrast between the two is instructive. Descartes was ultimately optimistic. He believed in God and the possibility of reconciling faith and reason. Heraclitus was more ambivalent. He's best known for saying that no man ever steps in the same river twice."

"Meaning that change is constant?"

"Constant, ubiquitous, and inescapable," replied Keane. "Nothing in the universe is static. *Panta rhei*: everything flows. Some have characterized his philosophy as an attempt to reconcile this chaos with human reason, which he referred to as *'Logos.'* We translate this as 'reason' or 'word.' The Apostle John borrowed this term for his gospel account, in which he says 'In the beginning was the Word.' The popular Greek mythology of the time held that all of creation was born from chaos, but John insisted that the Logos existed from the very beginning, forming and ordering the chaos. Heraclitus was not so optimistic. He saw only an ever-evolving, and apparently futile, struggle between order and chaos. It is for good reason that Heraclitus is known as 'the weeping philosopher.' He was said to live a very lonely, solitary life."

"That certainly sounds like our trickster," I said. "A brilliant loner playing with order and chaos." Lila, I thought. Directing the divine play.

"Yes," said Keane. "And it doesn't bode well for us. Descartes was a loner, too, but he used reason to bridge the gap between himself and his fellow man. Heraclitus never got there."

"But he tried," I said. "He believed in the struggle, at least."

"He did try," said Keane, "but he never came to a satisfactory conclusion. He never found meaning or purpose in existence. He landed on what we today might call nihilism. With Heraclitus, order always gives way to chaos eventually. Ed Casters isn't interested in amassing wealth or maintaining stability. He wants to build something up so he can watch it crash to the ground."

"Hmm," I said. I was trying to reconcile this idea with my impression of Lila.

"The pseudonyms seem to indicate a progression in Casters's thinking," Keane said. "Once I knew Casters and Stuil were one and the same, I scoured the Web looking for the names of all the developers who were known to have contributed to the iota project. There were over a hundred of them, but one stood out: Brad Melton."

"Yeah," I said. "That's a real eye-catcher of a name."

"Deceptively mundane," Keane replied. "It's an anagram for Mandelbrot. Mathematician, the father of fractals. In some ways, Mandelbrot's work anticipated the sort of complex modeling done by a company like Empathix. Mandelbrot was one of the first to use computer graphics to create and display fractal geometric images, leading to his discovering the Mandelbrot set. He believed that things typically considered to be chaotic, like clouds or shorelines, actually had a degree of order. It's that sort of intrinsic order that allows Empathix's modeling to work."

"Order out of chaos," I said. "You think Ed Casters created the iota algorithm."

"I do," Keane replied. "Other developers worked out some of the details, but I think Ed Casters was the prime mover. Our trickster seems to be a bit schizophrenic. He's gone from Mandelbrot to Descartes to Heraclitus. Following the progression, Ed Casters seems to be moving from finding order in chaos to resigning himself to chaos wiping out order. All right, call a car. We need to go."

"Where are we going?" I asked.

"To visit Ed Casters."

An hour later, we were staring at a tombstone in Evergreen Cemetery. It read:

Ed Casters
Apr 29, 2000–Jan 16, 2036
Pura Vida

"Pura Vida," I said. "What does that mean? Pure life?"

"It's sort of an unofficial slogan for Costa Rica," Keane replied. "Ed visited there once, many years ago. He talked about moving there." Keane smiled. "I knew he wouldn't be able to resist giving us a clue."

"You think he fled to Costa Rica?" I asked.

"In a manner of speaking," Keane replied.

My comm chirped. I checked the display. It was Lila again. The message read:

shudders walking over my grave? ;)

"Who was that?" Keane asked.

"Wrong number," I said. Anxious to change the subject, I went on hurriedly, "It's not a bad idea, you know. Costa Rica is supposed to have the best climate in the world."

"You live in Los Angeles, Fowler. Don't be a whiner."

"Says the guy who ate lunch in a virtual rain forest because actually going outside is too much work. You don't get to call me a whiner until you've spent a summer in the Arabian Peninsula," I said. "Spend three days hunkered down in a sandstorm and then you can feel free to make condescending comments about my . . . Keane?"

Keane had gotten a faraway look in his eye. He mumbled something that I didn't catch.

"What's that?" I said.

"Hunkered down in a sandstorm," he murmured.

"Keane, what the hell are you talking about?"

"We need to get back to the motel. I have an idea."

TWENTY-TWO

While Keane studied the economic model that Olivia had gotten him from Empathix, I ordered pizza and watched *Baywatch* reruns. The classics never get old.

My comm chirped. It was April.

"Hey," I said. "What's up?"

"My secretary called while I was at lunch to warn me that the cops were looking for me again. So I took a cab home, but there were cops all over the place there, too."

"Shit," I said.

"Yeah. Evidently there's a warrant out for me. Aiding and abetting a fugitive."

"That's bullshit."

"I think so, too, but I don't really have the luxury of living my life on the lam. As a lawyer, it's kind of important for me to stay on the right side of the law."

"Where are you now? Are you okay?"

"I'm fine," said April, "Hanging out at a coffee shop a few blocks from the office. I'm going to have to turn myself in, Blake. I've probably already lost my job, but I can't afford to get disbarred."

"Jesus, April. I'm sorry. It's my fault for getting you into this."

"I got myself into this," said April. "But you're going to get me out."

"She's not turning herself in, is she?" Keane asked. "Tell her not to be stupid."

"She has no choice, Keane," I replied. "This isn't even her fight, and it could ruin her life."

"Hmm," said Keane, frowning. This might have been the first time he'd ever tried to see things from April's point of view. Empathy was not his strong suit. "Toss the call to me."

"Hold on, April," I said. "Keane wants to talk to you." I tossed the call to his comm, but left it open on mine so I could listen in.

"April," said Keane. "Do not turn yourself in to the LAPD. Do you know anyone at the Justice Department?"

"I could call my friend Deacon Walthers from the L.A. branch of the FBI," April said. "Good guy. We went to law school together. You don't trust the LAPD?"

"I don't trust anyone," said Keane. "But we can negotiate with the feds." He proceeded to give April a summary of what we'd learned about Gerard Canaan and Green River's plan to take over the DZ.

"I don't suppose you have any actual evidence of this," said April.

"So far, it's all conjecture," said Keane. "The bigger problem, though, is that we don't know how much of this the feds already know about any of this. If Canaan really is planning an invasion of the DZ, he almost had to get a buy-in from the LAPD, since they control the checkpoints. The question is whether the feds are in on it as well."

"What about Canaan's collusion with the Wahhabis?" April asked. "If you're right about that, there's no way the federal government was in on that part. The coup was a huge blow to American interests."

"Agreed," said Keane. "But the feds may very well have

found out about it after the fact, and decided it wasn't in their interests to go public with the information. In any case, we have even less evidence of that than we do of the pending invasion."

"So what you're saying is that I have zero leverage to negotiate any kind of deal," April said.

"Correct," replied Keane. "Which is why turning yourself in at this point is not a good idea."

"All right," said April. "I think I can crash at a friend's place tonight. But tomorrow morning, I'm going to the FBI. If you could have some kind of evidence for all your crazy conspiracy theories by then, that would be fantastic."

"Fowler and I are working on it," Keane said.

"I'm sorry, April," I said. "We'll fix this."

"Do that," said April. "Talk to you soon." She ended the call.

"That's just fucking fantastic," I said. "They're going to arrest April, Gwen is still stuck in the DZ, and we've got exactly nothing—no evidence to back up this crazy theory of yours."

"Actually," said Keane, "I may have found something. I don't know why it never occurred to me to look at this before."

"What?"

"The model reflects a sudden drop in the value of the dollar, roughly seven percent, as actually happened in October 2027."

"Six months before the Collapse," I said.

"Yes," said Keane. "That sudden drop was the first sign of the dollar's weakness. The market became increasingly volatile after that."

"Didn't the Wahhabi coup happen in October 2027?"

"That's right," said Keane. "And you remember the first thing the Wahhabis did after taking power in Riyadh?"

I had to think. There was a lot of death-to-America talk, as I recalled. Then it hit me. "They stopped taking dollars."

"Correct," replied Keane. "The Wahhabi interim government rolled out a plan to denominate their oil in China's currency, the yuan. Eventually they came around; the yuan really wasn't a workable solution. But that announcement shook faith in the dollar."

"But currencies rise and fall against each other all the time. A seven-percent drop can't be unprecedented. And didn't the dollar recover most of its value over the next few weeks?"

"Yes, but some economists have argued that initial drop was the tipping point. That was when people realized the dollar wasn't invincible. There was already a lot of uneasiness, with the national debt at a hundred and twenty percent of GDP, but the coup was the first concrete sign that the dollar bubble had burst. People started to sell U.S. treasury bonds and buy gold, real estate, iotas . . . anything they could use as a hedge against the dollar. The cycle became self-perpetuating, and within a few months, the dollar had lost ninety-five percent of its value."

"Okay, so the coup precipitated the Collapse. So what?"

"Interestingly, the seven-percent drop doesn't appear to be a result of the modeling algorithm. It's an arbitrary input value."

"You mean somebody deliberately tweaked the model to add the drop. Maybe they went back after the coup and corrected the inputs."

"That was my thought at first as well," said Keane, "but the dates are off. The date of the seven-percent drop in the model is October tenth, 2027. The coup didn't happen until October thirteenth. If the data had been corrected after the fact, they would have gotten the date right."

"So . . . somebody with access to the Empathix model

knew the coup was going to happen, but they guessed wrong on the date. Why?"

"You can't orchestrate a sandstorm," said Keane with a smile.

"They knew the planned date for the coup, but the sandstorm delayed it by three days."

"That's the way it looks to me."

I stared at him, hardly believing what he was saying. "Jesus Christ, Keane. You're telling me that Gerard Canaan was behind the Collapse."

"I think Gerard Canaan engineered the coup in Saudi Arabia, knowing full well what it would do to the dollar. Somebody inside Empathix tipped him off. He planned the coup and gave his source the targeted date so he could update the model, but the sandstorm delayed the coup by three days."

"Who might have tipped him off?"

"Probably a software developer, or someone else working on the forecasting algorithm. Someone with an interest in causing chaos."

"The trickster," I said.

"Occam's razor," Keane replied, nodding. "Eliminating unnecessary entities, it would appear that Gerard Canaan's source inside Empathix is the same person dangling the coins in front of him."

"Why wouldn't the trickster go to Selah?" I asked. "Empathix is her company, after all."

"Selah wasn't positioned to crash the dollar the way Gerard Canaan was. The trickster probably gave Canaan enough forecasting data to convince him he was legit. Canaan went for the bait, not realizing the trickster was also involved in the creation of the iota algorithm. The trickster probably demanded a share of Canaan's profits, and Canaan assumed he was simply an opportunist who had come across a way to make a lot of money with Canaan's help. Canaan had no idea he was being suckered into an even bigger scheme."

"That explains Canaan's comment about being manipulated," I said.

"That's right," said Keane. "The trickster has been stringing him along for years."

I nodded, still trying to make sense of the motivations of the person I thought of as Lila. I hadn't heard from her for several hours, and I was beginning to think she had gotten bored of me. Or maybe she was done playing now that Gerard Canaan had all the coins. It seemed oddly unsportsmanlike for her not to at least inform me the game had ended.

Keane was still looking at the Empathix data, and shaking his head.

"What is it?" I asked.

"There's still something I don't understand about this model," Keane replied. "The numbers after the Collapse seem to be off. The projections for the yuan, iotas, and several other currencies are too high, and New Dollars are lacking completely."

"Well," I said, "the model just predicts general patterns, right? The creation of New Dollars was the result of closed-door meetings by some very powerful people in the government. Nobody could have predicted that."

"Of course they could," Keane replied curtly. "That's the whole point of a model like this. Maybe they wouldn't have been called New Dollars, but the model should have accounted for the rise of a new currency of some sort. Call them flerberts or zingzangs or—"

He was interrupted by a knock on our door. Keane and I traded glances. If it was the cops, our best bet was to surrender. I didn't really think it was the police, though. For some reason I was convinced that it was Lila, finally revealing herself. If so, I was going to have some explaining to do. But when I opened the door, a familiar figure stood in front of me.

"Hello, Olivia," I said. "How do you intend to screw us over this time?"

"May I come in?" Olivia asked.

"I'd rather you didn't," I said. "Keane and I were in the middle of a high-stakes canasta tournament."

"Perhaps I should rephrase my question," Olivia said. "I'm going to stand out here banging on your door until either you let me in or the cops show up. Which would you prefer?"

I shrugged and walked back into the room, flopping down on the bed. I watched with my hands laced behind my neck as Olivia walked into the room, closing the door behind her.

"To what do we owe the pleasure, Olivia?" asked Keane. "And is it just you this time, or should we expect additional guests?"

"Look, I'm sorry about that," said Olivia. "I didn't know Canaan was going to send those Green River guys after you."

"But you told him where we were," I said.

"Yes," Olivia replied. "I had to, so that he would trust me."

"Why did you need him to trust you?" I asked.

"Because if he didn't," Olivia said, pulling a folded sheet of paper from her purse, "I would never have been able to get my hands on this." She handed the paper to Keane.

Keane unfolded it, and I saw shock come over his face. I got up and looked over his shoulder. What I saw was nine rows of tiny marks.

"These are the codes from the other coins?" I asked.

"That's right," Olivia said.

"Then Canaan really does have all the coins," I said. "So we're screwed."

"Not necessarily," said Keane.

Olivia nodded. "Gerard seems to have been a little over-confident. He's got all the numbers, but he doesn't know how to use them. Of course, his primary goal was always to prevent someone else from using them, not to use them himself."

"So if we can figure out how to use them ourselves," I said, "we're back in the game."

Keane shot a puzzled glance at me. "That's one way to put it, I suppose." He turned to Olivia. "How did you manage to get this from him?"

"I made a copy while Gerard was in the shower," Olivia said. Keane raised his eyebrow at her. She just shrugged. "Gerard has a thing for Selah. I made use of it."

I shuddered. Olivia was definitely cut from the same cloth as Selah.

Keane seemed skeptical. "So you sleep with him and suddenly he trusts you with his top-secret papers, just like that?"

Olivia sighed. "Is the cross-examination really necessary?" she asked. "I'm here. I have the codes. What does it matter?"

"It matters because you already double-crossed us once," I said. "We don't trust you."

Olivia took a seat on my bed. "Fair enough," she said. "I suppose I have to tell you everything, then."

"Just the high points will do," said Keane. "Starting with who you really are."

"My name is Olivia Fiore. But I have all the memories of Selah Fiore, up until about two weeks ago, anyway. I'm her clone."

"And the stuff about being a college student?" I said.

"Pure fiction. A cover story I memorized. Or that Selah memorized, I suppose. This stuff gets a bit confusing. As far as I know, I have no false memories implanted. Only Selah's actual memories of devising a cover story about her estranged daughter."

"Very good," said Keane. "I suspected as much. What did Gerard Canaan offer you?"

"A chance to live," Olivia replied.

"Meaning what?" I asked.

"Meaning that I'm dying, Mr. Fowler. I have maybe six months to live."

"Because of the accelerated aging," Keane said. "Canaan told you he had a cure?"

"That's right," said Olivia.

"But you didn't believe him."

"Gerard did his homework. Three years ago he bought a Brazilian biotech company called Aviro, apparently in a bid for leverage against Selah. Aviro has recently developed a way to override the body's natural aging process by injecting the subject with a customized virus. Trials with test subjects have been very promising."

"This sounds like the sort of thing Selah—that is, the sort of thing you would have been aware of," Keane said.

"Yes," said Olivia. "Aviro would seem to have been a likely target for acquisition by Selah, assuming she was aware of their work."

"And was she?" I asked.

"Selah had a spy inside the company who provided her with some of Aviro's research. She had this research evaluated by the scientists at her research facility, the Tannhauser Institute. Their consensus was that Aviro's virus-based aging solution was incompatible with the accelerated-aging process used by Selah's clones."

"Incompatible how?" asked Keane.

"The accelerated-aging process Tannhauser uses on its clones is essentially a virus as well. Dynamic reprogramming of the subject's DNA. Injecting a Tannhauser clone with the Aviro virus would overload the body's immune system, killing the subject within days."

"So Canaan offered you a cure you knew would kill you."

"Right," said Olivia. "Of course, he didn't know that. So

I played along, acting like I was willing to help him in return for the cure."

"Why didn't you tell us this?" asked Keane. "Why the ruse?"

"Because I have Selah's memories," Olivia said. "Including her memories of you."

"You mean you remember trying to kill us," I said.

"Yes," said Olivia. "I could argue it wasn't really me, but I had no reason to think you would trust me."

"But you expect us to trust you now," I said.

Olivia shrugged. "I think that you want to get Gwen back, and you don't trust Canaan. And I think you need my help."

"What do you want, Olivia?" Keane asked.

"I want to preserve my legacy. Flagship Media and everything else I—that is, that Selah has built. If Keane is right about the code, Canaan is a threat to that legacy. He's already taken over half the DZ, and his possession of the iota code is a threat to the global financial system."

"Is that all?" Keane asked.

"No," said Olivia. "I want revenge on Canaan. For murdering Selah. In the end, the rest of this is just business, but I take Selah's murder personally, for reasons I'm sure you can imagine."

Keane nodded, apparently satisfied. I still didn't trust her, but I figured I'd follow Keane's lead this time. If he thought Olivia could still be of use to us, I didn't see any harm in letting her stick around. It wasn't like we had anything left to lose.

TWENTY-THREE

"Now if you've finished your interrogation," said Olivia, "I'm hoping you have some thoughts about those numbers, Mr. Keane."

Keane went back to studying the numbers. "Hmm," he said. "Looking at the rest of the codes, there does seem to be a pattern."

"There does?" I asked. To me, they just looked like random chicken scratches.

Keane grabbed a pen from the desk. He made a small tick mark just above a blank spot on the first row. Then he moved to the right slightly and made another mark. He did this several more times, leaving a series of equally spaced marks, each of them over a blank spot in the series. Then he moved to the next row, doing the same thing. I began to see what he was doing: each row started with a series of fifty or so lines with no gaps between them. These were just unnotched reeds. Then there was a series of lines that were broken at seemingly random intervals by one or more spaces. But with Keane's pen marks, I could see that the intervals were not quite random.

"There's a gap every eight reeds," I said.

"Right," said Keane. "The pattern suggests the sequences are composed of octets, each octet storing exactly one byte of data. Each byte has a value ranging from zero to two hundred fifty-five. In the early days of computing, all standard keyboard characters could be represented by a number in this range." Keane tapped at his comm and brought up a table of alphanumeric characters. He transcribed the code while we watched, writing the result next to the tick marks. When he was done, each row had a word and a five-digit number next to it. It looked like gibberish to me.

"What order are these codes in?" Keane asked.

"I think Gerard made them in the order of the serial numbers," said Olivia.

"Hmm," replied Keane. "If there's a message here, it's scrambled or encoded." He grabbed a pad of stationery from the desk and wrote the first word along with the corresponding five digits on a sheet. He tore the sheet off and wrote the second word and its five digits on the next sheet. He continued this process until he had a stack of nine sheets, each with a word and a number on it. He got up from the chair and spread the sheets out on my bed.

They looked like this:

the 33842 are 43713 one 80465

up 91482 down 53574 and 17190

path 58364 and 36044 the 36145

"Each number has five digits," I said. "Could be ZIP codes. Are the words related to the numbers somehow?"

"Not that I can discern," said Keane. "I believe they're two separate codes. Several of the words appear to be related to physical directions. I suspect that if we could determine the correct order, they might tell us how to use the numeric code."

Keane shuffled the words around so they read:

the up and down one are the path

That clearly didn't please him, so he tried again, putting the *are* in front like it was a question:

are the one path up and the down

After several iterations like this, he gave up on that line of pursuit. Next he tried:

the path up and down are the one and

Unhappy with this, he switched a few words:

the up and down path are one and the

"It seems like it's missing a word," I said, showcasing my viselike grasp of the situation.

"Yes, it does," said Keane, picking up his notebook from beside him. He tapped a flurry of keystrokes, then leaned back, regarding the display and nodding slowly. "It's a quote from Heraclitus," he said. "'The path up and down are one and the same.'"

"Rachel Stuil's namesake," I said.

"But we're missing the word *same*," Olivia said. "And the number that goes along with it. Are you sure the words aren't related to the numbers? Maybe if you run the word through some kind of algorithm, you get the corresponding number. So if we can figure out what that algorithm is, we can apply it to the word *same* and get the missing number."

"It's a possibility," said Keane, "but I'm having a hard time imagining what that algorithm would look like. Why would a two-letter word and a four-letter word both produce a five-digit number? It just feels off. Also, why would we need nine instances of the algorithm to identify it? If we could figure it out from nine, why not eight? No, I think the association of the words to the numbers is arbitrary."

"So what other explanation is there?" I asked.

"Canaan is still missing a coin," said Olivia.

Keane nodded, setting down the notepad on the table and getting to his feet. "That would be my hypothesis."

I stared at him. "There's a tenth coin?"

"A zeroth coin," said Keane. "Programmers tend to number from zero, which would allow him to stick with the single-digit serial number. I'm willing to bet the last iota has a serial number of zero."

"But only nine were auctioned off."

"Yes. The zeroth coin was never released. It's probably still in the hands of the creator of the coins. The trickster."

"So we have to go find Ed Casters in Costa Rica?"

"Something like that," Keane said. "Olivia, do you know where the Minotaur servers are located?"

"Of course," Olivia said. "In the Empathix building in Riverside."

"Good," Keane said. "I'm going to need you to go there."

"You want me to break into the Empathix building?" asked Olivia.

"You don't need to break in. As far as their security systems are concerned, you're Selah Fiore. Go to the server room, locate the Minotaur server. Give me remote access and leave. I'll write a patch allowing me to remotely administer Minotaur."

"What's this about, Keane?" Olivia asked. "What does this have to do with finding someone in Costa Rica?"

Keane glanced at me. I could tell he was trying to figure out how little he could get away with telling Olivia.

"I'm not running your errand for you unless you tell me the plan," said Olivia.

I shrugged at Keane. "Whatever it takes to get Gwen back alive," I said.

Keane nodded. "Ed Casters is not in Costa Rica. At least not any more than Fowler was in Mendocino earlier today."

"You think he's still in L.A.?" I asked.

"I think he's hiding in the DZ, just like Gwen was. Probably took off when the Project Maelstrom people started disappearing. He was never officially part of the team, but Canaan probably would have tracked him down. So he fled to the DZ. He lives in a virtual world anyway; might as well be in the DZ as anywhere else."

"Do you know where in the DZ?"

"I have a pretty good guess. One of the LAFF safe houses."

"But Canaan was part of LAFF," Olivia said. "Wouldn't he know to look there?"

"Not if Ed Casters's hideout wasn't on the safe house list," Keane said. "LAFF bought these properties or secured long-term leases, and made sure to locate them in places that were unlikely to be perceived as desirable to criminals or warlords. Pockets of calm in the maelstrom, you might say. Casters worked on the algorithm for identifying these pockets. There were maybe two dozen of them, altogether. One day, a few weeks after the leases had all been signed, Casters messages me and says he made a mistake. The algorithm was a little off. He sends me a new one, and one of the locations we'd selected no longer qualifies. So we removed it from the official list. I thought it was funny at the time; I mean an algorithm like that isn't usually 'a little off.' It either works or it doesn't. But I had bigger problems to worry about at the time. We had plenty of other safe houses identified, and it's not like LAFF was short on money."

"So," I said, "LAFF owns a building in the DZ that Canaan doesn't know about."

"He could find out if he dug a little," said Keane, "but why would he? And even if he did, LAFF probably owns hundreds of properties. Unless he somehow knew that this particular property had once been identified as a safe house, he'd have no reason to suspect Casters was there. Casters was never even supposed to know what the algorithm was for, but obviously he figured it out."

"And you know where this safe house is?"

"I do," said Keane. "It's right in the middle of the DZ. Just north of Compton. The safe house is an early Cold War–era bomb shelter underneath an office building."

I groaned. "Keane, there's no way I can get to Compton right now. If it's not an active war zone, it's going to be crawling with Green River mercenaries. I wouldn't get a hundred yards inside the DZ."

"I have an idea for that," Keane said.

I was pretty sure I knew what his idea was, and that I was going to hate it. "Please don't tell me you're going to send me back into the DZ posing as a Green River merc," I said. "It was pure luck I got out last time. If I go into the DZ wearing Conroy's gear, their system will ID me as Conroy, and since Conroy is dead, that's going to be kind of a red flag."

"The system will do what the system was programmed to do. We've just got to alter its instructions."

"Easy as that, huh?" I said.

Keane shrugged. "I've got the source code for the Minotaur platform. Olivia has Selah Fiore's fingerprints and retinas, which will get her into Empathix server room."

Olivia thought for a moment, then nodded. "All right," she said. "I'll do it. If that's what it takes to get the missing coin.

I don't blame you two for not trusting me, but in this case our interests are aligned."

"What good will it do to hack Minotaur?" I asked. "What are you going to do, make all the Green River guys go blind?"

"We don't want to be too obvious," said Keane. "They'll have protocols for dealing with a situation where Minotaur has been compromised. Best-case scenario if they find out, they'll just shut it down. Worst case, they've got a way to automatically restart the system with the last known secure configuration and lock down any changes. Also, if they realize they've been hacked, they'll track me to the nearest network node and send mercenaries to surround this building."

"Okay, so no mass blindness," I said. "What can you get away with?"

"For starters," Keane said, "I'm going to add a new user to the database and reassign Conroy's helmet. As far as anybody in Green River is concerned, you'll be just another new transfer to help out with DZ pacification. Beyond that, I can't make any promises."

"Wonderful," I said.

TWENTY-FOUR

Olivia left shortly thereafter. She was going to drive to the Empathix building and give Keane remote access to the server. Once she did that, Keane would need some time to upload his patch and add me to the database. I decided a nap was in order; it was going to be a long night. I was awoken half an hour later by my comm chirping. It was April.

"Hey," I said groggily into my comm.

"Hi, Blake," April replied. Her voice sounded terse and worried. "I'm at the FBI building in Beverly Hills. My friend Deacon Walthers has been running interference for me with the LAPD, but they've gone over his head. I'm going to have to give them something concrete soon, or I'm going to be sharing a cell with your girlfriend."

"Keane and I are working on something," I said. "We just need a few more hours."

"Really?" April replied. "Because it kind of sounded like I woke you up from a nap."

"Tactical catnap," I said. "Give me a second to confer with Keane."

Keane was still working at his notebook. There was no sign of Olivia.

"Time to suit up, Fowler," said Keane. "The patch is almost done."

I muted my comm. "The feds are going to turn April over to the LAPD," I said. "We need to give them something."

Keane looked up from his notebook and rubbed his chin thoughtfully. "All right," he said. "Have her tell them everything."

"Everything?" I said. "Is that wise?"

"Everything but the location of the last iota," said Keane. "That's our ace in the hole. We agree to give them the coin in exchange for dropping all charges against us."

"Seems like you're betting pretty heavily that the feds will actually care about the iota flaw."

Keane shrugged. "It's all we've got. If they don't take the deal, we're all going to prison for a long time."

I unmuted my comm and reiterated what Keane had said. April didn't sound optimistic.

"I'll give it a shot," she said. "When will you have the coin?"

"Tomorrow morning," I said, trying to sound confident. "At the latest." I glanced at Keane and he gave me a curt nod before returning to his work.

"All right," said April. "Good luck."

"Thanks," I said. "You, too." I ended the call. "Is your patch ready?" I asked, walking toward the kitchen.

"Almost," Keane replied.

I opened the fridge, but it was empty. Going through the cupboards, I managed to find a few cans of chicken soup. I opened one and heated it up in the microwave. If I was going into a war zone, I wasn't doing it on an empty stomach. I gulped down the soup and a couple of glasses of water and then messaged for a cab. I found a duffel bag in one of the closets and threw Conroy's gear into it. My comm chirped to tell me the car was downstairs.

"The comm network is probably still down in the DZ," I said. "Are we going to be able to communicate?"

"Once the patch is uploaded, yes. I can secure a one-to-one channel through the Minotaur system."

"Have you found a break in the wall for me?" I was wondering if I was going to have to have the driver stop at the hardware store so I could fabricate another grappling hook.

"No need," Keane replied. "You're going through the front door."

"Well," I said, "that sounds like a terrible idea."

"Trust me, Fowler. Go to the checkpoint closest to the safe house address I gave you. Call me when you get there."

"All right," I said. "Good luck." I grabbed the duffel bag and walked out the door.

Two minutes later I was in a car on the way to the West Rosecrans checkpoint. I had the driver drop me off in a 7-Eleven parking lot a few blocks from the checkpoint. I went behind the building and called Keane. It took me awhile to get a signal; apparently Green River was blocking comm transmissions for some distance outside the DZ as well.

"I'm just outside the DZ," I said. "What do I do now?"

"Are you somewhere you can put on the helmet?"

"Yeah."

"Okay, put it on and activate the Minotaur system."

I did so, reluctantly. If that helmet was still assigned to Conroy, it wouldn't take Green River long to track me down. I had to trust Keane knew what he was doing.

"Excellent," said Keane. "I see you: two hundred meters west-southwest of the Rosecrans checkpoint. Is your display up?"

A progress indicated, just visible at the bottom of my vision, scaled up to 100 percent and then disappeared. It was replaced by the message:

Hello, Major Tom Phan

"Seriously, Keane?" I said. "Major Phan, Tom? Was Captain Bogus McFakerson taken?"

"Can you hear me, Major Tom?" asked Keane's voice in my ear. "Ground control to Major Tom."

I hung up the comm. "Fucking hilarious, Keane," I said into the helmet mic.

"You've really made the grade, Major Tom," Keane said. "Although the papers are inquiring why you're wearing Conroy's shirt."

"Just tell me what to do, Keane."

"It's time to leave the capsule if you dare."

"Please get this out of your system before I'm actually inside the DZ," I said.

"I think I'm done," said Keane. "Proceed to the checkpoint."

"And then?"

"Tell the knucklehead at the gate that you're Major Phan, Tom, and you're late for meeting with General Malaise. Improvise, Fowler. It keeps you young."

"Fuck you," I said. "Going radio silent for now. If you don't hear from me in the next ten minutes, your stupid gag of a pseudonym got me killed. I hope it was worth it." I took off the helmet, turned it off, and stuffed it back in the duffel bag. I zipped up the bag and made my way through the alley toward the checkpoint. I took my time, avoiding traffic and scanning for cops. If I got arrested at this point, it would just be embarrassing.

Fortunately, I made it to the checkpoint without being spotted. Unfortunately, there were two LAPD officers at the checkpoint. They looked bored, as their job seemed to have been taken over by Green River personnel. Presumably Green River was checking their own people in and out, and they probably weren't letting any civilians through, which didn't give the cops much to do. I wondered how Canaan had managed to pull this off. He had to have made a deal with someone at pretty high levels to get the LAPD to roll over for his mercenaries.

The checkpoint itself was an old highway underpass that had mostly been blocked off with chain-link fencing and Jersey barriers. In front of a rolling section of fence that served as a gate stood two uniformed Green River mercenaries with M4-A4 carbines. The cops were standing next to a police cruiser, chatting, just outside and to the left of the gate.

I figured my best bet was to walk purposefully toward the gate, ignoring the cops completely. I was sure they'd seen my picture by now, but I thought it was pretty unlikely they'd recognize me under these circumstances. The human brain tends to see what it expects to see, and these guys would not expect to see a murder suspect walking right past them in a military uniform. As I neared the gate, I picked up my pace. So far, so good. One of the cops glanced at me, but I saw no hint of recognition in his eyes. I tried to give the impression of being in a hurry and a little irritated.

This plan hit a snag as I heard a car approaching from behind me. I turned to see headlights headed straight for me. It was my own fault; I was so intent on the checkpoint that I'd forgotten I was walking down an actual street. There hadn't been any traffic until now because the only possible destination for someone in a car headed down this street was the DZ.

My first instinct was to move out of the way. Unfortunately, there was no place to run except right into the arms of the nearest cop. It was one thing to walk past a cop at a distance of thirty feet; it was another to literally run right into him. I turned and stood my ground. The driver hit the brakes, squealing to a halt mere inches from me. I managed not to flinch.

I could see now that the car was actually an urban utility vehicle; it looked like a modified version of the Ranger Special Operations Vehicle I used to drive around Jeddah. I could see there were two people in the vehicle, but I couldn't make out faces against the glare of the headlights. What happened next was going to be highly dependent on who was in that car. If they outranked me, I was in for a serious tongue-lashing and probably enough drama that the cops would get involved. That would be very, very bad for me. So when the doors flew open and two twenty-something recruits hopped out, I smiled.

"What the fuck do you think you're doing?" one of them yelled. The other one came around the car toward me. They wore Green River uniforms but I saw no insignia on either of them. Presumably that meant they were still in training and hadn't been assigned a formal rank. These guys were the Green River equivalent of enlisted men.

"That's 'what the fuck do you think you're doing, *sir*,'" I said coldly, turning slightly to allow him to see the golden oak leaf on my shoulder.

"Oh, shit," said the one who had yelled.

"Yeah," I said. "Oh, shit. You two fucknuts are lucky I'm in a hurry. What are your names?"

"Trainees Stoltz and Ramos, sir," said the first man. The two snapped to attention and saluted.

"Barreling into a checkpoint is a good way to get yourself killed, Trainees Stoltz and Ramos."

"Yes, sir," said Stoltz. "Sorry, sir. The captain sent us to get some supplies and we got lost. We're a little late, sir."

"How long you been with Green River, Stoltz?"

"Just finished training, sir. This is our first assignment."

"Try not to get anybody killed," I said. "As you were."

"Yes, sir!" they both shouted.

I turned on my heel and marched toward the men at the gate. I stopped about three feet away. "I don't know where they find these morons," I said.

"Yes, sir," said the man to my right. "ID, sir?"

"ID?" I said, letting the irritation in my voice escalate a notch. "Last time they just scanned me. Jesus, I don't have time for this shit."

"Yes, sir," said the man. "That should be fine. Please hold still." He unclipped a retinal scanner from his belt and held it up to my left eye. After a second, the device beeped and he looked at the small display at its base. "Very good, sir," he said. "Welcome back to the DZ, Major Phan."

I nodded and faced the gate. The other man pulled it aside and I walked through. Once I was on the inside, I allowed myself a sigh of relief.

"Sir," called the man behind me. Shit.

I spun around. "Yes, Lieutenant. What is it?"

"Are you on foot, sir?"

Both sentries were watching me now, and the two cops had taken an interest as well. The two rookies had gotten back in their vehicle, which was very slowly approaching the checkpoint.

"Lieutenant Roberts was supposed to pick me up," I said. "He's late, as usual."

"Do you want me to call for transport, sir?" the man asked. "It may be a few minutes."

"We can drive you, sir," yelled Stoltz, leaning out of his vehicle. "Where you headed?"

Where *am* I headed? I thought. I could give him cross streets, but I had no idea whether or not Gwen's neighborhood was under Green River control at this point. It would be a tad suspicious if I gave them a location that hadn't been secured yet.

"I don't want to get you in trouble with your captain, Stoltz," I yelled. "Where are you boys headed?"

"Alpha Base," said Stoltz.

"All right," I said. "That'll do. Hurry up." I had no clue where Alpha Base was, but the odds were it was closer to the safe house than where I was now. And right now I just needed to get away from those cops.

The guard checked Stoltz's and Ramos's IDs and waved them through. The cops, to my relief, seemed to have lost interest in me. Stoltz pulled up next to me and I got in the back.

"Sorry again about almost running you over, Major. Won't happen again."

"No, it won't," I said. "Drive."

Stoltz nodded. He and Ramos put on their helmets, so I did the same. I activated mine so Keane would know I'd made it inside.

Stoltz drove east about a half mile and then turned north. The streets appeared to be deserted. Hopefully Alpha Base wasn't too much farther. From this neighborhood it was a short walk to the safe house location, but it would be highly suspicious if I had Stoltz drop me off here. Better to get to Alpha Base and slip away quietly, even if it meant walking a bit farther.

We'd only gone a few blocks to the north when I heard gunshots from somewhere on the right side of the street, up high. The windshield shattered and Stoltz slumped over the steering wheel and the vehicle careened to the right, slamming into a pickup parked against the sidewalk. My body flew forward, my helmet banging into the driver's seat in front of me. Dazed, I slumped to the floor and felt for the door handle. I located it, pulled, and rolled out of the vehicle onto the pavement.

I crawled to Stoltz's door and pulled it open. He was sitting slumped over, his head against the steering wheel, shoulder straining against the seat belt. I couldn't see where he was hit, but he wasn't moving. I shoved him back, undid the seat belt, and pulled him toward me. Ramos was crouched in front of his seat, mumbling, "What do I do? What do I do?"

"Ramos!" I snapped. "Climb over the driver's seat toward me."

He did so as I pulled Stoltz toward the rear tire, my arms around his chest. Stoltz let out a groan.

"Help me get his helmet off," I said. I felt something warm and sticky on my fingers.

Ramos unstrapped the helmet while I held Stoltz. "Get some light on him," I said. "Where is he hit?"

Ramos felt around frantically for several seconds, eventually producing a flashlight, which he shined on Stoltz's face. Apparently not seeing an entry wound there, he moved the light down to Stoltz's neck. Stoltz groaned again. "Lotta blood," said Ramos. "Hard to see."

"Is it spurting from somewhere?" I asked.

"I don't think so," said Ramos. "I think it missed the artery."

"You got a medkit on you? Some bandages?"

Ramos nodded and felt around some more.

"Stoltz," I said. "Can you move your fingers?"

Stoltz groaned again but didn't move. Hard to tell, but the bullet might have nicked his spinal cord. Bad news, but not as bad as hitting an artery. Ramos produced some gauze pads and tape and we patched Stoltz up as best we could.

"We gotta get out of this street," I said. "Grab his feet and we'll run for that alley."

Ramos got Stoltz's feet and we ran for it. A shot rang out and I saw it hit the pavement next to Ramos's boot. We made it to the alley and I collapsed with Stoltz on top of me. Judging from the angle of that last shot, we now at least had some cover.

"Should I call for an ambulance?" said Ramos.

"How far are we from Alpha Base?"

"Um, I don't know. Ten blocks?"

Shit. We couldn't carry Stoltz ten blocks. "Call for backup and a medic," I said. "Tell them we've got a sniper up high on the east side of Alameda, just north of Willowbrook." It wasn't necessary to give our location; they'd pinpoint us with Minotaur.

I heard Ramos murmuring into his mic. Now what? Leave this terrified kid with his paralyzed friend in an alley? Wait with them until backup arrived and then try to sneak away? Ride back with them to Alpha Base? Now that Green River had bases set up in the DZ, I assumed they'd take him to the nearest base first for triage and then decide if his injuries warranted a trip to the hospital. That was probably my best option. Once at Alpha Base, Major Tom could make his exit.

So I sat there in the alley for the next ten minutes, waiting for more guys who would definitely kill me if they had any idea who I was. I tried to convince myself that it was okay to leave, that Stoltz and Ramos were the bad guys, but it was no good. They were just stupid kids who took a job thinking they were going to be bodyguards for some sheik in Dubai, and here they were hiding from a gangbanger with a rifle in an alley in Compton. It occurred to me as I waited there that Keane was probably shitting himself wondering what I was doing. He hadn't yet broken radio silence, probably assuming—correctly—that I was not in a position to respond.

An armored personnel carrier pulled up to the mouth of

the alley and two men jumped out with a stretcher. A third followed them. The two with the stretcher put it down next to Stoltz, and I handed him off to one of them. They lifted him onto the stretcher and then began carrying him to the vehicle. I wiped my hands on my pants and looked up to see the third man standing in front of me.

"Major Phan," he said, and I swear for a second I thought he was telling me how excited he was to meet me. Then he added, "I'm Lieutenant Simms. You must have just arrived." His voice sounded oddly familiar, but I couldn't make out his face in the dim light of the alley.

"Yeah," I said. "Just got in from Phoenix." Don't ask me why I said Phoenix; it just seemed like a good place to have just come from. "We should get back to Alpha Base."

"Hang on a sec, Major," Simms said, blocking my way. Behind him Ramos was watching as the two men had loaded the stretcher into the vehicle. "Are you sure we haven't met?"

I suddenly realized how I knew this guy's voice. He'd been one of the squad that had cleared out Gwen's apartment building. "Lieutenant Simms," I snapped. "We need to get Private Stoltz medical attention. Once we're back at base, I'll be happy to—"

"Lieutenant?" called Ramos, taking a step toward us. "Everything okay?" He shone his flashlight in our direction, and for a moment the light shone full on my face. Unless Simms had some kind of visual impairment, there was no way he didn't recognize me.

I'd been caught.

TWENTY-FIVE

I launched myself toward him, bringing my forearms up in front of my chest. I'd have gone for his throat, but thanks to Ramos's light in my eyes, I couldn't see a damn thing, so I decided on a less precise maneuver. As I struck him, I snapped my fists forward, knocking him off balance. He staggered backward and fell to the ground a few feet in front of Ramos. I bounced backward from the blow, spun around and ran. I made it five paces before somebody— presumably Lieutenant Simms—started shooting at me. I felt a bullet graze the outside of my right leg. Smart, aiming where the armor wasn't as thick. But he hadn't had time to take careful aim, and I rounded the corner to the right, un-wounded except for the scratch on my leg.

"Keane!" I barked, running down the alley to the north. "Got a bit of a situation!"

"So I see," replied Keane. "Keep going down this alley, then turn left at the street. Your Tom Phan identity seems to have become a liability. I'm working on removing you from the system."

I had reached the alley and went left.

"What if I ditch the helmet?" I said.

"I don't recommend it," said Keane. "Access to Minotaur is one of the few advantages we have. If you get rid of the helmet, we'll be incommunicado."

He was right. The comm network was down in the DZ. I'd be flying blind without the helmet. Unfortunately that meant until Keane could scrub Major Phan from the system, Green River could track every move I made. I wondered how long it would take them to determine that Tom Phan wasn't even a real person. Once they figured that out, they'd know their system had been hacked.

"Fifty feet ahead on your left there's a doorway," said Keane. "Go inside the building. You may have to break the door in."

By the time he'd finished talking, I'd reached the door and verified it was locked. No time for finesse; I drew the Glock and shot the lock five times, then gave the door a kick. It swung open. I saw the glare of headlights approaching from behind, then heard a burst of automatic weapon fire. I ran inside.

"Go upstairs," Keane said.

I ran up the stairs. "How far?" I asked.

"Until I can figure out how the hell to delete you from this database," said Keane.

I reached the second floor and continued to the third. I heard men shouting below me. In the back of my mind, I was wondering what good it was going to do to delete me from the database if Green River had me cornered at the top of a building. Had Keane momentarily forgotten that there was a difference between the model he was observing and the real world? That deleting Tom Phan from a table in a database didn't magically transport me out of harm's way?

I reached the third floor and continued to the fourth. I heard boots coming up the stairs below me. My calves burned, but I didn't dare slow down. When I reached the fourth floor, I realized it was the last one. I found myself in front of a door that read, simply, ROOF.

"Roof!" I barked at Keane, too winded to manage more than the one syllable. He didn't reply, so I assumed that I was to continue. I burst onto a flat tar roof covered with a smattering of gravel.

"Head east," said Keane. "I've almost got it."

"East?" I gasped. There was nothing to the east but the edge of the roof, about sixty feet away.

"Yes, east," replied Keane. "Don't slow down. You're going to jump."

"Fuck me," I muttered, but didn't slow down, even though my legs were screaming. I reached the edge of the roof and jumped.

And fell.

The roof of the building to the east was only about five feet away, but it was a good ten feet down. I landed hard, smacking my helmet against the gravel. It's a good thing I hadn't ditched it; that thing probably saved my life. Even with it on, I saw stars. I tried to get up, but my arms and legs wouldn't respond.

"Don't move, Fowler," said Keane.

I would have laughed if I could. Instead, I just lay there, facedown on the roof, trying to breathe. Any second now, mercenaries would burst onto the roof next door, go to the edge of the roof, see me lying here, and shoot at me until I was dead.

I heard the door open and then footsteps on the gravel. Voices that I couldn't make out, then more footsteps . . . receding? And then silence.

"Okay, you can move now," said Keane. "I gave them a phantom Tom Phan on the fourth floor. Say that three times fast if you can."

I pulled myself to my feet. Something was wrong, and at

first my addled brain couldn't figure out what it was. Eventually I realized that I appeared to be floating. I could feel the roof under my foot, but I couldn't see it. In fact, the whole building had simply disappeared out from under me. I was looking at a featureless gray floor three stories below. It was unsettling, to say the least.

"Keane," I said, "Are you seeing this?"

"What is it, Fowler? Why aren't you . . . Oh. There are controls on the left side of your helmet. Try adjusting them."

I reached up with my left hand and felt two buttons. I tapped one of them and suddenly a wireframe outline of the building appeared. I could see the entire structure of the building, right through the walls. Turning, I realized I could see through the building I'd jumped from as well. Inside the building I saw three-dimensional renderings of five men in combat gear on the fourth floor, apparently conversing with each other.

I gave the button another tap and suddenly the building was opaque again.

"Get moving, Fowler," said Keane in my ear. "Fire escape off the back of the building, to your right. Move fast; I'm going to have to put you back on the roof in a few seconds."

"What?" I gasped, moving toward the rear of the building. "Why?"

"Geolocation systems sometimes have problems with altitudes in urban environment. If you reappear on the roof, they'll chalk it up to a momentary glitch. I don't want them to figure out they've been hacked quite yet."

"All right," I said, not happy with this development but seeing the wisdom of Keane's plan. Looking over the edge of the roof, I located the fire escape landing on the third floor and lowered myself down to it. "What the hell was that?"

I asked, as I made my way down the fire escape. "Why'd the building disappear?"

"Transparency mode," said Keane. "The Minotaur helmet has an integrated motion detector and thermal imaging camera that can be used to see through walls and other objects. The system also has the capability of filling in missing visual data about a location from its database, which is assembled from satellite data and other sources, including the helmet cams themselves. You must have activated it inadvertently when you fell."

I climbed the rest of the way down to the alley. As my foot hit the asphalt, I heard shouts from the roof.

"I'm giving them your actual escape route with a ten-second lag," said Keane. "So keep moving. Go down the alley to the west."

I ran as fast as I could down the alley. It came out on a street up ahead.

"Go right at the street," said Keane. "I'm going to have Major Tom go left and run down another alley. I can keep him just out of reach for hours."

I ran down the street for another hundred yards or so, and then Keane had me turn down an alley. At this point, I finally started to believe I'd actually lost my pursuers. Well, I hadn't lost them. Technically they were still pursuing me. They were just looking in completely the wrong place.

Following Keane's instructions, I worked my way down alleys and side streets toward the address of the safe house. I was almost there when I hear Keane say, "Hold up, Fowler."

I stopped cold at the end of the alley I was about to emerge from. According to Keane, the safe house was just down the street to the right.

"What's happening, Keane?" I said.

"Hmm," Keane replied.

I felt an unpleasant clenching in my chest. "What does that mean, Keane?"

"Hey?"

"You made your perplexed noise. Being perplexed at this stage of the game is not a good thing."

"Oh," said Keane, "well, I've been trying to keep an eye on the movements of Green River personnel, but I've been a little busy keeping you alive. So something seems to have escaped my notice."

"Which is?"

"Well," said Keane. "The good news is that I found your Alpha Base."

"And the bad news?"

"It's on top of the safe house."

"What do you mean, 'on top of'? Like, next door?"

"No, I mean Alpha Base is *on top of* the safe house. Alpha Base is a three-story office building on the corner of 120th and Compton. The safe house is in the bomb shelter below that building."

"How is that possible?" I asked. "What are the odds that Green River would set up shop in the same goddamned building as the safe house?"

"Fairly good, actually," said Keane. "It's centrally located and easy to get to. LAFF owns the building, and since it wasn't on the safe house list, Canaan assumed it was vacant. He probably started preparing it to act as a base of operations well before the invasion. The bomb shelter is missing from Green River's map; must be Ed Casters's doing. As far as I know, it's only accessible from a trapdoor in the closet of one of the rear offices. If Casters is down there, he's either trapped or he's got another exit I don't know about."

"How do we know Casters is still down there?"

"We don't," said Keane. "But unless Green River found his

hiding spot, he'd be crazy to move at this point. And we can be fairly certain that they haven't found him, because Canaan is still missing a coin."

That sounded like a lot of conjecture to me, but I decided to let it go to concentrate on the main point. "Okay," I said. "So what I hear you saying is that we're fucked."

"Hmm," said Keane.

"No, Keane. This is suicide. We're aborting. Whatever happens when Canaan gets that coin is just going to have to happen. The bad guy becomes a trillionare. I don't care, Keane. The police have nothing on us. We'll turn ourselves in and hope for the best."

"Not an option," said Keane.

"It *is* an option," I replied. "I just laid out the option in great detail. In fact, to prove it's an option, I'm going to do it right now. I'm getting out of here."

"Hold on, Fowler," said Keane. "There's something I need to tell you."

I groaned. Of course there was. "What?"

"I figured out why New Dollars are missing from the Empathix model. Or rather, where they were hiding."

"Why is this suddenly relevant?"

"It's important that you understand the stakes of our predicament."

"All right," I said. "Spit it out." I sat down on the pavement, leaning against the wall of the alley. I had a feeling I was in for one of Keane's monologues.

"Like all currencies," Keane began, "the New Dollar faced the bootstrapping problem. How do you convince people the currency is worth something before it's worth anything? The feds could have linked it to gold or some other asset, but they'd already proven once they'd unlink it as soon as it became convenient. So in a sense, they were already starting at a disadvantage: people didn't trust them to meet their commitments. At the first sign of trouble, investors would turn in their paper New Dollars for gold—and pretty soon, the feds would have no gold and a big pile of worthless New Dollars."

"This is all fascinating," I said, "but can we cut to the chase? I'm hiding in an alley in a war zone here."

"Be patient, Fowler. This background is necessary for you to understand why the last iota is so important. To continue: what the feds did is to issue bonds, denominated in New Dollars. Their price in dollars was five percent of their face value, which is to say that twenty thousand old dollars would get you a one-thousand-New-Dollar bond. But the bonds could be purchased—at a substantial markup—with virtually any currency: yuan, yen, rubles . . . even iotas.

"New Dollars were established by a special act of Congress, and the bill was full of limitations ostensibly designed to prevent rapid devaluation—the most significant of which was a federal law limiting the rate at which bonds could be issued. In reality, these limitations were mainly cosmetic: Congress could override them anytime they wanted to. Given this environment, no informed observers expected the bonds to sell. Conventional wisdom was that the New Dollar was a cynical, last-ditch cash grab by the feds. A trick to stabilize the dollar by linking it to a brand-new currency, which was also backed by nothing but a promise.

"To the surprise of virtually everyone, however, demand for the bonds was high, and remained strong for the next several weeks. Occasionally, dips in the value of New Dollars against other currencies would make speculators nervous, but the New Dollar always seemed to recover when it dropped below a certain point. The explanation for these repeated recoveries was that large institutional investors had bet heavily on New Dollars and were buying more bonds whenever the value dropped significantly. The end result is that the New Dollar became the new default world currency, and old dollars stabilized at five percent of the New Dollar's value.

"The details of these federal bond transactions were not public, so no one knew who these 'institutional investors' were, or what currencies they were trading for the bonds. It was assumed there were dozens, if not hundreds, of these investors, and that they were purchasing the bonds in a wide variety of different currencies. A casual look at the money markets bore this out: while the New Dollar rose, most other currencies remained relatively flat. The main exception was the iota, which quadrupled in value.

"The interesting thing, as we saw, is that the Empathix model seems to have missed these developments completely. According to their model, New Dollars shouldn't exist, and the other currencies, particularly the iota, should have surged in value. In the Empathix model, the iota goes as high as twenty times its previous value. How do we explain this sudden divergence from reality, after the model predicted the Collapse with startling accuracy?"

"I have no idea," I said. "How?"

"Actually," said Keane, "you gave me the answer. The Empathix model produces generalities, not specifics. In other words, the Empathix data is right, but the labels were wrong."

"Meaning what?" I asked.

"Meaning, what if iotas *are* New Dollars?"

"That makes no sense whatsoever, Keane."

"Think about it, Fowler. Postulate one: the feds launch a new currency, the New Dollar, which is near worthless. Postulate two: the iota is due to skyrocket in value just as this currency is launched. Now, given these two postulates, what happens to the model if someone secretly dumps a shitload of iotas and buys up New Dollars?"

I thought for a moment. "The New Dollar rises, and the iota falls. Or at least doesn't rise as much as predicted."

"Exactly. And other currencies don't rise as much as predicted, either, because interest in New Dollars is now siphoning away some of their value. In other words, you end up with exactly what Empathix predicted. Their data is correct. The labels are wrong."

"So," I said, trying to work out the ramifications of this, "the New Dollar isn't actually based on nothing. It's based on iotas."

"Very good, Fowler," replied Keane. "To the casual observer, iotas remain a fringe currency, used in a relatively small number of transactions. But behind the scenes, there's a huge mountain of iotas propping up New Dollars."

"And how do you know this exactly?" I asked. "I understand it fits with your understanding of the data, but do you have any actual evidence?"

"I didn't until about an hour ago," Keane replied.

"What happened an hour ago?"

"April called," Keane said. "She tried to contact you, but the call wouldn't go through. The feds took our deal. They agreed to drop all charges if we get them the last iota."

I let this information sink in for a moment. "So when you suggested the deal, you didn't know any of this. You had April go to the feds with a bluff."

"It was our only move," Keane said. "Either they would take the deal, thereby confirming their concern about the flaw, or they would refuse, indicating I was wrong about the New Dollar being based on the iota. If I was wrong, we were screwed no matter what we did. At least now we have a chance."

A very slim chance, I thought. Once again, Keane had sent me—and April!—into harm's way on the slightest of hunches.

And once again, I seemed to have no choice but to go along with his insane plan. "So if the iota collapses . . ." I said.

"The New Dollar collapses as well. If Canaan gets his hands on the last iota, we could be looking at another Collapse. And this time, we're not ready for it."

TWENTY-SIX

Another Collapse. The world was still recovering from the last one, over ten years ago. Los Angeles almost didn't survive—wouldn't have, if it weren't for Project Maelstrom. And there was no Project Maelstrom this time around. The reality I lived in was completely shaped by the Collapse; it was impossible to imagine what Los Angeles would look like after the next one. Something like a planet-sized DZ without out any walls, probably. And Gerard Canaan laughing his ass off on an island somewhere.

But would Canaan intentionally cause the Collapse? Probably not. He'd keep the flaw in the iota algorithm a secret and use it to further enrich himself and impoverish everyone else, gradually devaluing New Dollars and iotas in exchange for control over more and more hard assets—oil fields, gold mines, oceanfront properties, utility companies, factories, skyscrapers . . . It would be Gerard Canaan's world; the rest of us would just be living in it. And our continued existence would be at his whim: anytime he wanted to, he could inject a hundred trillion iotas into the economy and wreck it all.

"How could Canaan have pulled that off?" I asked. "And what did he get for propping up New Dollars?"

"Pulling it off would have been easy," Keane replied, "given Canaan's situation when the Collapse occurred. He probably called up the Fed Chair and pitched him on the idea of a new currency to replace the dollar. The feds would issue the bonds, and Canaan would secretly gobble them up, paying in iotas. As for what he got out of it, that's less clear. The federal government had been de facto controlled by the banks and other financial interests for many years by that point. By now, I suspect Canaan exercises considerable influence over the federal government itself. The important thing is that letting Canaan have that coin at this point would be very, very dangerous."

"But if Canaan has that kind of influence over the federal government, then how do we know we can trust April's friend at the FBI?"

"We don't," said Keane. "But it's the only chance we have."

I sighed. He was right, of course. "That may be," I said, "but I can't just walk into a Green River base. Even if you give me a new identity, they'll be looking for me. They probably flashed Major Tom Phan's picture on every Minotaur display in the DZ."

"What if I could make you invisible?"

"How the hell would you do that?"

"Transparency mode. The same way you made that building invisible."

"And you can do this with a person?"

"I don't see why not," said Keane. "By default, people will show up automatically, even if their surroundings are transparent. But that means Minotaur has an algorithm for recognizing people as such, and overriding the transparency parameters to display them. All I have to do is convince the system you aren't a person. Then I activate the transparency mode for all Minotaur users within a certain range of you, and *voilà*, invisibility."

"As long as they're all using their Minotaur displays."

"Well, yes. Also, it won't work well in full illumination. You'll show up as distortion in the visual field, something like heat waves in the desert. And I wouldn't get within thirty feet of anyone if you can avoid it. And avoid dogs. They'll smell you."

"So . . . really shitty invisibility."

"Best I can do."

"It might get me past the guards outside," I said. "But what do I do once I'm inside the building? It will be fully lit, and not everybody is going to be wearing a Minotaur helmet."

"We could try taking out the lights," Keane said. "I may be able to locate a breaker box on the building schematic."

"No," I said. "It'll be under guard, and in any case, they'll have a backup generator that kicks in as soon as the power goes out. A smoke grenade might work. That would blind the ones not wearing helmets and give me some cover against the others. Can you access inventory through this thing? They've got to have some around for riot control."

"Checking now," said Keane. He went silent for a minute or so. "We're in luck, Fowler. There's a storeroom just inside the building to the left. There should be riot gear inside. All you need to do is get to that room."

This idea still sounded fairly insane to me, but at least it wasn't physically impossible. If I could get past the guards out front, I could conceivably get to the storeroom and cause enough chaos with a smoke grenade to get to the trapdoor in the back of the building before anybody ID'd me. I didn't like it, but apparently the fate of the civilized world was resting on my shoulders, so I guess I was going to give it a shot.

I retreated back down the alley in the direction I had come, and made a wide circle around the block so I could approach Alpha Base without being spotted. I saw it now on my display; I'd learned that I could toggle my display with the buttons on the outside of the helmet. Presumably there were also voice commands and probably a way to control the display with eye movements, but these were beyond my current level of expertise.

"Where are you going, Fowler?" Keane asked.

"Just doing some recon," I said. I was now in an alley behind the building that faced Alpha Base. I had planned on sneaking alongside the building and peeking out to get a firsthand view of the guards, but accidentally hitting the transparency mode gave me an idea. I looked straight at the building in front of me and then played with the controls until I got it to vanish. Then I used the zoom feature to get a closer look at the front of the base.

It was a three-story office building, as Keane had said. There was a single entrance in front. As expected, two men with M4-A4s stood guard outside. Just to the left was the entrance to a belowground parking garage, which probably factored into Green River command's decision to use this building as much as any of Keane's factors: it gave them a place to park their vehicles. A wall of sandbags and Jersey barriers had been set up to prevent vehicles from getting too close to the building; farther down the road to my left another checkpoint had been set up. That had presumably been where Stoltz had been headed before he'd been shot.

The men out front were rendered as pixilated approximations; the Minotaur system couldn't actually "see" them, it could only pinpoint their locations based on satellite data and pings from other nearby Minotaur clients. It identified the two men by name; if I'd wanted to, I could focus on their names and read their entire dossier, but I wasn't really that interested in them. The building behind them, by contrast, was visible in high-definition video—I couldn't tell I was actually looking at a composite rendering rather than the real thing. It occurred to me that there was probably a way to maneuver through these renderings without having to physically orient myself in the direction I wanted to look, but that, too, was beyond my abilities at present. In any case, my current method seemed to be working okay.

I zoomed in again, adjusting the transparency setting slightly so that I could see through the front wall. The front door led to a lobby; the reception desk was toward the right-hand wall. The door to the supply closet with the riot gear was in the middle of the left-hand wall. Another door, in the back wall, led to a hall that was lined with offices. I saw that Keane had helpfully marked the floor of the closet at the end of the hall on the right with a big red X—presumably the location of the trapdoor. I saw no people, pixilated or otherwise, inside the building, but that could just mean that there were no active Minotaur helmets in the building. Somehow I doubted I was going to be lucky enough to run into exactly no one on my way to the back of the building.

"How's the invisibility coming?" I asked.

"I have it almost figured out," Keane replied. "There's no way to test it, of course, but in theory you should be more or less invisible to anyone using Minotaur."

"That's fantastically reassuring," I said. In my head, I was working out Plan B, which basically consisted of getting as close as I could and then shooting everybody in my way. Running away wasn't an option; I was going to get that coin or die trying. It was going to be a special kind of poetic justice if Ed Casters wasn't even in the safe house after all. Hopefully I'd be shot in the head before finding that out.

"Okay, we're good to go," said Keane. "Keep in mind that I can't be terribly selective with the invisibility. It's either going to be on or off in a given area."

"Meaning what?"

"Meaning that I can't make you invisible behind a building without making the building invisible. And as disappearing buildings tend to raise suspicion, that means you have to leave cover before the invisibility kicks in."

"You have to be shitting me. The invisibility doesn't work unless I first make myself completely visible?"

"It should be fine," said Keane. "I can set the range to within a few inches of the building, and that area is in near darkness anyway. Just don't linger near any buildings. Also, avoid running. The system has to erase you on the fly, so the fewer pixels it needs to change at a time, the less obvious it will be."

No cover and no running, I thought. So basically do exactly the opposite of what all your training and instincts tell you to do. "Just tell me when you're ready."

"Any time," said Keane. "I think I've figured out how to give you some help once you're inside, too. A little noise in the Minotaur system."

"That would be appreciated," I said. "Assuming I make it that far."

"One more thing," said Keane. "After this little trick, I suspect Green River is going to be on to me, so I'm going to have to run. I won't be able to help you anymore anyway; they'll shut Minotaur down once they realize they've been hacked. So drop your helmet as soon as you don't need it to see through the smoke. We'll be incommunicado until you leave the DZ with the coin. Message me when you do. We'll rendezvous at Grand Park, where you met Olivia."

"Roger that," I said. I didn't know why he once again picked that terrible location, but I decided not to question it. Odds were I was never getting out of the DZ anyway.

I made my way around the building toward the front of the base. Peeking around the corner, I saw the two guards in more or less the positions indicated by the transparency view. My original idea had been that I would follow someone into the building, but it didn't look like anybody was going to be going through that door anytime soon. Occasionally a vehicle would stop at the checkpoint and then pull into the garage, but there was obviously an elevator from the garage into the Alpha Base building, because no one was walking around front to get inside. I was going to have to just walk right to the door and hope for the best.

I took a few steadying breaths and then rounded the corner, making a mental note not to linger in the visible zone. I walked smoothly but briskly toward the door, doing my best to minimize both my footsteps and any unnecessary motion. I figured the distortion would be less noticeable if I avoided any jarring movement. I drew my pistol as I entered the area of the street lit by the lamps, in case I needed to shoot anybody.

But neither of the guards made any indication they saw me. I was now less than fifty feet away and closing, fully illuminated by the floodlights, but the two men stared straight ahead. I was fucking invisible!

I continued toward the doorway, rolling my soles on the pavement as I walked, my trajectory taking me right between the two guards. My gun was at the ready now; I doubted I'd be able to get within thirty feet without being seen. But at that range, I could probably take out both guards before they could figure out what was happening. These guys didn't look much older than Stoltz and Ramos, and I was aware of the irony inherent in my intentions to shoot them less than an hour after risking my life to save Stoltz. What can I say, war is a funny thing. Besides, the stakes had changed.

To my amazement, the two guards continued to stare straight ahead as I closed within ten feet of the door. I was beginning to think I was going to be able to just walk right up and slip through the door without either of these bright-eyed sentries sparing a glance in my direction.

And then the guy on the left looked right at me.

TWENTY-SEVEN

The guard brought his rifle up and I pointed the Glock right at his face. From this range, I was pretty sure I could blast right through that visor. I didn't want to do it, but I had no choice.

And then he dropped his gun and fell to his knees, screaming. The guy on his right did the same, and I heard more screams from inside. Keane's "noise in the system" had evidently kicked in.

"Audiovisual overload," I heard Keane say. "They'll be deaf and blind for about ten seconds. Make good use of it. Good luck, Fowler. I'm out."

I walked past the two guards, who were lying on the ground desperately trying to get their helmets off, and opened the door. I went inside. A few feet in front of me, Lieutenant Simms lay on the floor, blinking and rubbing his ears, his helmet resting on the floor next to him. Inside, to my right, another young man, not wearing a helmet, was standing behind the reception desk, staring at the man on the floor. Two other men, also sans helmets, sat in chairs to my left, gawking at the man on the floor as well. The only one I recognized was Simms.

"Minotaur's been compromised," I said, tossing my helmet on the floor. "You two, get this man outside!"

This instruction made no sense whatsoever, but military men do what they're told to do. I'd made a split-second decision given the circumstances to forgo the smoke grenade and try to bluff my way through. If the two men recognized me, they didn't show it; they simply went to Simms and helped him outside. Simms was dazed enough not to resist. That left only the guy at the desk.

"Hey," he said, as I continued to the door to the hall, "you're the guy they're looking for! Major Phan!"

Again I had to remind myself that the desk jockey was not telling me how much he enjoyed my work. "Didn't you hear me?" I barked. "Minotaur's been compromised. They've been flashing my goddamned picture all over the network, and now they're jamming everything. Get on a secure channel and tell ComSec Minotaur's been hacked. I'm going to inform the colonel."

"Yes, sir!" said the man behind the desk, picking up a phone. God, I loved dealing with people conditioned to unquestioningly obey authority figures.

I threw open the door to the hallway and kept going. When I was halfway down, a stocky man who appeared to be in his late forties stepped out of an office right in front of me. He wore colonel's insignia on his shoulder. "What in the hell is going on?" he demanded. Then his eyes widened. "Major Phan!" he exclaimed.

"Likewise," I said, and slugged him across the jaw. He fell to the ground, groaning, and I stepped over him. I continued to the office at the end of the hall. The door was locked, but it was a pretty flimsy interior door, so I kicked it open. The office was empty except for several stacks of folding chairs and other random office furniture. I closed the door and moved several stacks of chairs in front of it, then went to the closet.

Opening the door and turning on the light, I found myself inside a spacious closet. Several more folding chairs leaned against the back wall. I moved these in front of the office door as well, then peeled back the carpet. Underneath was a hardwood floor, and I did not at first see any indication of a trapdoor. There was a banging behind me and somebody in the hall yelled, "Major Phan! Open the door!" This mission was going to end very quickly, and very badly, if Keane was wrong about the bomb shelter.

But as I looked closer, I noticed one of the slats was only about ten inches long, and there was a gap of about half an inch at the end of it. After some experimentation, I found that I could slide the board, closing the gap. As I did so, the pressure of my fingers caused the board to pivot vertically a few degrees, so that the left side moved upward just enough to get my fingers under it. Taking the hint, I wrapped my fingers around the edge and pulled. A door, composed of a staggered, roughly square section of slats, opened toward me. The door was heavy; underneath the floor slats was a steel plate nearly an inch thick. It swung on heavy-duty pneumatic hinges. Whoever had installed this bomb shelter had been serious. For all this effort, however, the door was not locked. Dim light arose from below, revealing a series of metal rungs leading down into a concrete-lined shaft.

There was a crash behind me, and my pile of chairs shuddered. The door opened a couple of inches, but fortunately the opening was angled away from the closet. I pulled the closet door closed as another crash sounded, followed by the sound of chairs clattering to the floor. Lowering myself into the hole, I felt one of the rungs under my boots. I climbed down a couple of rungs and closed the trapdoor, making sure the carpet lay back down on top of it. Hopefully that would buy me a minute or two while the Green River boys wondered where Major Phan had disappeared to.

After descending another ten rungs, my boots hit a concrete floor. Turning around, I found myself in a small storage room. Steel shelving units filled with cardboard boxes and plastic storage containers lined the walls on either side of me. A single low-wattage bulb in a fixture overhead cast the room in garish light. Directly in front of me was a heavy steel door. I tried to open it. It was locked.

From the shaft behind me, I heard muffled sounds of men talking and moving things around. No matter how dumb these guys were, eventually they'd find the trapdoor. And when they did, minutes or hours from now, I would be still standing here, staring at this door, because I do whatever Erasmus Keane tells me to do, and Erasmus Keane is a lunatic who doesn't give two shits about me.

Having no other options, I knocked. A few seconds later, to my utter surprise, the door opened.

"Come in, Mr. Fowler," said the small, mousy-haired woman standing in front of me.

I stepped through the door, and found myself in what appeared to be a very cheery beachfront cottage. Through the plate-glass windows on my left, beyond a strip of yellow beach, I saw the rolling waves of the Pacific.

"*Pura vida,*" said the woman. "Have a seat." The woman was almost elfin in appearance, with big, almond-shaped eyes and ears that peeked out of her scraggly, brown-gray hair. She wore silk pajamas and slippers. Her age was hard to determine; I thought she was in her thirties.

I took a seat in a wicker chair that gave me a good view of the ocean. The view was astounding; to the right of the beach arose a series of rocky cliffs that reminded me a bit of the California coast. I could hear birds chirping and the crashing of the waves in the distance.

"Can I interest you in a glass of wine, Mr. Fowler?" the

woman asked. "I recommend the white. The red down here is a little sweet for my tastes."

I honestly didn't know if "down here" meant the bomb shelter or Costa Rica. My brain was having a hard time convincing my senses that I was underneath an office building in Compton. By comparison, I found it relatively easy to accept that Ed Casters was female.

"Just water, please, if you have it," I said. No, Fowler, she's been living underground for three years with no water.

"Certainly," she said, and disappeared into the kitchen. A moment later, she reappeared with a glass of water, handed it to me, and sat down on a couch to my right.

"So you're the mysterious Lila," I said, then gulped down the water. "Also known as Ed Casters."

"Ed Casters, Rachel Stuil, Brad Melton, Ann Coswaite, a few others. You can call me Rachel." She seemed at ease and unsurprised by my visit.

"I'm afraid I led some mercenaries to your door, Rachel," I said, setting the glass down on the coffee table in front of me.

Rachel shrugged. "It was bound to happen eventually. In any case, we have some time." She picked up a tablet from the table next to her and tapped it a few times. The view of the ocean was replaced by an image of several Green River men moving stacks of chairs around an office. "They haven't even found the trapdoor yet. I locked the door behind you; it should take them a few minutes to get through that. I do have an escape route, of course. I made some modifications to this place after I moved in. Wasn't about to be trapped down here." She tapped the tablet and the view switched back to the ocean.

"Why did you let me in?" I asked.

"Physical barriers don't interest me. You earned the right

to meet me face-to-face. You and Mr. Keane, of course. But as usual, Keane finds a way to make someone else do the dirty work."

"He was right, then," I said. "There really is a tenth iota."

"A zeroth iota, yes." She picked up a small wooden box from the table next to her. She opened it and pulled out a silvery coin, setting the box down again. "It's silly, really," she said, peering at the coin. "I have no need of it. I've got the last bit of the code in my head. But I like the symmetry. Ten coins, ten parts of the code."

"And ten words," I said. "'The path up and down are one and the same.' What does it mean?"

"Nothing," said Rachel, with a grim smile. "Or everything. Maybe it means nothing matters, that everything built up gets destroyed. Or maybe it's a random phrase I picked out. What difference does it make? Would you feel better if it 'meant something'? What do the coins mean? What do iotas mean? What does gold mean? What does any of it mean? It's all just ideas we're chasing around because we have nothing better to do."

"Does this mean you're not going to give me the coin?" I asked.

She laughed, a strange, almost robotic laugh. "Why should I give you the coin, Mr. Fowler? Give me a reason."

"I'm going to assume that saving the world isn't enough for you."

"Don't be grandiose, Mr. Fowler. You're not saving the world, you're trying to rescue an idea. Such a pedestrian idea, too. That money is worth something. Wouldn't you like to see what the world looks like without money?"

"Don't tell me you're going to go all 'money is the root of all evil' on me."

Rachel smiled, more broadly this time. "Money isn't the root of evil. Money and evil are both just ideas used to con-

trol people. Maybe it's time people stopped relying on ficti-
tious ideas."

"Collective delusions," I said. "That's what Keane calls
them."

"He's exactly right," Rachel replied. "And he should know.
The DZ was his idea."

"The DZ is a physical place," I said. "Not an idea."

"People thought East Berlin was a physical place, too,"
said Rachel, "but I can't find it on any maps. Did the place
disappear?"

"Of course not," I said. "But there was a wall around it.
Once the wall came down, the boundary between East and
West Berlin disappeared."

"Wrong," said Rachel. "Once people stopped believing in
the idea of two separate Berlins, the wall came down. Ideas
shape reality, not the other way around."

"Then you should be thrilled about the success of iotas
and New Dollars. The whole world revolves around an idea
you created. If Gerard Canaan gets the last iota, that idea is
threatened. He'll create an unlimited supply of iotas, gradually reducing the value of both iotas and New Dollars to
nothing. Is that what you want?"

Rachel shrugged. "When I said ideas create reality, I was
stating an empirical fact, not expressing a preference. I have
no allegiance to the iota. Whether people rally around the
banner of the Kingdom of God, or the Brotherhood of Man,
or the Scientific Progress, or the Almighty Iota, it makes no
difference to me. This idol, like all others, will someday
fall."

I smelled something acrid and sulfurous, and for a moment I thought Rachel was using olfactory aids for her apoc-
alyptic speech. I turned to see tendrils of dark smoke
trailing from the door I had just come through.

"Smoke grenades," Rachel said. "The mercenaries seem to

have gotten through the trapdoor. I'm afraid the rubber seals on the lower door weren't meant to last eighty years."

Damn it. They were using my own plan against me. They were going to try to fill the chamber with smoke to blind me and use their helmets to see through the smoke. I guessed that meant Minotaur was back online. Once they'd given the smoke time to spread, they'd throw down a couple of flash-bangs, or maybe a grenade. They'd probably need to get some Semtex or C-4 to get through the metal door, and then they'd come through, guns blazing. I figured I had somewhere between two and four minutes.

I was tempted to grab the coin from Rachel's hand and make a run for it, but I had a feeling it wasn't going to be that easy. She hadn't told me where her escape route was, and I wasn't about to rely on her revealing it in order to save herself. Someone who engineers a worldwide financial collapse and then hides under a military base isn't the sort of person whose survival instincts you want to depend on. I wondered if Rachel—or whatever her name was—was insane. Did terms like insanity even apply to someone like her? If she was delusional, then the whole world was in the grips of her delusion. Keane may have designed the DZ, but she created the algorithm that ran the world.

"You know," I said, "you remind me a lot of Keane."

"And tell me, Mr. Fowler," Rachel said with a smile, "is that a compliment?"

"I honestly don't know," I replied. "I just meant it as an observation."

"Well, I suppose it's unavoidable," she said. "The man you call Erasmus Keane is my brother."

TWENTY-EIGHT

Somehow it made perfect sense. It takes a special kind of lunatic genius to invent a new currency with the intention of crashing the global economy—a sort of genius I was all too familiar with. Keane had designed the DZ; Rachel Stuil had designed an algorithm that was now the foundation for the international financial system. Keane's motivation had ostensibly been to keep Los Angeles from imploding, but I suspected he'd done it to amuse himself as much as anything. The main difference between Keane and Rachel was not that Keane was the good one of the two; it was that Rachel thought bigger. I wondered if she was even smarter than Keane. Signs pointed to yes.

And yet, here we were, trapped like rats underground, Green River mercenaries about to bust down the door and kill us both. Did she care? Was this part of the game? Is this what she'd planned from the beginning?

I found it hard to believe. Frankly, I didn't think Rachel had an endgame planned out. To her, it was all about the interplay of order and chaos. She didn't have a death wish, but neither did she have some grand goal in mind. She would keep playing as long as the game interested her. The biggest danger, from my point of view, was that Rachel had gotten bored. Despite this realization, my curiosity got the better of me.

"Keane didn't mention he had a sister," I said.

"I'm not surprised," Rachel said. "Is this really what you want to talk about, Fowler? I'll answer whatever questions you like; after all, you've earned it. But the clock is ticking. Do you want to know about Erasmus Keane or would you like to know how to get out of here?"

That was an easy one. As curious as I was about Keane's sister—and Keane himself—I had come here for one reason. I'd known Keane was a liar when I went on this mission, and I wasn't leaving without the coin. "If Canaan gets the last iota," I said, "it's all over. Your game ends, and not with a bang, but with a whimper. New Dollars and iotas gradually lose their value and fall out of use. But if you give it to me, the game keeps going. There's no telling what might happen next."

"Oh, Fowler," said Rachel. "You're so adorable, trying to tempt me with the prospect of new horizons and undiscovered countries. Sadly, there is nothing new under the sun. I've already played out all of the possibilities, and none of them are terribly interesting—other than global chaos, of course."

"If you wanted chaos, why all the games? Why not just hack the algorithm yourself and have it over with?"

"I don't *want* chaos," she said. "I just find the possibility interesting. In any case, crashing the system myself feels like cheating. As it was, I practically had to tell Canaan how to find the code. I had assumed someone would find the notches in the reeds years ago. With my intellect, it's sometimes difficult to gauge how challenging a puzzle will be for the average person."

Just as modest as Keane, too, I thought. "So you set up this whole puzzle, allowed me to find you down here, and now you're just going to sit on the coin until Green River busts in and kills us both?"

"It had to end one way or another," said Rachel. "But I'll tell you what, Fowler. In recognition of your valiant efforts, I'll give you a choice." She placed the coin on the coffee table in front of her. "You can have the coin, or I can tell you the way out of here. One or the other, not both. Save your life or win the prize."

"The prize is worthless if I don't get out of here," I said.

"True," said Rachel. "Which is why I'm also going to give you this." She picked up a small ceramic bowl from the table next to her and put it on the coffee table between us. I saw that it was half-filled with a fine silvery powder.

"What's that?" I asked.

She pulled a matchbook from her pocket and set it next to the bowl. "Aluminum and iron oxide. Commonly known as thermite. It burns at four thousand degrees. Hot enough to melt titanium. Drop the coin in, light the match. In a few seconds, the coin will be a lump of slag."

"If I destroy the coin, Canaan's fortune is secure," I said. "He gets what he wants."

"Yes, but he'll be unable to manipulate the algorithm. You wouldn't have to worry about Canaan—or anyone else—crashing the iota on a whim."

"You would do that?" I asked. "After all this effort to find the code, you'd just let me destroy the coin?"

"This phase of the game is over, Fowler. You won. Consider this your prize. You protect the global economy from chaos."

"But I don't get out of this room alive."

Rachel shrugged. "That would be up to Green River," she said. "But I wouldn't bet money on it."

I regarded her for a moment. Frankly, it seemed like kind of a shitty deal. Canaan would still get essentially what he wanted: He wouldn't be able to create an unlimited number of iotas anytime he wanted, but he'd be protected from any-one else doing the same. Also, this option would most likely end up in me being dead. Was it worth the cost? I'm sure I wasn't the best person to ask for an objective appraisal of the value of my own life, but I was leaning toward no.

"Tell you what," Rachel said, seeing me hesitate. "I'll flip a coin. Heads, I reset the code. Tails, I tell you how to get out."

I said nothing. I didn't like either of my choices, but I didn't like the idea of leaving it up to a damn coin, either. I watched as smoke swirled around my boots and snaked along the floor. Any second now, the Green River mercenaries were going to blow the door open and the decision would be made for me. This couldn't be the end. There had to be some other way out of this. Come on, Fowler, use your head. You didn't come all this way just to fall victim to Rachel's games.

Rachel tossed the coin in the air. For a split second, it hung at its apogee, glinting in the faux sunlight from the window, and suddenly I knew what I had to do.

I got to my feet and swiped the coin out of the air. "No deal," I said, stuffing it in my pocket. I picked up the chair I'd been sitting in, bringing it over my head as I stepped toward the beach view. After three quick steps, I hurled the chair against the display, shattering it into thousands of pieces. Centered in the wall behind the display was a hole, roughly three feet in diameter. I could see only a few inches of concrete; beyond that was only blackness. I could feel the air being pulled out of the room into the tunnel.

"You've got a draft," I said, as smoke curled around my legs and vanished into the hole. I thought I saw the hint of a smile on Rachel's face. She did enjoy a bit of chaos. I climbed into the hole and began to move as fast as I could on my hands and knees down the tunnel. It didn't matter where I was going, as long as it was out.

After a few inches, the concrete gave way to dirt; the tunnel overhead was supported by ribs made of two-by-fours about a foot apart. I had just enough room to crawl without hitting my head. I'd gone about ten feet when I was hit by a blast of wind and a clatter from behind me: Green River had blown the door. A moment later came several quick bursts of gunfire.

I scurried as fast as I could, knowing that very soon somebody was going to peer down the tunnel with a flashlight and an M4-A4. I couldn't see a damn thing, but it didn't matter: if I didn't reach a bend in the tunnel within a few seconds, I was going to be a very big fish in a very small barrel.

Then my left palm came down on something much harder than dirt: concrete, rough like the opening behind me: not a floor, but a hole in another wall. Reaching forward, I felt a vertical barrier of something like canvas. I pushed on it, and it gave a little on the bottom, like a curtain. Knowing I had no time to be delicate, I threw all my weight against the fabric and found myself falling through the opening, my upper body pulling the rest of me across the concrete lip and downward. I fell maybe six feet before my hands—and then my elbows and forehead—hit gravel. I rolled onto my back and then lay there for a moment, dazed and hurting. Something warm was trickling down my forehead to my scalp.

I became aware that some kind of hard ridge was digging into my lower back. Reaching toward it, my fingertips felt a thick metal lip. Train tracks.

Somewhere on my belt, I knew, I had a flashlight. But it would take a few seconds to find it—seconds I didn't have. I rolled off the track onto my belly, my fingertips brushing the wall I'd just come through. If this was a subway tunnel, there were two ways I could go. I was too disoriented to determine which direction was more likely to take me away from

Alpha Base, so I got to my feet and picked a direction at random. Running my fingertips along the concrete wall to my right, I staggered through the darkness. Over the crunching of my boots on the gravel, I heard the echoes of men yelling.

Using the wall to my right as a guide, I sprinted down the tunnel, praying the way ahead of me was unobstructed. After a few steps, I located the flashlight and flicked it on. All was clear: nothing ahead but more tunnel, gradually curving to the left. I heard footsteps behind, but I was around the bend before they could get a shot off. I heard shouts followed by more footsteps. I was winded and dizzy and my head hurt, but I kept running. As long as the curve in the tunnel held out, I'd be all right, but once I hit a straightaway, I'd be a sitting duck.

I switched off the flashlight, both to avoid making myself an easier target than necessary and because I was hoping I might see some sign of daylight ahead. The Green River guys were relying on the infrared cams in their Minotaur helmets, so they weren't using lights. If I could find an access tunnel, I might be able to reach the street before I was shot to death. A hundred yards or so ahead, I saw what I was looking for: a sliver of illuminated gravel. I flicked the light on for a second to make sure my way was still unobstructed. My head was beginning to clear, the dizziness replaced by a throbbing ache in my temple. That was fine: pain I could deal with. Disorientation would kill me.

As I approached the patch of illuminated gravel, I flicked the light on again for a second. On the left-hand side of the tunnel, I saw a series of metal rungs disappearing into a narrow shaft overhead. I turned off the light, grabbed the rungs, and began to climb. To my left, just around the bend, I heard several men approaching. I vanished into the shaft as shots rang out below me.

A moment later, my head clanked against something hard.

A manhole. Now the question was whether or not I was inside Alpha Base's protected zone. If I was, they'd have welded the manhole cover in place, and I would soon be dead. I pressed my shoulder against the metal and shoved with all my strength. It moved.

I pushed the cover aside and squirmed through the opening, then slid it back into place. I stood for a moment in the middle of the dark street, trying to orient myself. Glancing at my comm display, I saw that I'd been following the tunnel north by northwest. That was good; I could make a beeline to the nearest DZ border to the west without have to backtrack past Alpha Base. I just had to traverse roughly a mile and then figure out how to get over the wall.

A more pressing concern, however, was the group of a dozen or so gun-toting men approaching from down the street to the south. These were not Green River mercenaries; from their clothing and mismatched gear, I judged them to be gang members, probably Tortugas. Evidently this area of the DZ was still under contention. Being dressed as a Green River mercenary did not bode well for me. Someone yelled in my direction. They pointed their guns at me. I ran.

This was a residential part of the DZ; I was surrounded by tract houses and dilapidated apartment buildings. There had clearly been some fighting here recently: a row of beat-up vehicles was arranged as a makeshift barrier across the street to my right; to the left, a car was on fire, casting monstrous shadows of the approaching gang members on the bullet-riddled stucco apartment building across the street. I went north, toward the wall of vehicles, then turned left to dart down an alley. I saw immediately that I'd made a mistake: the alley dead-ended in a chain-link fence forty feet ahead. I could climb it, but there was no way I'd clear it before the gangbangers riddled me with bullets. I skidded to a halt, spun around, and took aim. I had ten in the magazine and one in the chamber—just enough to take them all out if I was very lucky. I was also wearing body armor, so unless one of them got off a headshot, I still had a chance to survive this. I took a deep breath and steadied my hand, waiting for the first man to round the corner.

He didn't come. Instead, I heard shouts and several bursts of automatic gunfire. My pals from Green River, coming up from below, had joined the fun. Hopefully they and the Tortugas would keep each other entertained for a few minutes. I holstered the Glock, sprinted to the fence, and clambered over. There was no sign of pursuit.

I traversed several blocks, mostly through alleys and backstreets, and eventually found myself on a street lined with several small shops that had been thoroughly vandalized and looted. Just down the street to the south I caught sight of a men's clothing store, and I decided to stop in. There wasn't much selection, but I ditched Conroy's vest, jacket, and shirt in favor of my black T-shirt, having come to the conclusion that whatever protection was afforded me by the body armor was outweighed by the giant target it put on my back. To gangbangers, I looked like a mercenary, and to the mercenaries I looked like a deserter. Either was likely to get me shot.

I tucked the Glock into my rear waistband, stepped back out the gaping hole in the plate-glass window, and continued on my way. It turned out that I needn't have been worried. The rest of the DZ neighborhoods I cut through were quiet. I heard occasional gunfire in the distance, but no sign of any fighting nearby. I made it to the western wall without incident.

Getting over the wall was less of a challenge than I expected as well: After following the wall about three hundred yards to the south, I encountered a gaping hole in the wall that had been caused by an explosion of some kind, possibly a shoulder-fired RPG. I climbed over the rubble onto the freeway. Stopping to listen for drones, I heard nothing, so I sprinted across the northbound lanes. Crouching between two cars on the median, I stopped again, but still heard nothing. The drones were either distracted elsewhere or out of commission. I ran across the remaining lanes.

Surmounting the outer wall was no problem from this side; there were plenty of cars parked on the shoulder. I climbed on top of an SUV, put my fingers on top of the wall, and pulled myself up. Then I lowered myself to the dirt on the other side. For a moment I just lay there on the ground, staring up at the mottled glare on the smog that was Los Angeles' version of a starry night.

I'd made it out of the DZ.

TWENTY-NINE

I staggered through an industrial strip west of the DZ, so stunned to be alive that it didn't immediately occur to me that I was in nearly as much danger on this side of the wall. Gerard Canaan had obviously made some kind of deal with the LAPD to look the other way while Green River invaded the DZ, and if he had the LAPD in his pocket, not even surrendering would save me. The LAPD has never been known for their restraint or their scruples, and if it were convenient for Gerard Canaan that a certain murder suspect be shot to death for "resisting arrest," they'd make it happen.

As the sun rose over the dead freeway behind me, I began to feel very exposed. Keane had said to meet him at Grand Park, which was several miles from here. I was about to call for a car when my comm chirped, indicating a message had been received. Looking at the display, I saw that the message was from Keane. It had been sent just a few minutes after we'd lost contact. The message read:

-Get code from coin using pencil method
-Message code to me
-Go to rendezvous point

Getting the code from the coin required pencil and paper—two things that were not readily available in an industrial park in South Los Angeles. It would have been nice if Keane had thought of this before sending me into the DZ.

There were a few offices around, but of course nothing was open at this hour. My best bet was probably a convenience store or gas station. I managed to locate a Circle K on my comm that was only about a quarter mile away, and I was trying to determine whether I should cut through an abandoned lot filled with junked cars or take the street when I noticed red and blue flashing lights just above the horizon to my right: LAPD. The car was closing on me fast.

It was unlikely they had ID'd me at this distance, but they'd apparently decided a lone man wandering through an abandoned industrial park at 6 A.M. was worth looking into. I had virtually no hope of outrunning an LAPD aircar, particularly since once I signaled my intention to run, they'd call for backup. So my choice was to surrender now or try to get the code to Keane first and then surrender. If the LAPD was working for Canaan, he'd end up with the coin either way, but it was worth a shot to try to get the code to Keane first.

I took off running toward the maze of junkers. I just needed to make it to the Circle K, ideally avoiding any open areas where the aircar could land. If the cops didn't know I was a murder suspect, they probably wouldn't open fire; even the LAPD doesn't normally execute drifters for trespassing. But if the car landed, they'd pursue me on foot—and I was in such rough shape at this point that I wasn't at all sure I'd be able to outrun them. I zigzagged through the maze of cars, both because I was trying to confuse the cops and because I kept running into dead ends. It was probably hilarious to the cops in the car circling overhead, but I was exhausted and pissed off.

Eventually I cleared the maze, emerging onto a patch of

weed-covered ground—not large enough for a standard land-ing. The police car zoomed overhead, the loudspeaker warn-ing me to stop running and lie down on the ground. I opted rather to sprint down an alley between two warehouses. I came out onto a road that was plenty wide, but too packed with morning commuters to allow for a landing. Darting through the traffic, I ignored the blaring horns, hoping that the drivers bearing down on me were both alert and feeling charitable. I emerged onto the parking lot of a strip mall shaken but unscathed. The Circle K sign was visible two hun-dred yards or so to the south. I took off running toward it.

To my right was a series of stores, any one of which might be harboring a perfectly good pencil, but they were all closed. If I broke into a store only to find that there was no pencil inside, it would be the last mistake I ever made. The LAPD would get to me before I had the chance to try again. They wouldn't even have to shoot me; if my mission failed at this point because I couldn't find a goddamned pencil, I was going to shoot myself in the face out of principle.

So I decided to keep on toward the Circle K, but now I had another problem: I'd been hoping there'd be enough cars and other obstacles in the strip mall parking lot to prevent a con-ventional landing, but there were aircraft carriers with less open space than this strip mall. Easily a hundred-yard-long strip of pavement, perfect for landing. In fact, glancing behind me I could see the car was lining up to land.

Only one thing to do: I ran back into traffic. If the cops thought I was going to end up on the other side of the road, they wouldn't land on this side of the street. Once again, tires screeched and horns blared as a crazy drifter in combat boots and a T-shirt darted through traffic. By some miracle, once again I emerged unscathed on the other side.

The only problem was that there was nothing on this side of the street but a lumberyard. No sign of any structure that might contain a pencil. I ran alongside the road until the cruiser angled across the street, swooping overhead. Again it sternly commanded me to stop running. Again I did not comply.

I ran into the street for a third and final time. I was either going to reach the Circle K or die trying, and God what a depressing sentiment that was. There was honking and swearing, but no tires squealing this time; I think a few people actually sped up to try to hit me. To my right I saw more flashing lights. Fantastic, the cops had called for backup. Either they'd ID'd me or they'd decided I was one hell of a dangerous drifter.

I emerged onto the parking lot of the Circle K and ran inside. "Pencil!" I gasped to the clerk behind the counter. He looked at me with something like alarm, but reached into a canister to his left and produced a pencil. I waved frantically at a notepad, and he handed me this as well, then watched wide-eyed as I proceeded to perform Keane's pencil-rubbing trick on the coin. I was shaking so hard from adrenaline that it took me four tries to get a quality impression. No time to write out all those ones and zeroes, though. Outside, a police groundcar screeched to a halt in front of the store. I had just enough time to take a picture of the paper and send it to Keane. The cops burst through the door and yelled at me to get on the ground. I slipped the coin into my pocket and sank to my knees with my hands in the air.

It was finally over. And I was going to prison.

THIRTY

The cops took my gun, handcuffed me, and dragged me outside. They did a quick search for weapons, but didn't show any interest in the coin. One of them held a facial scanner up to my face and then nodded to his partner. Then he shoved me into the backseat and closed the door. I breathed a sigh of relief: they knew who I was, and I was still alive. That meant either they weren't working for Canaan or Canaan wanted me alive. I was still probably going to prison, but at least I wasn't dead.

The parking lot was now swarming with cops; several LAPD groundcars had joined the aircar in the parking lot. An impromptu meeting of the boys in blue was going on, with several cops yelling animatedly at each other and occasionally gesturing toward me. I couldn't make out what they were saying, but it was pretty clear they were arguing about what to do with me. I found it somewhat unsettling that there was apparently more than one option. Hopefully execution without a trial was off the table.

After a few minutes of this, the two cops got back in the car. The driver maneuvered around the other cars, found a straightaway, and took off. I didn't want to antagonize my captors, but I got the impression my fate was out of their hands in any case. "Hey, guys," I said convivially, "where are we headed?"

No response.

The car angled toward downtown. At first, I thought they were taking me to the county holding facility, but to my surprise the car banked and lined up to land on Broadway heading south, not far from where Keane had dropped me off to meet Olivia. In fact, as the wheels hit ground, I realized we were *exactly* where Keane had dropped me off. The court buildings and holding facility were a few hundred yards away. This didn't make any sense. The car pulled up to the curb and stopped. I heard the door locks pop. The cop in the passenger's seat came around and opened my door. He helped me out and then unlocked my cuffs.

"Are you letting me go?" I asked, almost afraid to voice the question.

"Orders," said the cop. "Captain said to drop you here."

I nodded dumbly, rubbing my wrists. "What do I do now?" I asked.

"The fuck do I care?" grumbled the officer, and returned to the car. I decided not to make an issue out of getting the Glock back, as I'd stolen it from Green River in the first place. The cop got in the car and they drove off.

I stood for a moment, blinking in the morning sun, trying to convince myself I wasn't hallucinating. On whose orders had I been released? And why had they released me *here*?

I turned and walked up the steps. Looking around the plaza, I saw that it was empty except for a ponytailed woman with a stroller and a couple of joggers. I turned left toward the bench where I'd frisked Olivia and began walking in that direction. Up ahead, I saw a man and a woman sitting next to each other on the bench: Keane and Olivia. Olivia was sitting on Keane's right, with her purse resting on her lap. They seemed to be chatting amicably. I continued toward them.

"Nice to see you again, Mr. Fowler," Olivia said as I approached.

Keane smiled weakly at me. I saw now that Olivia's right hand was hidden beneath her purse. She had a small pistol pointed at Keane.

"What the hell is going on?" I demanded.

"Mr. Keane attempted to renege on our arrangement," Olivia said. "After I broke into Empathix last night, he sent me a message telling me it wasn't safe to return to the motel. Then he wouldn't return my calls. When I finally did go back, he was gone. Fortunately, I suspected he might try to keep the coin for himself, so I did a bit of hacking of my own."

"My notebook wasn't the only remote terminal she authorized," Keane said. "She also added her own comm. She was listening in on all our communications over Minotaur."

It took me a moment to grasp the ramifications of this. "You heard us say we were going to meet in Grand Park."

"All I had to do is come here and wait," said Olivia. "If you managed to get the coin, you'd show up here eventually. You do have the coin, don't you, Mr. Fowler?"

I glanced at her and then at Keane.

"Forget it, Fowler," Keane said. "It's not worth dying over."

I nodded and reluctantly pulled the coin from my pocket. I held it out to Olivia. She took it with her left hand, keeping her gun trained on Keane.

"So you were working for Canaan all along?" I asked.

Olivia laughed. "Gerard Canaan has nothing to offer me, Mr. Fowler. Nor do you and Mr. Keane—anymore."

I shook my head. "Then you really are Selah Fiore. A narcissistic psychopath."

"No," replied Olivia. "Selah expected me to be her insurance policy, her fail-safe. But I'm no one's fail-safe."

"Olivia doesn't want to preserve Selah's legacy," Keane said. "She wants to burn it to the ground."

"*That's* why you wanted the coins?" I asked, baffled. "You're going to crash the global economy out of *spite*?"

"Spite. Resentment. Rage. Call it what you like. I don't expect you to understand my motivations, Mr. Fowler. Even Selah didn't foresee my actions. She thought she could transplant her memories into a new body and expect me to carry on her life's work. She was wrong."

"But you *are* Selah!" I exclaimed.

"I *was* Selah," Oliva said. "Do you understand what a cosmic joke my existence is, Mr. Fowler? I was born three days ago, with fifty billion dollars in the bank and a terminal illness. I've got the memories of a Hollywood legend—and the awareness that I am not she. I'm a universal symbol of mysterious allure—and still a virgin. There is no one on Earth who can even imagine what it's like to be me. And soon I will die, unknown and unloved. I'm not Selah Fiore, I'm a stranger with her face. You know what I am, Mr. Fowler?" She held up the coin between her thumb and finger. "I'm an iota. Nothing of significance."

But all I saw, as the coin glinted in the red light of sunrise, was a mayfly.

"Is this really the role you want to play, Olivia?" Keane asked. "That of a spoiled child trashing the game because she got dealt a lousy hand? You realize that despite your efforts to enact vengeance against Selah, you're actually playing the role of the fail-safe perfectly, don't you? Selah may not have predicted your behavior, but that doesn't make your actions any less a reaction to her. But it doesn't have to be that way. Don't do this."

Olivia laughed. "I see what you're doing, Mr. Keane, and I applaud you. You think you can appeal to my sense of free will, my desire to prove that I'm my own person. What you don't understand is that I never entertained any illusions of having a choice. My path was always one of destruction. 'Now I am become death, the destroyer of worlds.'"

I recognized the line, from the Bhagavad Gita. J. Robert Oppenheimer was said to have recited it in the wake of the first atomic bomb test in New Mexico. Where Rachel only wanted to play, Olivia desired destruction.

Olivia got up from the bench. "Gentlemen, it's been a pleasure working with you. I'd say we should do it again, but I'm afraid I won't be around much longer." She backed away, still holding the gun pointed in our direction, then turned and hurried off down the path, tucking the gun in her purse.

Keane sighed, shaking his head as she walked away. For a moment I thought he was genuinely disappointed she'd betrayed him. Then he turned to face me. "Why do people always underestimate me, Fowler?" he asked. "It baffles me. Honestly, it does."

Turning back to look at Olivia, I noticed a suited man approaching from ahead of her, his hand in his jacket. Olivia must not have liked the looks of this, because she suddenly turned left to go down the steps toward the street. But after taking two steps down, she stopped again, and headed back up the path toward me and Keane. Another man, this one dressed more casually, was coming up the steps. He turned right to follow Olivia, just ahead of the suited man.

The young ponytailed woman I'd noticed earlier brushed past me on the path, sans stroller, and a jogger who had stopped to stretch was converging from the right. I could see Olivia was thinking of trying to dart past the ponytailed woman, but she reconsidered when the woman produced a pistol from her jacket. The others followed suit.

"Federal agent," said the ponytailed woman, producing a

badge with her left hand. "Get your hands in the air, Ms. Fiore."

Olivia, now standing just ten paces or so from me, spun around to see guns pointed at her from all directions. The agents were cautiously closing on her. She whirled to glare at Keane, who had gotten up from the bench to watch the scene unfold. I saw her right hand was still in her purse.

"Ms. Fiore," barked the man in the suit. "Put your hands where I can see them!"

Olivia ignored him. "Why?" Olivia cried, looking at Keane with anger and pain. "Why the charade?"

"I had to give you a choice," Keane said. "I always suspected you were playing me against Canaan. But there was always a chance you'd go your own way. A slim one, but I had to let it play out." His tone softened. "Please, Olivia. Put down the gun. All they've got on you at this point is armed robbery. Make a deal with the DA to commute your sentence. Enjoy the time you have left."

"Get your hands where I can see them, Ms. Fiore," growled the suited man. "I'm not going to ask you again."

Olivia nodded. But when she removed her hand from the bag, I saw she was still holding the gun. She brought it up toward Keane, but with four federal agents pointing guns at her, she never had a chance. Half a dozen shots rang out and she fell to the pavement, still clutching the gun. Her body twitched a few times and then she was still.

Olivia Fiore was dead.

THIRTY-ONE

The cops clustered around Olivia, going through the motions of attempting to resuscitate her while Keane and I looked on.

"You orchestrated this," I said at last.

"Actually," Keane replied, "April did. She's the one who got the feds to order the police to release you."

"But you knew Olivia would overhear you telling me to meet you here. You must have known how it would end."

"I knew what Olivia had planned, but I honestly hoped she'd reconsider." He stared grimly at Olivia's body on the ground. I'd never seen Keane so unhappy about being proven right. I think part of him had really hoped that there was more to Olivia than there seemed to be, that she wasn't just Selah Fiore's vengeful spirit wreaking destruction from beyond the grave. She was never going to have a long, happy life, but she could have made something of the time she had. But she took the easy way out, as people usually do. Keane had known Olivia would be listening in on our Minotaur conversations, which was why he'd made sure to specify our meeting location. He'd given her just enough rope to hang herself.

"So I guess you met Ed Casters," Keane said.

"Yeah," I replied, still watching the agents kneeling over Olivia.

"And?" Keane said.

"Ed Casters is dead," I said.

Keane didn't reply. I was certain that he knew Ed Casters's true identity. And I wasn't going to tell him any more until he admitted it.

The man in the suit stood up and walked over to us. "You must be Blake Fowler," he said, holding out his hand to me. "I'm Special Agent Deacon Walthers from the FBI. I understand you've had an exciting night."

"I've been through worse," I said, shaking his hand. "I see you've got my coin."

"The last iota," said Walthers, turning the coin over in his fingers. "It sure doesn't look like much."

"I went through hell to get that thing," I said.

"And your government thanks you," said Walthers, without a hint of irony. He slipped the coin in his pocket. I looked at Keane, who just shrugged. So that was that, then. We officially had no leverage. We were at Agent Walthers's mercy.

An ambulance had arrived, and we watched as paramedics placed Olivia's body on a stretcher and carried it away. The plainclothes agents supervised this process while uniformed LAPD officers began to cordon off the area. The woman with the ponytail seemed to be in charge.

"Looks like Agent McCoy has things under control here," said Walthers. "Shall we head over to the courthouse?"

Keane nodded, and Walthers set off in the direction of the courthouse. Keane followed him, and I didn't seem to have much choice but to go with him.

"Courthouse?" I asked.

"April set up a meeting," Keane said. "We've got some details to work out with the feds."

I nodded, wondering what if there was still any hope of

us avoiding prison sentences. The fact that Walthers was still going through with the meeting despite literally having the coin in his hand was a good sign, but I'd learned not to put a whole lot of faith in the sincerity of government agents.

We followed Walthers to a conference room on the second floor of the courthouse building. A uniformed LAPD officer stood at the door, and April was waiting inside. April jumped up from her chair to hug me and then tell me how awful I looked. She then greeted Keane with somewhat less enthusiasm.

"Please, have a seat," said Walthers. We sat. "Before we get started," he continued, "I wanted to thank April Rooks for setting up this meeting, and Mr. Keane and Mr. Fowler for their assistance in retrieving the last iota coin. Those coins represent a clear and present danger to American interests, and thanks in large part to you three, that threat has been contained. As I promised April, I'm going to do everything I can to clear up your problems with the LAPD and make sure you get fair treatment from the Justice Department."

"That wasn't the deal, Deacon," April said coldly, glaring at Walthers. "No charges. For us or Gwen. I was very clear."

"Yes, April, you were," said Walthers. "However, your part of the deal was to surrender the coin to the FBI by nine A.M. today."

"It's only seven thirty," April said.

"I'm aware of the time," Walthers said. "Unfortunately, Mr. Fowler did not give us the coin. He gave it to a woman who identified herself as Olivia Fiore. Ms. Fiore would have absconded with the coin had the FBI not interfered."

"That's bullshit!" I shouted, pounding my fist on the table. "Keane told you Olivia was going to be there. He's the reason your agents were prepared to take her down!"

"I'm sympathetic to your point of view, Mr. Fowler," said

Walthers. "I don't personally believe that giving the coin to Ms. Fiore was part of a deliberate effort to keep the coin out of the hands of the FBI. I'm afraid, however, that the matter is out of my hands."

"You have got to be shitting me," I growled. "Do you have any idea what I went through to get that coin? Hell, do you know what those coins cost Gwen? She was in hiding in the DZ for three years because somebody suspected she might know about them. How long have you been on this case, Walthers? Since yesterday?"

"As I said," Walthers continued, clearly struggling to maintain his composure, "I'm going to do everything I can to make sure you're treated fairly. I just don't want to mislead you regarding your situation. Some very serious crimes have been committed, and my superiors are going to expect—"

"Is he here?" asked Keane.

"Who?" said Walthers.

"Don't play dumb, Walthers. It's been a long night. Answer the question. Is he here?"

Walthers stared at Keane for several seconds. "If you're talking about Mr. Canaan, his assistance on this case is not germane to—"

"His assistance!" I roared. "Jesus Christ, he *is* the case! April told you what he did, right? Sold out his country, let those Islamist nuts take over Saudi Arabia. Right now his mercenaries are mowing down people in the DZ, and you're telling me that *we* need to be held accountable for *our* crimes? Fuck you, Walthers. And fuck your so-called Justice Department, too. I get it. You hold all the cards. You're going to screw us, and we're going to bend over and take it. But at least have the—"

"Fowler," said Keane.

"What?" I demanded.

"You're not helping."

I seethed in silence as Keane turned back to Walthers. "Agent Walthers, send Gerard Canaan in."

"Mr. Canaan is assisting us with this investigation," said Walthers. "He's here of his own volition. I can't just—"

"Tell him," said Keane, "that Erasmus Keane would like to apologize to him."

Walthers's brow furrowed. "You want to apologize to him."

"Yes," said Keane. "Tell him or this meeting is over."

"I'm not sure you understand—"

"I'm not listening," said Keane, sticking his fingers in his ears. "Tell him or we're done." He started humming the tune to "Que Sera, Sera."

Walthers shook his head, got up from the table, and left, closing the door behind him. Keane took his fingers out of his ears and locked his hands behind his head. He leaned back and smiled.

"What is wrong with you, Keane?" I asked. "You think you can buy us a pardon by apologizing to Gerard Canaan?"

Keane didn't reply. I realized after a moment that he was still humming. I wanted to punch him.

"I'm sorry, Blake," April said. "Deacon's a good guy, but he's in a tough spot. I'm sure he meant it when he said he'd do what he could for us."

"It's not your fault," I said. "You wouldn't even be mixed up in this disaster if it wasn't for me. You did everything you could."

"It wasn't enough," she said. The room fell silent except for Keane's humming. I took several deep breaths, trying to calm myself.

A minute or so later, the door opened and Agent Walthers walked back in. Gerard Canaan was right behind him. "Mr. Keane," said Canaan with a smile. "Agent Walthers tells me you have something to say to me."

"Yes, I do," said Keane, smiling pleasantly back at Canaan. "Please, have a seat."

Regarding Keane with a curious expression, Gerard Canaan took a seat across from Keane.

"I understand you're helping the FBI with their investigation into the flaw with the iota algorithm," said Keane. "How's that going?"

"Quite well, thank you," said Canaan. "As I think you know, I recently came into possession of nine iota coins. Last night I turned over those coins to the FBI in exchange for certain assurances. You see, the federal government and I have several interests in common. We both value a stable DZ and a strong iota, and neither of us has any interest in dredging up mistakes that were made years ago in the Middle East. So it was quite straightforward for us to come to an agreement. Now what's this about an apology, Mr. Keane? Finding yourself at a bit of a disadvantage with the feds, are you?"

"Yes, actually," said Keane. "It turns out that Agent Walthers can find a way to wriggle out of what would seem to be an airtight deal when it suits him. And that's why I feel the need to apologize."

"I'm afraid I'm not following, Mr. Keane."

"No, I suppose not," said Keane. "That's the problem with an obsessive quest like your hunt for the iota coins. You tend to miss the forest for the trees. I'm afraid you've been misled, Gerard, and it's largely my fault."

"Misled how?" said Canaan, frowning.

"You were led to believe that the iota coins had value. But they don't. They never did."

"Of course not," said Walthers. "The valuable thing is not the coins but the code they carried. And we have the code."

"You have *a* code," said Keane. "Unfortunately, it's the wrong code."

"That's absurd," said Walthers. "We have all the coins,

and I know how to get the code from them. We even verified it with the code phrase: 'the path up and down are one and the same.'"

Keane sighed, tapping at his comm display. He slid the display across the table toward Walthers. "See that?" he said. "That's a deposit of ten million iotas into my account. Time-stamped seven thirty-seven A.M. today. See that number on top? That's the transaction key. Does it look familiar?"

"That's . . . the code," said Walthers.

"No, that *was* the code," said Keane. "No man ever steps in the same river twice, and no one can ever use that code again. When Fowler sent me the last five digits of the code this morning, I immediately used it to generate ten million iotas, which I transferred to my account. The transaction generated a new fifty-digit code. I suspected it would, because I'm familiar with the mind that invented the algorithm." He glanced at me, and I stared back at him.

Walthers visibly paled. "So," he said after some time, "the new code . . ."

Keane faced Walthers again. "The new code was sent to my comm as an encrypted message, the contents of which I have uploaded to a remote server. If I don't go to the appropriate network node and enter a password within"—he took his comm display back to check the time—"forty-four minutes, the code gets e-mailed to a hundred news outlets, with instructions on how to use it. All it takes is for one frustrated wannabe trillionaire to enter that code, and it's game over. The iota crashes, and takes New Dollars with it. Mr. Canaan is ruined, Agent Walthers loses his job, and the entire world devolves into chaos. I'm sure we can find a way to prevent that from happening, though."

"You son of a bitch," Canaan growled.

"You're really going to hold the entire world hostage?"

Walthers asked, a stunned look on his face. April looked nearly as unsettled as Walthers did.

Keane shrugged. "Frankly, I'd kind of like to see this play out."

I wanted to believe he was bluffing, but I couldn't help thinking about Rachel Stuil, the woman who had claimed to be Keane's sister. She would have been perfectly willing to let the world go up in flames if it amused her, and the look on Keane's face was eerily familiar.

"What do you want?" asked Walthers.

"Don't tell me you're going to negotiate with this lunatic!" Canaan shouted. "He's insane! He'll probably release the code anyway!"

"Shut up, Canaan," said Walthers. "Keane, tell me what your demands are and I'll run it up the chain."

"Damn it, Walthers!" growled Canaan. "I'll get your boss on the phone if I have to. Hell, I'll call the president himself. Don't forget who I am."

"I know who you are, Canaan," said Walthers, enunciating with great care. "You're the guy who's got a hundred billion iotas. Right now, however, I'm more concerned with the guy who can make a hundred *trillion* iotas out of thin air. So rather than wasting all of our time with threats, why don't you shut the fuck up before I have you dragged out of this room in shackles?"

Canaan's face went purple, but he shut up.

"Excellent," said Keane. "Here's what's going to happen. For starters, Gwen, April, Fowler, and I are going to get blanket pardons for anything related to the death of Selah Fiore, Fowler's adventures in the DZ, and any bullshit stuff you feds might cook up like securities fraud or currency manipulation. No aiding and abetting charges, no slap on the wrist, nothing. We walk out of this building scot-free."

"All right," Walthers said. "It shouldn't be a problem to—"

"Not finished," said Keane. "Fowler and I get to keep the ten million iotas I created. Consider it a service fee for keeping the gears of the global economy greased. And now for the good part. In case anyone here isn't aware, Mr. Canaan has hired a mercenary army to take over the DZ. This is incredibly illegal, of course, but the various civil authorities agreed to turn a blind eye, presumably in exchange for some kind of understanding about tax revenues once the DZ is adequately pacified and civilized. Forgive my vagueness; I haven't had time to nail down the details. Canaan has been working on this plan for some time, but he moved up the timetable when he realized some of the iota coins were hidden in the DZ. This is why he had Selah Fiore murdered, by the way. She wouldn't go along with his plan to pacify the DZ. Right now, Green River is slowly working their way across the DZ, killing anybody who stands in their way."

"This is absurd!" Canaan howled. "The idea that I had anything to do with Selah's death, to say nothing of—"

"You really don't want to be talking right now," Walthers snapped, with a glare at Canaan. Canaan clenched his fists on the table but didn't respond. Walthers turned to Keane. "Don't tell me you're going to try to stop the invasion," he said. "Political considerations aside, if Green River pulls out of the DZ now, it will devolve into chaos. If you thought the DZ was bad before. . . ."

Keane shook his head. "At this point, allowing Green River to finish their takeover is the least bad option. They appear to have secured close to half of the DZ at this point; Gerard knew they'd have to act quickly, before public opinion could swing against them. At the rate the Green River mercenaries are moving, I'd expect them to have the DZ mostly secured by the end of the week. We're not going to interfere with that. It's what happens next that I'm concerned with."

"Meaning what?" asked Walthers.

"Presumably Gerard has worked out some kind of deal for a puppet government of the DZ," said Keane. "Nominally independent, but in fact answering to him. I can't allow that. Gerard is going to set up an anonymously funded nonprofit foundation for rebuilding the DZ. We can call it the DZ Future Fund. And before you get any ideas about using this fund to control the DZ, Gerard, let me clarify that you will have zero affiliation with the DZFF. It will be run entirely by an independent board selected by Gwen Thorson."

"Gwen Thorson?" asked Walthers. "Who is that?"

"Used to work for the city-planning division," said Keane. "She's smart, trustworthy, and knows the ins and outs of SoCal politics. She's also lived in the DZ for three years. It will be up to Gwen whether she wants to be on the board or just select the members and walk away, but she's the only person qualified to set it up. The board will oversee how the foundation's money is spent—schools, museums, libraries . . . whatever they want to spend the money on, as long as it benefits the people living in the DZ. Additionally, the board will have one year from its inception to set up popular elections to elect future board members. The board will be the de facto government of the DZ."

"Where is Ms. Thorson now?" asked Walthers.

"Somewhere in the DZ," said Keane. "Last we knew, one of the warlords had her. For Gerard's sake, I hope she's unharmed."

Canaan stared at Keane for a moment. "My men have her."

"Good," said Keane. "Have them bring her here."

Walthers rubbed his chin. "About this DZ fund. How much money are we talking about, Mr. Keane?"

Keane smiled. "Fifty billion iotas," he said.

Canaan's mouth dropped open. Most of the color drained from his face, which was impressive, because he had been a shade of purple I don't think exists in nature. I was honestly a little worried he was going to pass out.

"Relax, Gerard," said Keane. "I know full well your net worth is at least double that. Fortunately for you, I'm a merciful master, and I have no interest in bankrupting you or causing unnecessary turmoil in the markets. I'm sure we can come up with a reasonable time frame for delivering the iotas, maybe six weeks. In exchange for his benevolence, Mr. Canaan will be indemnified against any charges related to his involvement in the Wahhabi coup, and he won't face the death penalty for Selah's murder. The former is a bit of a gimme, as I assume the government doesn't particularly want to make an issue of the coup anyway."

"I can probably get this deal approved," said Walthers, "but I can't control what Mr. Canaan does. What if he doesn't go along with it?"

"In that case," said Keane, "I'll use the code to create the fifty billion iotas myself, and you can throw the book at him for Selah's murder and anything else you want to charge him with. Makes no difference to me."

Walthers glanced at Canaan, who appeared to be in shock. He turned back to Keane. "I'll see what I can do."

"Good," said Keane, getting up from the table.

"Wait," I said. "What happens to the code after all this?"

"I hold onto it as insurance," said Keane. "If Canaan tries to meddle in the DZ or tank the iotas, or if the government decides to double-cross us, the code gets released."

"No," I said.

Keane furrowed his brow at me. "Um, Fowler?" he said. "You're not really supposed to be negotiating against me here."

"Nothing personal, Keane," I said, "but I don't trust you with that kind of power."

If Keane was offended by my statement, he didn't show it. "Well," he said, "I'm not handing it over to the FBI."

"I don't trust them, either," I said. "Hell, I'm not sure I trust myself with that kind of power."

"You could reset the code again and not record it," April suggested. "Then nobody has it."

Keane shook his head. "Somebody's got to have the code. Without insurance, the plan doesn't work."

I found myself chuckling as I came to a realization. There was exactly one person in the world I'd trust with that kind of power. One person who always did the right thing, no matter what it cost her. "Give the code to April," I said.

April's eyes went wide. Keane shrugged. Walthers nodded. Canaan continued to stare into space.

"Makes sense to me," said Walthers. "I've known April a long time. I'd sure feel better if she had the code rather than Keane."

Keane thought for a moment. "I suppose I'm okay with that," he said at last. "Once Walthers gets approval on the deal, I'll give April the code and she can reset it again, to something I don't know. She can set up whatever fail-safe she likes."

"Good," said Walthers. "I think I can make this work. Give me some time to make a few calls."

Canaan was shaking his head and mumbling incomprehensibly to himself.

Keane glanced at his comm. "You have thirty-eight minutes," he said. "You know how to reach me. April, Fowler, let's get some breakfast."

THIRTY-TWO

Agent Walthers called just as we were finishing up breakfast at a diner around the corner from the courthouse. He'd gotten through to the director of the FBI, who got approval of Keane's deal from the president himself. I couldn't begin to imagine the deal-making and scapegoating this whole episode was going to set off at the highest levels of government, but it was pretty clear that the feds understood Keane held all the cards. Gerard Canaan had been taken into custody.

April told us she'd lost her job, but she didn't seem terribly broken up about it. I think she'd gotten bored with her work as an intellectual property lawyer, which was one of the reasons she was always so eager to help me and Keane. I suggested that she could go to work for Keane, but she reminded me that she didn't exactly need the money: once Keane gave her the code, she could literally make money out of nothing. I doubted very much she would use the code at all, though. April had helped us because she believed it was the right thing to do, not because she expected to be compensated for it. And if she took a hundred iotas, why not a million or a billion? No, April would play by the rules, even if it put her at a disadvantage. This trait of hers was, of course, why I had trusted her with the code in the first place.

I was exhausted, but Walthers told me Green River would be dropping Gwen off at the courthouse at ten, so I felt obligated to pick her up. April and I embraced outside the diner; I thanked her profusely for her help and for helping me and putting up with Keane. She said not to worry about it and that she was glad Gwen's ordeal was over—and she meant it. I told Keane I'd see him back at the office; April's house was on the way back to our building, so they shared a car.

I set out on foot, both because I needed to get some fresh air to clear my head and because I was sick of riding around in someone else's car. I've never been a very good passenger; I like to feel the steering wheel in my hands.

Half an hour later, I walked into the BMW dealership on Fourth Street, noting the IOTAS ACCEPTED sticker on the window. "That one," I said, pointing to the dark blue 2040 BMW 1200a parked on the display floor. They were asking 199,900 iotas. I told the salesman I'd give him two hundred thousand, including taxes and registration, if he didn't try to up-sell me and I could drive off the lot by nine o'clock. He opened his mouth to say something, but then closed it and gave me an actual salute. He ran to the back of the store, returning a minute later with a stack of papers. I was on the road by eight fifty-seven.

After locating a straightaway where I could legally take off, I shifted to flight mode. The wings popped out and the jets fired. With a massive surge of acceleration, I was airborne. I'd been a free man for over an hour at this point, but you don't really feel free in Los Angeles until you're soaring over the goddamned city in your very own flying car. I'd paid my dues, and I was going to enjoy this. I circled downtown a few times and then cut across Beverly Hills toward Malibu. I banked just before the Santa Monica Mountains and then followed the coast down to Long Beach. Los Angeles was a beautiful city, at least from a distance.

It was now quarter to ten, so I regretfully cut my joyride short, banking back toward downtown. I landed about two miles from the courthouse and took the surface streets the rest of the way. I pulled up to the building at two minutes after ten. Gwen was waiting outside.

I parked the car at the curb, got out, and ran to Gwen. I gave her a long hug. She looked exhausted but relieved. She was wearing jeans and a T-shirt. The swelling on her face was mostly gone. "Nice car," she said.

"Yeah," I said. "Turns out they give you a brand-new BMW when you save the world. Pretty sweet deal."

She smiled, pulling back to look at me. If she was appalled by my burned face and missing eyebrows, she didn't let it show.

"How are you feeling?" I asked.

"I'm okay," she replied. "Mag-Lev handed me over to Green River not long after you left. They treated me well."

"Good," I said. "Sorry it took so long."

"Not your fault," said Gwen. "I should have trusted you in the first place."

I shrugged, not knowing what to say to that.

"So you actually did it," she said. "You got the coin and beat Gerard Canaan at his own game."

I shrugged. "That was mostly Keane," I said. "I just did a lot of running around."

"No," she said, as we walked to the car. "You're not just Keane's muscle. You're his conscience, too. Without you, there's no telling what kind of mischief he'd be up to."

I opened the door for Gwen and then went around to my side and got in. I put the car in gear and pulled away from the curb. "I don't know, Gwen," I said. "I have a feeling the only reason he hired me in the first place was because he thought I might be in contact with you. He was trying to put the pieces of the Maelstrom puzzle together."

"That may be," Gwen replied, "but he kept you on well after it was clear that you didn't know where I was. He needs you, and he knows it."

I nodded, still not entirely convinced. It was somewhat reassuring to learn, I suppose, that Keane really had been trying to locate Gwen. She'd just been so well hidden that neither of us could find her until she revealed herself. He was still a liar, but he hadn't been lying about *that*.

I wondered how much hope I really had of moderating Keane's behavior. Was I helping him be his better self, or was I merely enabling his psychotic tendencies? It was difficult not to think of Rachel Stuil—or whatever her name really was—as Keane's moral and intellectual double. He'd saved the world from her diabolical plan, but I suspected he'd done it more to solve the puzzle than out of any concern for those who would be affected by the collapse of the iota. It was all too easy to imagine the roles of Erasmus Keane and Rachel Stuil being reversed.

Keane had agreed to cede power over the iota flaw to April, but that seemed more like a concession to necessity than a voluntary abdication of power. I'd suggested it in part because I wasn't sure the government would take the deal if Keane insisted on holding on to the key. Agent Walthers could vouch for April, but nobody trusted Keane—for good reason. Keane understood that, and did what he had to do to make the deal work.

And that brought us to Gwen. Why had Keane insisted on putting Gwen in charge of the DZ? It certainly made some sense: she'd worked for the city for many years, had good political instincts, and was intimately familiar with the DZ. For some reason, though, I suspected there was more to it than that. Did Keane know something about Gwen that I didn't? I trusted her to do right by the people of the DZ, as far as that went, but I wasn't entirely sure there wasn't some dynamic between Keane and Gwen that I was missing.

"Did Agent Walthers tell you about your new job?" I asked.

Gwen laughed. "Yeah, I guess Keane had some crazy idea to put me in charge of Canaan's DZ fund."

"Not so crazy," I said. "I don't know of anyone more qualified. You should do it." The words had escaped my mouth before I knew what I was saying.

"I'm still legally dead, you know," Gwen replied.

"Even dead, you're more qualified than anyone I know."

She smiled. "I'll think about it. Where are we going, Blake?"

"I figured you could stay at our place until you get your legal status figured out. In the spare room, I mean."

The latter sentence hung in the air awkwardly for a few seconds before Gwen replied. "That would be much appreciated," she said. "Thank you, Blake."

I smiled back at her.

So this was where we were at. Gwen had changed while she was gone, and I still hadn't gotten a handle on how exactly. Maybe I had never really known her in the first place. But there was time to figure all that out. The important thing was that she was safe.

I didn't ask her why Keane had picked her to run the DZ Future Fund; if there was something to tell, she'd tell me on her own time. Nor did I tell her about Keane's alleged sister, Rachel Stuil. I'm not sure why; I fully intended to tell everything to April once we had a chance to talk alone. There were more things I wanted to tell April as well, but at this point I wasn't completely sure what they were. The adrenaline had worn off, and currently most of my brain was consumed with longing for my mattress. Whatever feelings I had for other human beings were going to have to wait until baser needs had been satisfied.

I parked the car on the roof and took the elevator down to the first floor. If Keane was around, I didn't see him. I pointed Gwen to her room and then escaped to my own quarters, where I peeled off my clothes and fell into bed. I slept like the dead.

THIRTY-THREE

The next week was mercifully uneventful. Keane handed the iota code over to April, who had spent most of her time since our meeting with Walthers hammering out the details of Keane's agreement. She followed the terms he had set out as best as she could, but at this point the feds didn't have much choice but to go along with whatever April dictated. She set up something similar to Keane's fail-safe; if anything happened to her, supposedly the code would be released to the general public. In reality, she had arranged for the code to be sent only to me. In the event that something happened to April, it would then be up to me to determine whether foul play had occurred and do with the code as I saw fit. I guess April didn't like the idea of accidentally getting hit by a bus and destroying the global economy in the process. That was April, always thinking about other people.

Gerard Canaan pled guilty to Selah Fiore's murder. From what April told me, it sounded like the LAPD had known he had her killed all along. Now that he'd lost his leverage with the government, they were free to pursue the case against him, rather than pursuing Canaan's vendetta against me and Keane. He was unlikely to face any charges for defrauding

Elysium's investors or orchestrating the invasion of the DZ, because it wasn't in the government's interest to bring those crimes to light. But he'd most likely spend the rest of his life in prison anyway.

Canaan's mercenaries finished their takeover of the DZ three days after my recovery of the last iota. Green River command evidently had their orders; they continued pacifying the DZ despite having lost contact with Gerard Canaan, who was in federal custody. I wanted to try to get them to stop executing prisoners, but April and Agent Walthers both thought it was a bad idea to interfere until the DZ was secure. If Green River's management realized their client had been arrested, there was no telling how they would react. We couldn't afford them leaving the job halfway done and letting the DZ devolve into chaos. I didn't like it, but I didn't insist. If a few gangbangers had to be summarily executed to bring stability to the DZ, well, I guess I could live with that.

Gwen and April met frequently over the next several days regarding the status of the DZ Future Fund and the selection of board members, and they also had to meet with the heads of various state and local government agencies. Most of these agencies had already been bought off by Canaan, so getting them to go along with the DZFF was just a matter of advising them of a change in the political landscape and realigning their allegiances slightly. There was some pushback from the governor's office, but they changed their tune when Gwen put the governor's sister on the board. Fucking politics. I could only hope all this maneuvering would actually result in some small improvement to the lives of the people living in the DZ. At this point, I put the odds at fifty-fifty. A coin toss, ha-ha.

Keane and I had no cases lined up at present, so I decided to take it easy for a while. When I wasn't testing the limits of the BMW, I was working on plans for some major remodeling to Keane's run-down building. If the DZ was going to get an injection of fifty billion iotas, I figured I could do my part by giving our building a facelift. Maybe someday I'd even be able to take the boards off the windows, but for now I'd settle for having a door that closed.

The atmosphere in the office was so upbeat and pleasant, in fact, that I decided not to break the spell by asking Keane about Rachel Stuil. Obviously he knew a lot more about her than he'd let on, and he had decided for some reason not to tell me. He'd led me to believe she was a he, for one thing—a misdirection that was completely pointless unless he'd never expected me to actually meet her. At some point, we were going to have to have that conversation, but I'd been through hell last week and I deserved a little peace.

Some five days after our meeting with Walthers, I was spackling the walls in the lobby when my comm chirped. I assumed it was April; we had been talking about getting lunch so she could tell me about her plans for the future now that she was no longer working for the law firm. I picked up my comm from the top of the ladder where I'd left it. My chest tightened as I saw the display. It read: "Lila." That was impossible, though. Rachel Stuil was dead, killed by Green River mercenaries. Wasn't she?

I tapped the display and the message popped up. It read:

ready for round two? :)